Crew

Anderson Billionaires, Book Five

By Melody Anne

Printed and published in the United States of America.

Published by Melody Anne

Editing by Karen Lawson and Janet Hitchcock

Dedication

This is dedicated to my Uncle George. Yet again another loss too soon. But you get to live on forever in my heart, and the hearts of all of the family. I miss you so much. I'm also glad you're up there with Dad in Heaven. I'll see you both in the blink of an eye. And now I have more angels watching out for me. I love you.

Note from the Author

This is the final book in my newest Anderson series, and dang, it's so hard for me to write! I hate ending a series. I hate letting these characters go, but then I always find ways of bringing them back for visits. I love this story of Crew and Darla. I love it because there isn't some big emotional conflict, but outside forces instead. When I met Mike, who someday I hope to have a wedding with if the world heals sometime soon, I just knew. It was so strange to me. But within a month of dating him, I told my best friend I was going to marry this man. She laughed because I am very trusting, but at the same time, I didn't think I'd ever marry again after getting a divorce. But I just knew with Mike. And I still know. Do I get irritated with him? Yes. Do I panic sometimes? Yes. But do I know I'll be with him for the rest of our lives? Definitely, yes! I love him. We've been together for two years and the man has never yelled at me, and let me tell you, I am a brat sometimes. But he loves me, and he's patient and kind, without being a pushover. He's made me a better person. The bottom line is that I knew without a doubt I was going to marry him. I knew before he did, and I probably scared the hell out of him because I came in like a wrecking ball, but he's my person, and the one I'm glad to be with while we're locked inside far too often. So I wanted to do that with some characters. I didn't want them afraid of love. Love is beautiful if it's with the right person. It's also frustrating, and annoying, and about compromises. But ultimately, it's beautiful.

There are a few things I wanted to share with you guys in this story. I like to use real places. And I'm seriously wanting to travel! So I sent my characters to Italy. I will go to this place sometime. I've been to Venice but didn't get to explore nearly enough. I really have to go to some of these other places too. I included a link so you can check them out.

I also used a real place for maple syrup in one scene. And when I can travel again, I'm so going there and getting a bottle. I support small, local business any chance I can get. I grew up poor in a small town. I know it's these small businesses that make a community operate and I want to make sure they survive all of this craziness.

The story I wrote about Baily made me sob. It is fictional, but I based it on my youngest nephew Jesse, who is adopted. My sister was seriously stressed out until those papers were sighed. He was never taken from her, but it did take two years for them to adopt him. Agencies give the birth parents so many chances to take kids back. And just as the kids were doing in this scene, my niece and nephews love Jesse. There is ZERO doubt that he's their brother. And if someone came in to take him, they'd probably bury them. He *is* my sister and brother-in-law's son and my niece and nephews' brother. He's a holy terror at three years old now and an escape artist, and he's also a very, very happy boy. His story turned out very well. But there are a lot of stories for kids that don't turn out too well. I, myself, spent a year in foster care before my dad was able to get me out. I don't talk about it, but I do remember it. It was awful for half the time. I was in some terrible homes. Then I was in a beautiful, loving home when my dad rescued me. We all have a story, and we should all take the time to listen to each other's stories. I think the entire world would come together and heal if we learned to listen again.

I love you all so much! I love that you support me through my many journeys. I love that you want my books and love my characters. I live in these worlds I create and I always bring a piece of me into them. Thank you for helping me do that. Thank you for being a part of my world. I hope you are safe, healthy, and happy. Call your mom and dad, call your grandma, and grandpa, and don't always listen when a person tells you they're okay. None of us are fully okay until we get back to a better time. Don't stop visiting people. We aren't meant to be alone all the time. We can be safe and still have others. I don't care if you do have to sit ten feet apart, make human contact. We're not meant to be alone, and depression is a real thing. Don't be afraid to call out to others. I love you guys and here's to a beautiful 2021.

https://www.momandpopsmaple.com/#
https://www.cntraveller.com/gallery/prettiest-small-towns-italy

With Love,
Melody Anne

Books by Melody Anne

Romance

BILLIONAIRE BACHELORS
*The Billionaire Wins the Game
*The Billionaire's Dance
*The Billionaire Falls
*The Billionaire's Marriage Proposal
*Blackmailing the Billionaire
*Runaway Heiress
*The Billionaire's Final Stand
*Unexpected Treasure
*Hidden Treasure
*Holiday Treasure
*Priceless Treasure
*The Ultimate Treasure

BABY FOR THE BILLIONAIRE
*The Tycoon's Revenge
*The Tycoon's Vacation
*The Tycoon's Proposal
*The Tycoon's Secret
*The Lost Tycoon
*Rescue Me

THE ANDERSON BILLIONAIRES
*Finn – Book One
*Noah – Book Two
*Brandon – Book Three
*Hudson – Book Four
*Crew – Book Five

BECOMING ELENA
*Stolen Innocence – Book One
*Forever Lost – Book Two
*New Desires – Book Three

FINDING FOREVER SERIES
*Finding Forever

TAKEN BY THE TRILLIONAIRE
#1 Xander – Ruth Cardello
#2 Bryan – J.S. Scott
#3 Chris – Melody Anne
#4 Virgin for the Trillionaire – Ruth Cardello
#5 Virgin for the Prince – J.S. Scott
#6 Virgin to Conquer – Melody Anne

SURRENDER SERIES
*Surrender – Book One
*Submit – Book Two
*Seduced – Book Three
*Scorched – Book Four

UNDERCOVER BILLIONAIRES
*Kian – Book One
*Arden – Book Two
*Owen – Book Three
*Declan – Book Four

FORBIDDEN SERIES
*Bound – Book One
*Broken – Book Two
*Betrayed – Book Three
*Burned – Book Four

HEROES SERIES
*Safe in his arms – Novella
*Baby it's Cold Outside
*Her Unexpected Hero – Book One
*Who I am with you – Book Two – Novella
*Her Hometown Hero – Book Three
*Following Her – Book Four – Novella
*Her Forever Hero – Book Five

BILLIONAIRE AVIATORS
*Turbulent Intentions – Book One (Cooper)
*Turbulent Desires – Book Two (Maverick)
*Turbulent Waters – Book Three (Nick)
*Turbulent Intrigue – Book Four (Ace)

TORN SERIES
*Torn – Book One
*Tattered – Book Two

7 BRIDES FOR 7 BROTHERS
#1 Luke – Barbara Freethy
#2 Gabe – Ruth Cardello
#3 Hunter – Melody Anne
#4 Knox – Christie Ridgway
#5 Max – Lynn Raye Harris

ANDERSON SPECIAL OPS
*Shadows – Book One
*Rising – Book Two
*<u>Barriers – Book Three</u>
*Broken – Book Four
*Reborn – Book Five

Young Adult / Fantasy

PHOENIX SERIES
*Phoenix Falling – Book One
*Phoenix Burning – Book Two
*Phoenix Ashes – Book Three
*Phoenix Rising – Book Four

*All links part of Amazon Affiliate Program.

Prologue

An uproar sounded in the hospital as a thunderous voice echoed through the hallways. Several people jumped, then a few started laughing.

"He's at it again," Dr. Spence Whitman said.

"Can we please, for the love of all that's holy, discharge that man today?" a nurse asked, clasping her hands together in a prayer motion.

"I don't think he's going to give us a choice," another nurse said. "That man just ripped out another IV and told me I'm a blood-sucking vampire who's paid by the mob to make his life a living hell."

"Ah, are you guys afraid of a little old man?"

They all turned, and Crew Anderson gave them a smirk. He'd heard his uncle from the second he'd stepped from the elevator. The man had managed to chase away veteran staff in a matter of seconds.

"Little . . . old . . . man? Really, Crew?" Spence asked.

Spence had been a family friend of the Andersons from the time he was in diapers. He'd been a part of their lives longer than Crew, who hadn't known he had extended family until his mother confessed all on her deathbed.

"Isn't he like a hundred now?" Crew asked.

"I don't think anyone knows his actual age," Spence said.

"Dammit, I want out of here. I'm perfectly capable of walking on my own. Where's my wife?" Joseph shouted. Then the man of the hour stepped from his room, his hospital gown hanging on him, only reaching the middle of his thighs. If he turned around, Crew was sure they'd all see a show.

"Crew, my boy!" Joseph said, his eyes lighting up as soon as he saw his nephew. "I knew you'd come take me home. I don't know why these idiots are insisting on keeping me here. I'm just fine."

Joseph walked over, all six foot five, two hundred fifty pounds of him.

"It might be the fact that you were shot in the chest a week ago and had to undergo emergency surgery. If that bullet had been just a tad to the left, we wouldn't be having this conversation right now," Crew said.

"Exactly," Dr. Whitman added.

Joseph's smile faded as he glared at both of them.

"A tiny little bullet can't stop me," Joseph said. He opened his hand, revealing the mangled piece of metal that had pierced his flesh.

"How in the world did you manage to get your hands on that?" Crew asked.

"It was in my body, therefore it's *my* property. I want it as a reminder anytime my Katherine wants to do something so foolish as to release a criminal again. I'm making it into a ring so all I have to do is hold up my hand."

"You petty old man. I don't think that poor soul did what he did on his own. I think he was being forced," Katherine said as she came around the corner. "I'm not happy with you, Joseph Anderson. I found a sweet little nurse back there crying, talking about the very difficult man in room three-o-three."

Katherine was the opposite of her husband in every single way. While he was a giant of a man with a voice that could speak to an entire stadium without a microphone, she stood just a few inches above five feet with stunning blue eyes that watched them all, a gently weathered face, and a very petite frame. But it didn't matter; the two of them fit together. It was odd to see them apart.

Joseph didn't yell at his wife. He instantly dropped his chin.

"I'm sorry, Sweetie. I just want to go home with you," he said, his voice very much subdued. "I certainly didn't mean to make a sweet girl cry. I'll buy her a house."

Crew laughed . . . hard, which was a shock; he hadn't done that in a while. The funny thing was, he could see Joseph doing just that. Most people apologized with a card, maybe some flowers and chocolates. Not Joseph. Nope, he'd buy someone a new house or vehicle.

"Joseph Anderson, you can't buy your way out of this," Katherine told him. "Your behavior has been unacceptable."

Her petite hands were firm on her slender hips. He looked so sheepish and contrite Crew *almost* felt sorry for him.

"I disagree, Katherine," Spence said. "I think he *can* buy his way out of this. I expect him to send a five-star catered dinner for the entire hospital staff and a floral bouquet to every nurses station." He paused, his grin growing. "And chocolate. He owes every single one of my nurses a nice high-quality box of chocolates."

Katherine laughed at Spence. Dr. Whitman was her hero since he'd been the leader in fighting for the care she'd needed to remove a nearly inoperable tumor from her brain.

"I think that's a good start," Katherine told him.

"It's done," Joseph said. He pulled out his phone and handed it to Katherine as if he expected her to make the calls. "Then can I go home?" he pleaded.

Crew turned so Joseph wouldn't see his chest shaking from his silent laughter. It felt good to laugh. It felt good to focus on someone other than himself.

"It's all up to Spence," Katherine said. "You don't get to leave until *he* says you can." Joseph looked up in panic at Spence. He'd have given him a much meaner stare if his wife hadn't been standing there.

"Hmm," Spence said, quite liking the power he was wielding. He knew it wouldn't last long, so he had to act quickly. "If *all* of the nurses accept your apology and there's no more trouble, *and . . .*" He paused and looked pointedly at Joseph. "*You're* the one to order all of the stuff instead of brushing it off on someone else, then, and *only* then, will I'll sign your release papers."

There was a gleam in Joseph's eyes that told Spence his payback would be hell. But it was totally worth it. Not too often did someone get one over on Joseph. It felt damn good.

"Did you hear that, Uncle? *If* you behave you get to leave," Crew said.

Joseph's entire attention focused on Crew and he lost the smug look on his face.

"Since we're confessing our sins and apologizing, are you going to tell us why you've been acting like such a horse's ass?" Joseph asked.

"Nope," Crew told him. He wasn't ready, not yet. He had Darla Winters helping him. He was a mess right now. He knew it, but he was determined to solve the problem himself.

"You do realize I have ways of finding information. I'm about at the end of my rope, boy," Joseph told him.

"Let me try to handle it," Crew insisted.

Joseph paused for several tense moments. No one spoke. Patients in other rooms didn't even cough. They were all listening. Joseph being in the hospital was better than an episode of *Grey's Anatomy*.

"Fine, Crew. But my patience has run out," Joseph told him.

"Joseph, you have some phone calls to make. Why don't you leave this boy alone?" Katherine asked.

"Of course, my sweet wife. Can I have my phone now so I can get this over with?" Joseph asked.

"I don't know where it is," Katherine said. She smiled at him. "Why don't you go find it?"

Joseph's eyes softened with concern as he looked at his wife. Spence and Crew also looked at her. No one spoke for several seconds.

"You're holding it, Katherine," Dr. Whitman said. "How have you been feeling lately?"

Katherine looked down at her hand in confusion. Then she laughed. "Oh, I'm just fine, Spence, just fine. I thought this was my phone," she said.

Spence looked at Joseph, and Crew watched them both. It had only been a minute or two since Joseph had handed the phone to her. It wasn't until that moment that Crew realized his aunt was forgetting things a lot more lately. Had the tumor done something to her brain?

"Of course you are," Spence said without missing a beat. "But it's been a while since your last scan. I'd like to do another one."

Katherine laughed, and Joseph's face paled. "You're okay, right, Katherine? You aren't hurting?" he insisted. If Joseph could will his wife into perfect health he would. For a man who could do or get anything he wanted, it was a tough pill to swallow to not be able to do enough for his wife.

Joseph had been shot the week before by a madman, along with Jon Eisenhart, who was running a special operations team for Joseph. Both of them had pulled through. Crew's problems seemed minor compared to that.

He'd figure it all out — and maybe they'd figure out what was wrong with Katherine too. Then again, maybe there was nothing wrong. In this strange world they'd found themselves in, nothing seemed to make much sense anymore.

Chapter One

Crew Anderson had been going through absolute hell for months.

He was a psychologist, dammit! Crew told himself over and over again to stick to the facts, to not let speculation get to him. He tried giving himself the same advice he gave his patients — he needed to remain rational, in control, and look at the facts . . . only the facts. Yep, he also watched too many old black and white films if he couldn't think that thought without Jack Webb's voice from *Dragnet* filtering through his mind.

Three months ago Crew had received a cryptic note telling him he had a daughter and more information would soon come his way. He'd searched his mind, wondering how that was possible. He wasn't a saint, that was for sure, but he was a careful man and had been his entire life.

Crew had great respect for women. He also believed in honesty. He'd yet to meet anyone who'd swept him off his feet. He treated women well, took them on nice dates, and when he did bed them, he always made sure they were both protected. So, the logical part of his brain told him this was nothing but a smokescreen. There was no way he could have a daughter.

Protection fails!

That thought had stayed with him with each subsequent note he'd received.

Crew had finally asked Darla Winters to help.

Though Crew was miserable, the thought of Darla brought a bit of warmth to his seemingly frozen heart. She was unlike any woman he'd ever met, full of love, laughter, energy, and optimism.

She was the best friend of his brother Hudson's fiancée. The girls had been friends since grade school and had a bond as strong as Crew shared with his brothers. He'd been drawn to Darla the moment he'd met her, and because she was a social worker, he'd finally decided to share his story with her. He'd been keeping it from his family for months.

"Hey, cowboy, what are you doing?"

As if thinking about her had pulled her from thin air, Crew turned to see Darla approaching, her usual smile firmly in place, her walk confident on her long, toned legs encased in a pair of jeans that seemed to have been made just for her.

His gaze traced her luscious body as he admired the sweet curve of her waist where the fitted, bright pink, buttoned blouse she wore tucked into those pants, giving him a great view of her breasts and a peek at her cleavage.

"Getting a good look? Do you want me to pose for a picture?" Darla asked as she stopped a few feet from him. "Take it from my left side. It's much better." Then she turned slightly, put a hand on her hip, tucked her chin down the slightest bit, and looked up at him with blazing green eyes that took his breath away. After a second she laughed as she stopped her pose and closed the distance between them.

He gave her the slightest smile. Damn, she had a way of pulling him from his brooding thoughts.

"Ah, there's that almost smile I love so much," Darla said before reaching out and chucking his chin. She leaned against the fence he'd been standing at for the past hour. "I see your new arrivals are here safe and sound. I was hoping to get here earlier, but I had a mother who needed to talk."

Crew knew Darla would share only what she could and nothing more. She'd never break confidentiality, just as he wouldn't. "I hope all is okay," he told her.

"It's never okay in my world, but once in a while I see miracles, and I see families truly fight for one another. That's what keeps me going back again and again," she said.

They stood side by side as they both gazed out at the field. "I don't know what the hell I'm doing," he finally muttered.

"Well, it looks like you're adopting horses," she told him.

That morning, four horses had been brought to his home. He wasn't quite sure how he'd gotten roped into it. A couple of years earlier he'd bought the fifty-acre ranch with a barn, indoor arena, and an attached fenced field. He'd felt called to the property. But he'd never expected to fill it with animals.

This morning his uncle had called, saying there was an emergency. A group had been busted for animal abuse and they needed homes for two grown horses and two foals. Crew had said he couldn't do it, that he knew nothing about horses. But somehow, in a matter of minutes, his uncle had convinced him to accept taking charge of these probably-abused animals and have them dropped off ASAP.

As soon as he'd finished speaking with his uncle, he'd called Darla. He hadn't known why he'd called her instead of his brothers, but it seemed to be what he'd been doing for the past few weeks as the two of them tried to solve the case of whether he had a daughter or not.

After his call to Darla, Crew had rushed out to buy supplies, made phone calls to arrange a vet visit, then spent the remaining time making sure the fences were secure and there was nothing in the unused barns that would hurt the animals.

Now he was gazing out at the beautiful green field with fencing that needed some updating and the four horses that huddled together, sending suspicious looks his way.

"I'm just housing the horses," Crew said after a long pause at Darla's words.

"Mm-hmm," she said before chuckling.

"I won't get attached to them," Crew firmly said.

"I don't know," Darla said as she gazed with fondness at the animals. "That dark beauty over there keeps looking at you with a challenge in his eyes. I think you might be meant for one another."

"I've never ridden a horse, nor have I ever had the desire to do so," Crew told her.

As they spoke, the young tan foal with white highlights and skinny legs began taking steps toward them. There was no distrust in its eyes, only curiosity.

"Come here, baby girl," Darla crooned in a voice that made the horse's ears perk up as it took another step.

The female horse behind the foal neighed, making the young one turn its head, but then it looked back to Darla and took another step.

"That's it, baby girl. Come here," she said as she pulled out a bag of cut-up apples and held one out through the fence. The horse picked up its step. "What a pretty girl you are," Darla cooed.

Crew had been standing there for an hour, watching the horses, and they'd barely glanced at him, other than the large male whose evil eyes told Crew he wanted to kill him. Within seconds Darla was enchanting the animals. He knew how they felt.

"What's her name?" Darla asked as the foal made it to the fence and gingerly moved her head forward to smell the treat in Darla's hand. She took the small piece of apple and chewed it while Darla reached through the fence and gently petted her nose.

"They don't have names," Crew said. "I don't plan on naming them. They're only here temporarily."

"That won't do at all," Darla said. "I'm going to call you Pixie," she said. "You definitely look like a sweet little fairy princess."

The horse seemed to smile at Darla as she held out another piece of apple. The foal gladly took it then leaned against the fence munching it and enjoying the sweet caress of Darla's fingers. Crew wouldn't mind her caressing him with as much attention.

The other young horse that seemed a few months older had noticed what was happening at the fence and trotted over, butting the female out of the way so he could get his own piece of apple. He was black, lanky, and absolutely beautiful with soulful eyes that told Crew he'd seen a bit too much in his young life.

"He's a little edgier, but I think with a lot of love and attention he'll be as sweet as a purring kitten on your lap," Darla said as she gave him another piece of apple and scratched his neck. "Are they siblings?"

"No. I didn't get a lot of information, but they said they believe those two are the mom and dad of the one you're calling Pixie, and this boy is an orphan."

"Hmm, we'll call you Shadow," Darla said. Shadow seemed to like his name because he gave a whiney at Darla's words, then nudged her hand for more apple.

"Don't get attached," Crew told her. "They *really* aren't staying." He made sure his voice was firm. He had to keep his resolve.

Darla smiled at him. "Your uncle Joseph set this up?" she asked innocently.

"Yes, but he assured me it's temporary," Crew said.

Darla laughed, the sound full of joy. "Oh, Crew, I've only known your family a short time, but if your uncle got the horses here, they aren't going anywhere," she informed him.

Crew felt the color drain from his face. "I don't know anything about horses. They can't stay," he said, feeling near panic. "I have this mystery to solve about a possible daughter, I have a practice to run, and I don't want pets."

"We all need animals in our lives. They remind us we aren't alone and that we're loved. When people let us down, animals are there to pick up the pieces. No matter how much an animal might be abused, they'll crawl back to you to love them. Are you really going to turn these babies away when they have a secure home here? Would you do that to them when you can help them?"

"That's low," he said. "I can't help if I don't know what I'm doing."

"I've been around horses my entire life, so it's a good thing we're friends and I'm looking for a new adventure," she said.

"A new adventure?" he asked. He was confused and it wasn't a feeling he enjoyed.

"Yep. We have a mystery to solve and I have vacation time. So we'll take care of these horses and solve the mystery of your daughter. It's a win-win."

"How is any of this a win?" he asked, throwing his hands in the air. The horses moved away from him, feeling his agitation. "Sorry," he mumbled, realizing he was apologizing to animals. This woman changed his reality too often.

"You win no matter what, Crew. Don't you realize that? If you have a child out there, you'll get to know her, love her, and protect her. If you don't, then you'll know it's inside you to be a father. Your protective instincts have already emerged. And taking care of these beautiful horses will help you heal. There's nothing more therapeutic than horses."

"I thought *I* was the psychologist," he told her with a raise of his brows.

"You know you aren't allowed to doctor yourself. It's a good thing I'm around to help you out," she said.

The woman was so full of confidence. It was certainly a turn-on.

"They aren't going away, are they?" he finally asked.

She laughed again, the horses drawn to her pureness. "Nope. I'm glad you're realizing it. I think you should name that beautiful stallion out there. He's obviously yours."

"He's not mine," he said. She just raised a brow. "I guess it doesn't hurt to name him though."

"That's a first step," she said.

"Let me watch him for a couple of days. I don't know how you came up with names so quickly."

"Are you getting all sentimental on me?" Darla asked. The older horses hadn't come up to the fence but they had moved closer. The babies were still nudging Darla. "I'm all out of food. You'll have to wait until later," she told them. They actually seemed to look irritated with her.

There were a couple of people working in the barn, and Darla waived to them.

"It didn't take you long to get people here," Darla said.

"My cousin Mark was on it. He loaned me some of his help until I hire my own. I think my uncle had this planned for days; as soon as I reluctantly agreed, it was all good to go. He gave me phone numbers to call and the vet and hoof person are on their way now."

"Hoof person?" Darla said.

"You know, that guy who trims their feet."

Darla threw back her head and laughed. "I might have to stop calling you cowboy," she told him. "You mean the farrier."

"I told you I know nothing about horses," he said as he threw his hands in the air. "And I'm not even close to being a cowboy."

"Oh, Crew, there's a bit of cowboy in all men," she said as she shocked the hell out of him and slapped his ass — hard — before she turned and began walking toward his house.

He stood watching the sway of her hips as she moved forward, unaware she'd left him stunned in place. He didn't know what in the hell to think about this spitfire of a woman who had his insides twisted in a million directions. He wanted to chase after her and give her his own smack on her tight ass. Just the thought of that had him painfully hard beneath his jeans. He shifted as he tried to get more comfortable.

"Are you coming, cowboy?" she called.

"I thought I wasn't a cowboy," he fired back as he began walking after her.

"And I told you *all* men have a bit of cowboy in them. Want to show me your lasso?" she threw back at him with a wink before facing forward again.

Hell yes! He almost shouted that right at her. The thought of her in his bedroom, wearing nothing but a cowboy hat while he slapped his hand with a rope flashed inside his head. His arousal throbbed with need, and he felt his heart thunder in his chest.

What in the hell was wrong with him? He was a damn psychologist, for goodness sake. He didn't have fantasies of tying up women, and he didn't need kink in the bedroom to have a good time. What this woman did to his head should be illegal.

She turned and looked at him as he practically limped to her, his erection so painful it was difficult to walk. A gleam shone in her eyes as her gaze burned him from head to toe, and then back up again. When their gazes met this time, there was some definite fire in her eyes.

"Hmmm, I can practically read your thoughts," she said with a husky laugh. "Are you fantasizing about ropes and spurs?" she purred.

He took a step closer to her. "That mouth of yours is going to get you into some seriously hot water one of these days," he warned. Crew would've never considered himself a rough and tumble alpha male, but this woman seemed to be bringing it out in him. He had the strong desire to pull her against him and show her what teasing a man would accomplish.

"Promises, promises. Don't make an offer you aren't willing to back up, cowboy," Darla said in a taunting voice. She reached out and ran her finger across his lips, down his chin and over his chest. Then she laughed again before turning and once again walking away.

Crew stood rooted to the spot for several long seconds. Then he grinned. "I'm your huckleberry," he called.

Darla turned, stunned. And then she threw back her head and laughed, pure joy escaping her.

"Damn, you're fun, Crew Anderson. It's too bad I'm smart enough to know you're a *love 'em and leave 'em quick* kind of guy. Otherwise, we'd rock the hell out of your bed."

And then she was gone. She stepped inside his house. They had a lot to do that day. But Crew suddenly didn't want to do anything other than haul her into his bedroom. Should he do just that?

Maybe . . .

Chapter Two

Darla took some deep breaths in and out while she walked into Crew Anderson's home. She'd always been a confident woman, knowing who she was and where she wanted to go in life. She'd been knocked down a few times, but she'd never allowed that to keep her on the ground.

She'd get right back up, put a smile on her lips, and try again. That didn't mean she didn't have moments she wanted to give up, or moments of self-pity, it just meant she was human and had real emotions. She'd wallow for a few hours, eat a pint of ice-cream, and then tell herself in twenty-four hours she'd be in a better place — and she always was.

Because Darla was who she was, she'd been very unlucky in love. She'd dated quite a lot, more than the average person. But none of her relationships survived for long. She couldn't seem to find a man strong enough to handle her.

The men she dated couldn't seem to accept that she didn't need them. Yes, she *wanted* them, but she didn't *need* them. That was the key. She wasn't some princess in a tower who needed rescued. She wanted a partner who'd love her, appreciate her, spar with her, and stand next to her. She wanted her equal — not someone better or worse, but someone to walk beside her.

From the moment she'd met Crew, she'd been in lust. He was gorgeous, and not in an understated way. He seemed all calm and brooding on the outside, but she'd instantly recognized that burning desire in his eyes he didn't think anyone else noticed. He was intense, but managed to mask it with his calm demeanor and nerdy clothes. Even on Saturday the man wore business casual. She'd been shocked to find him in a pair of jeans for the first time she could remember. The man had every color and style of suit pants known to mankind. That was another thing that turned her on.

He kept his dark hair perfectly cut, like seriously perfectly cut. The man had to go to the barber at least twice a month. She'd only seen his strands out of place once and that had been the night she'd come to a family barbeque at his place and monopolized his time. They'd ended their night with a scorching kiss that had led to her fingers curling up in that beautiful silky hair and messing it up quite sexily.

His blue eyes were so bright and knowledgeable she knew she could get lost in them for an eternity, and the thick muscles he hid beneath his business attire were firm and cut. She wanted to run her fingers and tongue over every single inch of them.

So instead of leaping into his arms and taking what she wanted so desperately, Darla was even more cocky than normal, enjoying throwing him off-kilter, enjoying saying things to shock him, to make his hot body all tense and hard.

She knew she was playing with fire. She knew that when the man went off, it was going to be an eruption of raw need and power unlike anything the world had seen before. But she wasn't sure if she could hit the right buttons to cause the explosion. Did she want to? Hell yes, she wanted to. But she also knew he might be one more man in a long line of men who could put out the right vibes then sizzle and extinguish just when she needed to be ignited.

And that led Darla right back to where she always started, feeling enormous need and no satisfaction. So, she put on her armor and taunted the man until he was a mess. She knew she was safe with Crew, knew he'd never fully lose it. But damn wouldn't she love to be the woman if he did! She could always fantasize. She already had — quite often when it came to this man she'd only known a couple of months.

She'd poured herself a cup of coffee and was sitting at his kitchen island when Crew stormed into his kitchen, his eyes intense, his body strained.

"What took you so long, cowboy? I was beginning to wonder if you'd gotten lost," Darla said before she sipped her coffee. He always had the best creamers in his house. The man knew how to please a woman . . . in the kitchen at least.

He didn't say a word as he moved to his coffee pot and poured himself a cup. She smiled, wondering how much further she was going to push him that day. She was feeling good. She'd been late because she'd been with a mother who'd turned her life around and was getting her daughter back the next day after a year of foster care.

Darla dealt with so many cases where the parents didn't even try to get their kids back, so when she found a parent who truly wanted to correct their lives and give their child a better home, she fought tooth and nail to help them. Her first priority was always the children, but she knew a child was so much better off with parents who loved them — whether blood or not. Sometimes that was with their adoptive families, and sometimes that was with their biological families.

In her current case the mother had been severely abused, and when she'd lost her daughter, she'd finally had the strength to leave the man who'd attacked her and her child. Then she'd gotten the help she'd needed, going to counseling and back to school. She was on her way to becoming a social worker herself, and Darla knew she'd make a wonderful one.

Nobody was better at doing a job than one who'd gone through hell and back to get where she was. This woman would be a great mother, and she'd help many other children. There was no better ending to a long job, and Darla's mood couldn't be dampened that day. It was also making her a little spunkier than usual.

Crew faced her as he pulled over a box that held everything they'd been going over for the past week. He took out files and laid them out before the two of them. He looked exhausted, but she knew it was better for her to pull him into the moment than to allow him to sink into a pit of despair.

"Crew, it's time we bring your family into this. I know I've said that before, and you agreed with me, but you still haven't done it. I never keep anything from my best friend, and I hate that I can't discuss this with Daisy. Your whole big family loves you, and I know we can all solve this together."

"But what if this is all a lie? What if I bring them in and it ends up breaking their hearts?" he asked.

She reached over and took his hand. "It would break their hearts more knowing you don't trust them enough to share with them. This is a huge deal for you and your family. Whether you have a child out there or not, they need to be walking by your side."

"Are you done with this? Are you needing to step back?" he asked. By his tone, she could tell he was trying to keep it casual as if her answer didn't matter, but she could hear the vulnerability in his voice. He tried doing a lot alone, but like all humans, he needed other people.

"Wild horses couldn't drag me away," she assured him. "I just think we need to work as a team. These notes haven't stopped, but they aren't giving us clues. We need to find out if there's even a child out there, and if there is, we need to find out if she's yours."

"I did what you asked and really looked back at who I'd . . . um . . . been with . . . um . . . sexually over the last ten years," he began, unable to look her in the eyes.

She felt a little clench at his words. The thought of him in the arms of another woman made her want to scratch some eyes out. That was a new reaction for her. She knew most people weren't saints, that they had itches and scratched them, so it was very odd for her to feel jealous of women Crew had been with long before he'd known her.

For that matter, they didn't have a sexual relationship anyway. They had chemistry, that was for dang sure, but they'd only shared a single kiss. She knew he was attracted to her, just as he knew she was attracted to him, but hell, she was also half in love with Sam

Elliot. That didn't mean she was going to hunt him down and jump his bones. People could be attracted and never have sex. It happened all the time.

"What did you come up with?" Darla asked as she pushed the image of him with other women as far from her mind as possible. She was trying, for once, to be clinical about this conversation.

Crew shifted as he looked down at a piece of paper. Then he sighed. "There's only one woman on here who's a possibility. It was a one-night stand," he said with a little disgust. "Contrary to what my brothers might think, I don't normally have one-night stands. But I was at a conference in Southern California, and it was the last night, and we were all in the bar at the hotel. There was a lot of drinking."

"Do you know who she is?" Darla asked, no judgement in her tone.

He looked up miserably. "No. And I swear I used protection. I remember her name was something like Mandy or Sandy or something like that because I gave some cheesy-ass line about her being sweet as candy."

"Wow. Yep, that's certainly cheesy," Darla said. "I didn't know you had it in you."

"I don't!" he insisted. "I don't use lines and I don't like casual sex. I'd rather be in a short-term mutually satisfying relationship."

Darla sat there for a second before bursting into laughter. "Oh, be still my heart," she said as she put a hand against her chest. "That line makes me want to jump into bed with you right now."

Crew glared at her. "You're just a riot a minute," he said.

"I'm thinking maybe I need to take you to a hotel bar and meet this other Crew Anderson," she told him.

Those intense blue eyes nailed her to the seat as they burned into her. "Careful, Darla. I'm not always so controlled. A man can be pushed just so far before he takes what's being offered."

Her thighs clenched as heat flooded her. "I keep waiting," she said with a wink. She'd swear she saw flames flare up in his deep blue depths. His fingers gripped the counter and she figured she'd pushed him enough. She laughed. "Slow down there, cowboy. We're not at the bar, remember?"

"You are so unlike any woman I've ever known," he blurted as he ran a hand through his hair. She was mesmerized by the suddenly messy strands. Dang, she'd pushed him enough to make him forget about his perfect appearance. She wondered how crazy she could make him. Did she really want to find out?

Maybe.

"Thank you. I'll take that as a compliment. But back to Candy. Is there any way for us to track her?" she asked, her voice going professional, the tone she used with unruly parents in her office.

"The event was nearly six years ago. I don't know," he said.

"Okay, then we bring in the big guns," she said as she reached over and picked up his phone, holding it out to him. "It's time to call your brothers . . . *and* your uncle Joseph."

Crew groaned, looking as if he wanted to argue. Finally, though, his shoulders sagged. "I think you're right," he said.

"Do it now. I'm not moving until you've made the call. I want to get this mystery solved. I have horses to play with, and we can't do that if we're stressed over whether you're a father or not," she insisted.

He dialed the phone . . .

Chapter Three

Crew was no longer surprised by how quickly his family moved.

Joseph Anderson had taken some getting used to when he'd first met the giant of a man who was his uncle. Technically, Crew's father had been Joseph's uncle which made Joseph his cousin, but that was too weird to comprehend, so it was easier for all of them for Joseph to be his uncle and for all of his many cousins to be his cousins.

He hadn't wanted more family at first. The loss of his mother had been devastating for him and his brothers. She'd been the rock of their family through all of their rough times in life. Their father had been a monster, who'd abused his power over and over again, and their lives had improved dramatically since he'd died.

But losing their mother a few years earlier had nearly destroyed them, especially Crew. He'd been incredibly close to his mother. She'd encouraged his dream of becoming a psychologist. That dream began when he'd discovered how much he wanted to know about the human psyche and why people acted the way they acted. Why had his father been such a monster when he'd literally had the world at his fingertips?

Neilson Anderson had come from an incredible loving family who encouraged each other to reach for their dreams. They weren't handed things on a silver platter, but were expected to earn them. Neilson had wanted it all for free, and when he hadn't gotten what he'd demanded he'd decided to punish his family over and over again. The main victims had been his children, who'd been deprived of a life with their family. They were now making up for lost time.

Finn was the oldest of the brothers, and he'd had the roughest life. Their father had taken out a lot of his anger on him. He'd also shouldered the burden of caring for his younger siblings. He was now a happily married man to Brooke with twin daughters he couldn't possibly love any more than he did. All of the family loved them immensely.

Noah had been a bit of a lone wolf with his dreams of design. He'd been by Finn's side all of their lives and had held their family together. He too was married and happier than Crew had ever seen before. He'd almost blown it, though. Crew loved Noah's wife Sarah, and was glad Noah had pulled his head out of his ass.

Both Brandon who was married to Chloe, and Hudson who was with Daisy, were comedians, Brandon more than Hudson, but nonetheless they were goofballs. They hadn't witnessed nearly what the three older siblings had, growing up, and they'd used humor to try to bring light into the house when it was too dark. Crew had always enjoyed spending time with the youngest siblings.

And then there was Crew. He'd been the lone wolf brother. He'd always felt a bit like an outsider, sitting on the sidelines and observing while the rest of his family was action oriented. His mother had told him there was nothing wrong with taking time to analyze a situation. His other brothers were likely to act first and think later, while he was a man to think and think and think. She'd said that's why he was so special. He was sure she said that to each of her children.

Crew frowned when he thought about Damien. Having another brother was so new to him that he still had a difficult time accepting it. Neilson, the man who didn't deserve to be called their father, had lived two separate lives before Damien or Finn had been born. He'd had two women in his life, living about a hundred miles apart.

Crew's mother gave birth to Damien at the same time as Nielson's other woman gave birth to a child who died. Neilson had taken Damien, told Crew's mother he'd been killed, and given him to his other woman. Then he'd left the other woman and gone back to Crew's mom. None of them had found this out until recently. It was quite confusing and still a shock to all of them.

And now, on top of all of that, Damien had just gone through hell and back with some very high people on the food chain trying to frame him for money laundering. When was life going to be easy and normal? Probably never for them since they were a part of this elite family.

"Crew Anderson, I have a bone to pick with you." The booming voice echoed in Crew's kitchen as Joseph walked in, his eyes blazing. Crew smiled. The man was all talk. He might scare those who didn't know him, but his family knew he was a giant teddy bear who got tears in his eyes watching Disney movies with his grandchildren.

"I know, Uncle," Crew said. "I'm sorry I took so long to bring this to you."

"We all knew you were going through something, but none of us had a clue it was *this* big," Joseph thundered.

"Seriously, Crew? What in the hell were you thinking?" Finn asked, stepping in right behind Joseph.

"I've been telling him that for a week," Darla said with a smirk.

"I can't believe he told you first," Daisy said as she stepped in next beside her fiancé, Hudson. "Well, then again, you are pretty amazing, so I tell you things first too."

Daisy rushed up and hugged Darla. They were far more sisters than best friends, and Crew was happy his brother had found a woman he wanted to spend the rest of his life with. Crew was sure it wouldn't happen for him. He didn't stay interested long enough to make anything last.

Even as he had that thought his eyes sought out Darla's. She'd just let go of Daisy and turned to look at him. He wasn't sure what was written all over his face, but whatever it was made her tilt her head and study him. He didn't like feeling as if he was the patient on the couch and she was his doctor. He narrowed his eyes a bit, and she blew him a kiss and winked. He turned away with a little growl that shocked him. Her laughter at his back mocked him.

When he got her alone . . .

What? What exactly was he going to do? Nothing! He was more controlled than to act first, he reminded himself.

"I'm not shocked you're in a baby scandal," Brandon said as he moved into the room. "Leave it to the most conservative of our group to knock a woman up and run for the hills." Brandon laughed hard at his own words.

"Really, Brandon?" Crew said with a glare.

"That isn't what happened," Hudson said.

"Thank you," Crew told his brother, a bit shocked it was Hudson standing up for him.

"No problem," Hudson said before a sly smile flitted across his lips. Crew had thanked him too soon. "Nope, not with Crew. He just got freaky with a stripper and forgot to call in the morning."

Crew had to give Finn and Noah credit because their lips just twitched instead of outright laughing at Hudson's words. Brandon roared with laughter. Even Joseph's lips twitched before he turned away to hide it.

"Are the jokes finished? This is serious," Crew said in his best doctorly voice.

"The jokes won't be finished for a long time, but we can pause for a bit," Brandon said as if he was bestowing a great gift on his brother.

"Thanks so much," Crew told him.

"You're so welcome. Do you have anything better to drink than coffee? When I find out I have a lost niece out there I need something stronger than caffeine."

"Agreed," Hudson said.

Crew pulled out the Scotch and soda, and Joseph took over pouring drinks. Soon, they were all seated around his island as they looked through the letters that had come in.

"This is the last one?" Joseph asked, his tone now serious.

"Yes," Crew and Darla said together.

You have a five-year-old daughter, Crew, and if you ever want to see her, you'll pay us five million dollars. Tick tock, the clock is about to strike midnight.

"What have you found out?" Joseph asked.

"Nothing. Absolutely nothing. This was the last letter about a week ago. I haven't heard a thing since."

"Then how in the hell are you supposed to pay?" Joseph thundered.

"I'm not paying a dime," Crew said, his eyes narrowing.

"Fine, then I'll pay," Joseph said.

"I don't even know if I have a kid," Crew said. "Darla and I did a lot of research and I looked into my past. There's only one slight possibility from that time frame as I told you on the phone. I can't even remember the woman's name. I don't know if she was part of the conference or simply in the bar. I have no idea how to even find her. There won't be video tapes from that long ago, and I have no idea if there are records."

Crew was pacing as he spit out his words.

"I think the first thing we need to do is get a list of all of the attendees and guests at the conference. Then we can get pictures and maybe something will jog your memory. We don't need to wait for these extorters. We can jump into action," Finn said.

"Yes!" Joseph shouted so loudly everyone jumped. "I have just the man to track and trace every single person at the conference."

"Who's that?" Crew asked.

"You've met him. Just call him Brackish," Joseph said with a grin.

Crew knew a little about Brackish. They all knew a little about him. Joseph wasn't good on the secret front, not when it came to his family.

When Katherine had been attacked last year, Joseph had gone out of his mind with worry and wanted action taken. Suddenly things were happening, and problems were being solved. Chad Reddington, who was married to their cousin, Bree, had shown up at a paintball event with five men who looked as if they'd stepped off an AH-64E Apache Guardian Helicopter.

It hadn't taken Crew much probing to find out Joseph had a Special Ops team he and several of the Andersons were funding. Crew had insisted on being in. Any team that was willing to fight crime and take down the bad guys was a team he wanted to be part of.

"Well, I guess having Brackish help could've saved a ton of sleepless nights," Crew said with a sigh.

"Who's Brackish?" Darla asked.

"A friend of the family," Crew quickly said. "He's a computer genius."

"Why in the heck didn't you talk to him before?" Darla asked in exasperation.

"I didn't think about it," Crew said. "The Anderson world is still new for me and my brothers."

"That's for dang sure. I'm getting real used to having a private jet at my disposal though," Brandon said.

"Hell yeah," Hudson agreed.

"You do realize you've always been Andersons, right?" Daisy said with a laugh.

"Yeah, but Anderson a common name. It's only been a few years that we've been *those* Andersons," Brandon said. "I don't mind it a bit." He leaned back and took a sip of his drink.

"You're so full of crap. We were perfectly happy before," Crew said. "But it is very nice to have family so willing to step up and help."

"Don't knock being one of *those* Andersons," Joseph said with a laugh. "I've gotten used to the little smirk you guys use with that word. But *those* Andersons work their asses off to get what they want in life, and that's pretty impressive in my book."

"You do realize only we can say *those* Andersons, right, Uncle? You're *the* Anderson of *those* Andersons."

Joseph boomed with laughter. It was good to see he wasn't irritated with Crew anymore. The man loved his family, all of his family. He might get mad at them at times, but he'd still go to bat for them. It was a good feeling to know there was always someone who had their backs, no matter what.

"Let me call Brackish. We can have this situation solved within days," Joseph said as he lifted his phone.

They were all quiet as Joseph spoke to Brackish. They waited when he hung up. No one said a word, but Joseph was beaming as he held up his glass.

"It's done. Now let's make a toast. We either get a new family member, or we put this behind us. Either way, I'll kick your ass, Crew, if you ever hold something this big back from your family again."

All of Crew's brothers laughed at Joseph's words.

"Okay, I'll agree to an ass-kicking," Crew said as he shrugged.

They toasted. And as Crew lifted the glass to his lips, his eyes sought out Darla again, and he was more than pleased when their gazes collided. They had some unfinished business to attend to and as much as he loved his family, he wanted them all out of his house ASAP. He wanted to get Darla alone.

Maybe there was one more problem he could solve tonight.

His thoughts must've shown in his eyes because hers widened before she looked away. It was the first time they'd played chicken and she'd been the one to blink. His body stirred. What was he going to do next? He'd soon find out.

Chapter Four

Darla was sitting at a table enjoying a warm summer day outside with her best friend. Since Daisy had gotten engaged to Hudson Anderson, Darla didn't get to see her as much as she was used to. She sighed to herself but couldn't blame it all on Daisy. For the past couple weeks Darla had either been working or with Crew Anderson.

Daisy was the single best person Darla had ever known. She was kind, considerate, and always thought about others before herself. She was out to save the world, and nothing was going to stop her. It inspired Darla, making her want to be less selfish.

"How's the school project coming along?" Darla asked. "I know it's only been a couple weeks, but it feels like a year since we last talked."

Daisy beamed at her. She'd been glowing since she'd stopped fighting her feelings for Hudson, and Darla truly believed they were going to go to the finish line together.

"I've been dying to meet up with you for the last two days. You'll never believe what Hudson did," Daisy said.

"Hmm, do I get three guesses?" Darla asked. Before Daisy could answer, the waitress stopped and took their orders.

"Nope, I don't have enough patience for guesses this time," Daisy told her when they were alone again. "He moved the farmhouse to the school grounds." Tears spilled over Daisy's eyes.

"Wait? What?" Darla exclaimed.

"He moved my childhood home to the school grounds and made it into a museum!" Daisy was beaming.

Daisy's grandfather had sold the land that had been in Daisy's family for three generations to Hudson. Darla had a feeling Daisy's gramps had been matchmaking with Joseph Anderson. If Darla hadn't thought the match was so dang perfect she never would've gone along with them. But from the first time Darla had met Hudson Anderson she'd absolutely loved the man and knew he was perfect for her best friend.

The two of them had started off a bit rocky after a plane ride and some serious hanky-panky, but in the end it had been a match made in heaven.

"When did this happen?" Darla asked. "I'm going to kill Crew for not telling me."

"Hudson didn't tell Crew. He did it all on his own and surprised me two days ago. I was so sad when Gramps moved into the senior community and I walked inside our empty home. I started crying and wrapped myself in Hudson's arms. He promised me it was all going to be okay, but I couldn't stop crying. I knew the farmhouse had to come down for Hudson to continue his project, and it was killing me. But he'd already planned it all. He'd hired a house-moving company the month before and they got it moved to the school grounds in two days. There are framed newspaper articles on the walls from different projects that both my parents and I have done through the years. He told me there was plenty of space for me to add to the museum."

Daisy was crying all over again, happy tears streaming down her flushed cheeks.

"I don't even know what to say about that," Darla said. "That might be the single most romantic and thoughtful thing I've ever seen done for a woman."

"I know! I can't believe it myself," Daisy said. "I love this man so much. I want him to live every dream he's ever had. And what's an absolute miracle is he feels the same toward me. He believes in what I believe in just because he loves me. He's not only stood by my side as I've fought for the school, but he quietly slips in once in a while and brings his own magical touch to the project."

"I never would've thought you'd be happy with an Anderson billionaire, but it's easy to see how in love you are. I couldn't be happier for the two of you," Darla told her.

"I know. You've liked him from day one even when I was irritated with you for it," Daisy said with a laugh. "Sometimes it's easier to look at something from the outside than when you're in the situation."

"That's for dang sure," Darla said.

Their drinks and soup arrived and they took a moment to have a taste. This place had become their favorite ever since Hudson had brought Daisy there on a date, and then Daisy had brought Darla. It overlooked the river, giving them a view of activities all around them and the happy noise of people enjoying beautiful weather.

"Now," Daisy said with a mischievous smile, "why don't you tell me what in the heck is going on with Crew."

Darla held her hands in the air and laughed. "Don't get that gleam in your eyes, Daisy," Darla insisted. "I'm not going to lie. Crew Anderson is one helluva hot tamale, but the man has issues, serious issues. The chemistry between us is hot enough to power up a small city, but that means it will be even more disappointing if I try to do anything about it."

"I don't know, Dar. Being in the room with the two of you is hot enough to make me sweat. I've never seen you act this way around a man. You're always confident and ready to make men sweat, but this is the first man I've seen who's made *you* sweat," Daisy pointed out.

"I know! It's absolutely driving me crazy," Darla admitted.

"Why don't you do something about it?" Daisy asked.

Darla leaned back as the waitress came closer. "Can I get you two anything else?"

"No thank you," Daisy said.

"Yes!" Darla practically shouted. "Can you get me a double Bloody Mary. Make it strong and you'll be my best friend."

"Sure thing," the waitress said with a laugh. "I've had a few of those days myself."

"Amen," Darla said while Daisy chuckled.

"Well, when in Rome. Make that two," Daisy told the waitress.

"I'll put in a rush order," the waitress told them with a wink.

"Okay, spill all. What's making us drink doubles for lunch?" Daisy asked.

"The man's driving me absolutely insane. After our meeting yesterday, I could see how intense he was being, and for the first time I can remember, I totally chickened out."

"What are you talking about?" Daisy asked.

"I totally ran from the house before the last of the Andersons left. You and Hudson had to make a quick exit because of your appointment, but then I rushed away while Joseph and two of Crew's brothers were still there. I could see by the light in his eyes that something was going to happen. I'd seriously been goading him all day, well, actually for a couple of weeks to be truthful, and then when I felt as if he was going to do something about it, I ran like a little girl."

"You ran?" Daisy exclaimed.

"Here's the drinks. The bartender says he's on standby if you need more," the waitress said as she set the large glasses in front of them.

"You're a goddess," Darla told her. "Check back in five minutes."

The waitress laughed as she walked to another table. "So . . . don't leave me hanging. What happened after you ran away?" Daisy asked as she took a sip of her drink.

"He texted me," Darla said.

"What did he say? Why in the world are you dragging this out?" Daisy exclaimed.

"Partly because I'm nervous, which totally confounds me, and partly because I . . . I . . . well, hell, I love it," she admitted.

"Spill all now, or I'm taking back your best friend status," Daisy informed her.

Darla handed over her phone.

Daisy gasped.

Why did you run away, Darla?

I didn't run away, I had another appointment.

Liar. I think you didn't want to carry through with what you've been taunting me with for the past two weeks.

I have no problem carrying through on anything, cowboy.

Prove it. Come back right now . . .

"This is from Crew?" Daisy asked.

"Yep, from Crew. And I stopped answering, unsure what to say next. What in the hell should I do now?" Darla asked.

"I think you should go get your freak on," Daisy told her.

"Who in the hell are you, and what have you done with my best friend?" Darla asked.

"I don't know. I'm just having the best sex in my life, and I want everyone to experience it, I guess," Daisy told her with a shrug.

Both of the girls were a bit mystified when the waitress appeared again, and they found their glasses empty. "Do you want a refill?" she asked.

"Why not?" Darla said with a shrug.

"Sure," Daisy confirmed.

"I guess we better order an Uber and stay a while," Darla said.

"Nah, I'll just text Hudson, tell him he's going to get very lucky, and ask if he can also pick up our car," Daisy said as she lifted her phone.

"Tell him not to come for at least an hour," Darla said, feeling much better now that she was sitting there with her best friend.

"I'm going to tell him to make it two. We might need to order some nachos and sit a while."

"That's true. You can't really have Bloody Marys and skip the nachos," Darla told her.

The two women giggled as Darla's phone dinged.

"That one was yours," Daisy told her.

"Did you just text Hudson?" Darla asked.

"Yep, and he said no problem, but your phone just went off."

Darla lifted her phone then felt her cheeks heat. "Oh my gosh. What do I do?"

Daisy took the phone from her best friend and her own cheeks heated. "Say hell yes," Daisy told her.

"I'm going to need another drink," Darla said just as their waitress appeared with their second round. "And some nachos." Their waitress laughed as she put in their order.

Then Darla looked at her phone again.

I'll be the one picking you up. This time there's no escape.

"Hot damn. Let's have another drink and then maybe jump into the river," Daisy said. "It's a good thing I have Hudson or I'd seriously be jealous of you right now."

"I'm going to admit that I was a little jealous when you and Hudson were first together. The way he looked at you was something I'd dreamed of my entire life," Darla told her.

"What do you mean?" Daisy asked.

"I don't want to change who I am to make a man love me. I want to be strong and confident and in control. But I want a man to not be afraid of me. You're more like me than you realize, yet Hudson was never afraid of you. He loved you from the start even if it scared him a bit, and he never saw your strength as a threat. I don't think I'll ever find that."

"Dar, I think you've found that with Crew," Daisy said as she reached across the table and took her best friend's hand.

"What if it's just the chemistry? What if it all falls apart once the chase wears off?" Darla asked in a rare moment of vulnerability.

"Holy cow, Dar, I love to see that you're actually human. I didn't think anything could penetrate your thick skin," Daisy told her.

"To tell you the truth, I didn't either," Darla said.

"Just be yourself and everything will work itself out," Daisy assured her.

"I don't think it's possible to be anything else. I've been like this too long," Darla said.

"Then let's sit back, enjoy the view, get a little tipsy and wait to be picked up by some very sexy men," Daisy suggested.

"That might be the best idea you've ever had," Darla said.

Their nachos arrived and they ordered a third Bloody Mary.

Darla wasn't sure what was coming next, but she wasn't too worried about it. The drinks helped, but the message from Crew helped even more. That man had her head spinning and her body on fire. What did that mean? What was coming next?

Chapter Five

The second Hudson had texted Crew asking if he wanted to help get Daisy and Darla safely home, he'd called his brother and asked what in the hell was going on.

Hudson laughed. "It seems Daisy and Darla have decided to have a Bloody Mary lunch and now they need picked up and Darla's car to be driven home," Hudson said. "I called Brandon first but he's busy. I can try Finn next. Daisy rarely lets go and I'm very much looking forward to some afternoon delight," Hudson said with a chuckle.

"You really are in love," Crew said, a bit in awe at how much his brother loved his fiancée.

"I'd walk across coals or nails, or through a firing squad, the dessert, or across an iceberg to be with her," Hudson said with complete seriousness. "I don't know how I survived without her this long."

"Damn. I'm truly happy for you, brother. That's fantastic," Crew told him.

"So, does that mean you're in?" Hudson asked.

"I'm in. I'll take Darla and her car home," Crew said. He had to keep the eagerness out of his voice. He hoped like hell she wasn't too drunk by the time they got there. The woman had been driving him crazy for weeks now and he wanted to take her home and see if she really wanted what she'd been offering.

He knew it was probably a mistake. Hell, she was the best friend of his brother's fiancée, but she was on his mind 24/7. With all of the stress he'd been feeling the past few months, having Darla in the room with him was like taking in a deep breath after not breathing for days. How could he allow her to escape without fighting for her? He couldn't.

He'd been pacing in front of his house for five minutes when his brother arrived.

"Are you okay?" Hudson asked.

"I'm fine. I'm waiting to hear back from Brackish, but other than that I'm great," Crew told him.

"I don't know. You've been off for a while, but yesterday I saw something shift. I figured it's because you finally let us all in. Now, I'm not so sure," Hudson said.

"I like Darla," Crew blurted out.

There was total silence after that statement. Crew waited for the laughter. When none came, he turned and looked at his brother.

"Hot damn, that's amazing," Hudson said. "Darla's an incredible woman. I can't believe I didn't think of the two of you together, but now that you mention it, I can't think of a more perfect couple. She's so confident, full of fire, and probably the only woman on the planet who can pull you out of your damn suits and ties and make you laugh. This is amazing. I'm so glad I called you instead of Finn."

"Don't get too excited," Crew warned. "I like her, I'm not offering to marry her."

"Yeah, that's what Finn, Noah, Brandon and I all thought too," Hudson said with a laugh. "Once these women sucked us in, it was all over. I think Mom's up in heaven sitting beside the Fates and pulling our strings."

"I don't believe in magic," Crew said. "I'm a scientist."

"Hell, Crew, I've always been a pretty logical person myself, but from the moment I met Daisy, she consumed me body, heart, and soul. I think that proves there's a little bit of magic in the world. For four out of five brothers to fall so madly in love with these incredible women has to prove something," Hudson said.

"It could just be lust," Crew said, clinging to some semblance of sanity. Besides that, he could be taking on a daughter soon. He wouldn't have time for anything serious.

"Or it could be love and lust mixed together. What's better than that?" Hudson asked.

Crew didn't answer. They pulled into the parking lot by the restaurant, stepped from the vehicle, and walked around to the outside patio. Crew heard Darla's laughter ringing out across the river, and he felt the twist in his gut and the stirring in his blood he always felt at the sight and sound of her.

"Yep, you have it bad. Just accept it and deal with it as best you can. I'm not going to push you because I didn't want to be pushed. I'm just going to tell you that it'll all work out in the end. Be patient and hope for the best while she puts you through hell," Hudson told him while laughing.

Crew followed his brother onto the back patio. Daisy jumped up at the sight of them and slid into Hudson's arms. "Mmm, you smell amazing," she said as she kissed his neck.

"You're my dream woman," he replied. He kissed her a little longer than comfortable for the people around them. Then he pulled back and the two of them grinned at each other like lovestruck teenagers.

Darla stood, her eyes slightly glassy, her lips turned up in a smile. "Hello, cowboy. Are you here to give me a ride?"

And just like that Crew was rock solid and ready to haul her over his shoulder, take her to any secluded place he could find, and give her the ride she'd been taunting him with for weeks.

"I sure am," he said, looking deep in her incredible green eyes. She was obviously buzzed, but there was no doubt in his mind she was reading his message loud and clear. He wanted to give her a ride for sure, and it had nothing to do with her car.

For the first time since he'd known her she seemed speechless. He sort of liked that. He liked taking her breath away. He pulled out his wallet and threw a few hundred dollar bills down on the table, figuring that would cover their check, then held out his arm. "Are you ready to leave?"

"Mmm, okay," she said, accepting his arm. A tingle of electricity surged between them.

"You got Darla and her car?" Hudson asked as they walked from the patio.

"Yep, you worry about getting your fiancée home," Crew said as he kept Darla close to his side.

"I'll get right on that," Hudson said. Both Darla and Daisy giggled as they made their way toward the parking lot.

Crew was tense as Darla clung to his side and the two of them approached her car. His hand fluttered over her back as he opened the passenger door and helped her inside. She looked up, grinning, as if she was quite pleased with where she was.

"Where's the horse?" she asked. He stood there confused.

"At home," he told her.

She giggled. "When you rescue a woman, you're supposed to come riding up on a white horse with your shield and sword," she told him.

Crew couldn't help himself, he laughed. Sober Darla was like a burst of sunshine on a rainy day. Drunk Darla was even more infectious.

"I'll remember that the next time," Crew assured her. Then he carefully closed her door, making sure all of her limbs were safely inside the vehicle.

He came around to the driver's side and slipped into the too-small vehicle. After making some adjustments, he started it and began driving. He nearly jumped out of the seat when Darla reached over and ran her painted nails along his thigh.

"Are you trying to get us in an accident?" he asked, his voice tight. Her fingers were moving dangerously close to the bulge in his pants.

"I'm just fascinated by the sparks that fly off of you," she told him. She was looking over at his leg, her face curious as she made a pattern on his thigh.

"Yeah, I'm pretty damn curious about that myself," he said, his voice a low growl he didn't recognize.

"It's fascinating. I've felt attraction before, but with you, it's as if I'm getting hit by lightning over and over again whenever we're in touching distance." She was saying the words like she was a scientist trying to figure out a complicated formula.

"Do you have any theories on that?" he asked. Those slim fingers moved an inch from his throbbing arousal and he had to be very careful not to slam his foot down on the gas pedal as his leg twitched. He should move her hand away before they had an accident, but he couldn't bring himself to do that. Instead, he reached down and took her fingers in his, entwining their hands and resting them on his leg. She didn't fight him.

"No. I was talking to Daisy about it, and she thinks we should just get naked and sweaty," Darla said so matter-of-factly, he jerked a bit. He quickly gained control of the vehicle while letting out a little swear word.

"I'm thinking that wouldn't be such a bad idea," he told her.

"I'm afraid the second clothes come off though, whatever this is will simply fizzle and die," she told him.

"I don't see that happening," Crew said, very sure the sparks they set off would increase not diminish when they were together as one.

"I've felt attraction before. I've even felt sparks while I'm kissing a man, but when it gets a little hot and heavy it suddenly fizzles and dies," she told him.

The thought of her being naked with another man made him want to put his fist through a wall. What in the hell was wrong with him? "I think I'm broken," she quietly added. Those words stopped what he'd been about to say.

"What are you talking about?" he asked as he squeezed her hand.

"I think I'm broken," she repeated. "I can't . . . um . . . well, this kind of sucks to admit, but I can't really achieve orgasms." She finished the words while looking down at her lap.

This confident, self-assured woman who swept the rug out from beneath him on a continuing basis was insecure in the bedroom? It didn't make sense to him.

"Did some asshole tell you you're broken?" he gasped after several seconds of stunned silence.

"Yeah, I've been told I'm all talk and no action," Darla said with a shrug. "In a couple cases, I can't really blame them. I do come across pretty wrecking-ball style, but then I get all of these thoughts in my head and pull from the moment, and well, then I lose interest in what we're doing."

Crew laughed. The sound seemed to shock her. She looked up at him, her beautiful face turned, her eyes curious.

"What?" she asked.

"If you check out during sex it's because your partner's doing a piss-poor job," Crew said.

She grinned at him, that sparkle he'd come to know and admire back in her eyes. "Are you saying I wouldn't check out with you?" she challenged.

"Baby, I guarantee you that not only will you not check out, but you'll have multiple orgasms," he promised her. "I've never been a slacker. I believe in hard work, and in lots of pleasure, so my skills in the bedroom will exceed your expectations." His arousal was now pulsing as he pressed down on the accelerator, wanting to get her home.

She seemed to consider his words as if they were in the middle of a business deal. Crew wasn't exactly a stranger to drawing clear lines before jumping into bed with a woman, but this felt odd with Darla. He didn't want to plan something out with her, he wanted to push her up against a wall and make her scream over and over again.

"I don't know. You're pretty clinical," she said after a moment. "And you don't even like to mess up your hair."

He pulled up to a light then turned and gave her a glare. "I can mess up my hair," he insisted.

"Hmm, there's not a strand out of place right now," she pointed out.

"There's nothing wrong with caring about your appearance," he said.

"I care about my appearance too, but I like to get messy," she countered.

"I'll take great pleasure in messing *you* up," he growled. The light changed and they surged forward. Darla laughed again.

"Am I getting under your skin, Crew Anderson?" she asked.

It was his turn to laugh. "Darla, you've been under my skin from the first moment we met," he said honestly.

"Maybe it's time you get into my skin then," she said with a wink.

Hudson slammed his foot down on the accelerator. They were close to home, and he was more than ready to show this woman what all of her bold talk had been doing to him.

Darla chatted about her and Daisy's lunch for the last ten minutes of their drive, and she didn't blink when he pulled up to his house. She simply climbed from the car and wobbled a bit on her feet.

"Coffee," he said as he took her arm and pulled her toward his front door.

"I was thinking another Bloody Mary would be nice," she said with a giggle.

"Nope. I want you right there with me when I take you to my bed," he insisted. "And I *am* taking you to my bed. This teasing has reached its crescendo."

"Oh, really. What if the coffee changes my mind?" she challenged as they stepped into his kitchen. He started the coffee, then grabbed her, pulling her tight.

"Trust me, nothing's going to change your mind. What's going to happen is a lot of screaming and pleasure," he assured her.

Her eyes flared at his words, and Crew decided he'd talked long enough. He needed a taste of her while her coffee brewed — just one little taste.

He leaned down and took her lips, the sparks between them zapping all over his body as he traced his tongue along her bottom lip. She groaned against his mouth as she stretched her body out and lifted her arms, her fingers tangling in his hair.

He deepened the kiss, his tongue caressing her mouth as his hands ran up and down her back before settling on the sweet curve of her ass. He tugged her closer, pressing his pulsing arousal against her sweet core while he lifted a leg up and pushed her back against the counter. He was going to taste every sweet inch of her body.

He was rethinking taking the time to sit and drink coffee.

Suddenly, though, Darla pulled back from him, her eyes going wide, her skin turning a little green.

"Uh-oh," she said as her body twitched.

"What's wrong?" he panted.

"I'm going to be sick," she told him.

His desire instantly deflated as concern washed over him. He went right into action and lifted her in his arms as he rushed to his bathroom. They barely made it in time before Darla bent over the toilet and made some very unladylike sounds.

Crew stepped from the bathroom and grabbed a washcloth from his linen closet, then came back inside as Darla leaned against the rim of the toilet and groaned — and not in pleasure.

He wet the washcloth with cool water, then sat on the floor next to her and brushed it against her heated face.

"I'm so mortified," she said.

He chuckled. "Well, Darla, nothing's been normal since the two of us met, so this shouldn't be any different," he told her. He was shocked at how calm he was. He liked being with this woman; he liked taking care of her.

The cloth grew warm and he stood and rinsed it off just as she turned and let go of more of her stomach contents. He decided it was far wiser for him not to see what was coming out of her so he focused on washing her face between bouts of throwing up.

When she seemed stable, he helped her rinse her mouth out and brush her teeth, then he lifted her and carried her through his house, straight to his room. He set her on his bed and removed her shoes.

"This wasn't how I envisioned you coming to my bed, but at least I got you here," he said as he rubbed her face again.

"My stomach feels as if a nest of rats moved inside and have set up a fight ring," she said with a groan as she tossed on his bed.

"You'll feel better soon. I'll get you some Sprite and crackers."

"I'm sorry, Crew. You're stuck with me right now because there's no way I can drive," she told him.

"I'm glad you're here and not alone," he insisted.

She opened her glassy eyes and gazed at him, wonder in her expression. "Who are you?" she wondered aloud.

"This is what anyone should do," he said, brushing her words aside.

"But not everyone would, especially when I did this to myself," she told him.

"We do all sorts of crappy things to ourselves. It doesn't mean we shouldn't have someone ready to help us pick up the pieces."

She leaned back and closed her eyes and Crew left the room. He put Sprite and ice in his favorite Yeti cup so it would stay cold for hours, then grabbed crackers. By the time he made it back to his room, she was fast asleep on his bed.

He gazed at her a while, wondering why he wasn't upset, why he was so content to take care of her. Maybe because she'd been taking care of him for weeks as he tried to solve the puzzle of whether he had a child or not.

He set her items on the nightstand next to her, then carefully pulled off her jeans, taking note of her silky red panties before covering her up. Now wasn't the time to ogle the poor woman. Then he changed into sweats and an old college tee, grabbed his laptop, and climbed into the bed next to her so he could do some work while keeping his eye on her.

That wasn't how he'd planned to spend his afternoon, but he found he didn't mind it at all. What in the heck was this woman doing to him? Was it too late to stop it? It most likely was. At this point, he might as well just enjoy the ride the two of them were on. He wasn't sure he'd be able to get off anyway, not at this point — maybe not at any point.

Chapter Six

Crew shot awake, turned his head, and looked at the nightstand. The clock read 4:06 AM. He shook the cobwebs from his brain and was shocked when he realized he'd been asleep for at least ten hours.

Unlike his brothers, Crew enjoyed a solid night's rest. Letting his brain reset seven or eight hours made for a far more productive day. Too many people worried they were sleeping their lives away. The true tragedy was people who were only half awake. How productive could someone be if they were only half there mentally?

Still, he never slept for ten hours.

Crew was warm and comfortable other than his overly full bladder. Even though he'd fallen asleep at about six the night before, he didn't want to move, not when he had Darla's body wrapped around his.

She shifted in her sleep, her leg rubbing along his, waking up the rest of his body. She murmured something in her sleep, then snuggled her face a bit more against his neck, her lips whispering on his skin.

He froze.

Was she awake?

She murmured something else, shifted once more, and a tiny adorable snore escaped her mouth. Nope. She was definitely sleeping. He really liked that she wanted to be close to him in her most vulnerable moments. She might be a flirt, but she still had a bit of armor around her when she was with him or others — everyone except her best friend, Daisy.

In her sleep she was all his. She couldn't get close enough to him it seemed. He lay there for several more minutes enjoying the little sounds she emitted while she slept.

He'd stayed over with women before, sleeping in the same bed. He didn't go into relationships just for sex. He wanted them to have something in common, to be able to have a conversation at dinner, and be able to sleep in the same bed. He preferred to sleep alone, but he hadn't minded sharing a bed.

He'd never quite shared one like this before, though, and he realized he'd never had a woman stay at *his* house. When he'd stayed with women in the past, they'd each maintained their half of the bed, not crawled on top of each other. Once the sex was over, they'd each turn and go to sleep. The next morning, their days went on in their solo ways.

He wasn't sure what made Darla so different from other women in his life. He just knew he was drawn to her, and she seemed to be drawn to him as well.

He finally had to rise. She grumbled in her sleep as he reluctantly walked away from the bed. He moved into his bathroom and took a long, hot shower, shaking the cobwebs from his brain. When he dressed and stepped back into his room he found Darla sitting up in the bed.

He wasn't sure what to expect from her as their gazes met.

"Well, good morning, cowboy," she said as she stretched out her arms. "I guess yesterday didn't quite go as planned." Her deep, throaty chuckle at the end of her words left him speechless. He wanted to strip off the clothes he'd just put on, climb back into his bed, and make both of them so sated they'd never want to leave the warmth of his blankets again.

"What did you have planned?" he finally asked.

"I don't know if I had a clear plan, but I know it didn't include drinking too much, then puking, then passing out," she told him with a shrug. "I guess things happen."

Crew stared at her for a moment. He never knew what to expect from this woman. She was such a refreshing breath of fresh air in a world full of games and lies.

"Yes, sometimes the real world has a way of kicking us in the ass," he told her. He found he wouldn't mind waking up next to this woman on a daily basis. That scared the crap out of him.

"My mouth tastes as if a swarm of locusts dove in and died, and my body is all achy," she told him with a frown. She quickly smiled again. "And I feel as if I could eat a gourmet meal I'm so dang hungry. I hope you're planning to feed me."

Crew laughed — hard. She wasn't in the least embarrassed about the situation. She also didn't seem to be at all disturbed to find herself waking up in his bed. She was still dressed in her shirt and panties, and it was pretty obvious nothing had happened between them, but he'd still expected her to be at least a bit uncomfortable. But nope, not this woman.

"I can make some food if you want to use my shower," he told her. "I'll drop off a toothbrush on the bed while you're in there too."

"How about some clothes?" she asked. He looked at her petite frame. Her lower half was covered, but he didn't see any of his clothes fitting her.

"Um, I guess I could try to find something while you shower," he finally said.

"A pair of sweats and tee would be great as long as there's a tie on them. I could wash my clothes and change before I have to do the walk of shame." She paused. "Or I guess the drive of shame."

Crew laughed again. "Is it still a drive of shame if we didn't have sex?" he asked, sort of shocked he was standing there joking with her.

She cocked her head to the side as if she was really thinking about his words. "Only if someone sees me, I guess. I'd assume a couple got down and dirty if I saw a woman crawling away early in the morning," she told him.

"Then I guess you'll just have to stay for the day so you aren't slinking out of here," he said. He didn't want her to go. It was nearly five in the morning now and the day was only just beginning.

"What would we do for the day?" she asked.

He thought quick. "Maybe you can help me with the horses. I know nothing about them and you seem to know a lot."

Her eyes lit up. "Yes, that sounds wonderful. Okay, get out of here and wrestle up some clothes and some food while I shower.

Don't forget the toothbrush. The locust taste won't go away without some strong mouthwash and paste."

Crew laughed as he walked from his room to get the toothbrush. When he came back she was already in the bathroom and he could hear the shower running. He instantly hardened as he went into his closet and tried to find something that wouldn't fall off of her petite frame.

After some digging he found an old pair of college sweats that still had ties and a tee that would hang on her, but not too ridiculously. He whistled as he set the items on the bed then made his way to his kitchen and began pulling things from the fridge.

Crew wasn't even close to being a great cook. But he enjoyed breakfast so he could make a few things that would sate at least one of their hungers. He mixed up pancakes, prepared a batch of cheesy scrambled eggs, and fried some bacon. He was finishing up when Darla walked into the room, her trademark smile on her lips.

Damn, she completely took his breath away. Even in his oversized clothes, she walked with confidence. Her eyes had a hungry glint in them, but this time he didn't think it had anything to do with him. She was gazing at the simple meal he'd prepared as if it were a gourmet feast. She snagged a piece of bacon and began munching on it while she poured herself a cup of coffee and dumped a generous amount of creamer in the cup.

"You are a god," she told him as she leaned on the counter and sipped the coffee. "I love the brews you have. They're always different and taste great."

"I like to try different brands from regions around the world," he said as he handed her a plate. "Dish up before it gets cold."

"You don't have to tell me twice," she assured him. She grabbed two pancakes, a large scoop of eggs, and five slices of bacon. It was a good thing he'd fried the entire pack. "I hate throwing up. I'm always ravenous the next day," she said after munching on another slice of bacon. He was shocked she didn't seem to have a hangover.

"I know what you mean. I had the flu last year and couldn't eat for two days. On the third day when all of the pain was gone, I ate an entire large pizza. I was bloated and moaning, but I had no regrets."

"Amen to that. I work dang hard so I take immense pleasure in food," she told him.

She sat at the kitchen island and lathered butter on her pancakes before dousing them with the maple syrup that was his favorite. It was from a little mom and pop place in Vermont that was literally called Mom and Pop's. He'd fallen in love when he'd visited the area several years earlier. He ordered it in bulk now and gave it as gifts.

"Delicious," Darla purred as she placed a piece of bacon on her pancake then scooped the syrupy bite into her mouth.

They chatted a bit more as they ate their breakfast, surprisingly eating all of the food he'd made — and it had been a lot. Darla scooped up her last bite, then laughed as she leaned back and rubbed her belly.

"I guess now I'm grateful for your baggy clothes. I'm stuffed and that was fantastic."

"I like breakfast so it's really the only food I cook decently. I do a lot of takeout for dinner," he told her.

"I'll make you dinner. I have a few dishes I'm super good at. Other than that, I don't like cooking much. When I'm stressed I enjoy baking. I make some killer cinnamon rolls."

"I love cinnamon rolls. I think you'll have to make them and let me judge if they're worthy of killer status," he told her, his mouth watering. He didn't see how that was possible with the amount of food the two of them had just consumed.

"That's a challenge I'm more than willing to take on," she said. She leapt down from her seat and took her plate to the sink before she grabbed his. She quickly washed their dishes, her cheeks slightly flushed from the heat of the water. Crew was fighting his desire to simply grab the woman and kiss her — again and again and again.

"Are you ready to see the horses?" she asked.

"They're probably hungry. My cousin sent some hands over the other day, but I need to hire my own people," he said.

"I like taking care of horses. You might just want to take it on yourself," she said as they left the house together and moved toward the barn.

"I'm gone a lot, and as long as they're here I'll take an active role in taking care of them, but I do need to have at least one fulltime person to make sure I don't kill them."

Darla laughed. She did that often and it was just one of the things he truly liked about the woman. The list of her assets was so long it would take all day to name them.

They stepped into the barn together, the smell of fresh hay quite nice. Walking in front of him, she immediately crooned at the horses who looked up at her with interest and a little suspicion. Her long, thick hair hung down her back, still damp from the shower, and even in baggy clothes she couldn't hide the gentle swell of her hips as she took steps forward. Even if the woman wore a potato sack, he'd be turned on.

"Where do you keep their feed?" she asked as she looked around.

"Over here," he told her, opening a door with enough supplies to take care of the horses for a couple of months, not that he'd have them that long. But he could give the new owners all of the items he'd bought.

Darla grabbed a wheelbarrow and began filling it with grain. "You grab some fresh hay," she said as she moved from the room, her scent sweeter than the hay he reached for. It was a good thing his hands were full.

He followed her from the room and smiled when the horses hung their heads from their stalls and nickered at them. They clearly knew what was in the wheelbarrow. The foals were with mama, and the large stallion was next to them, not looking too pleased to be separated from the other horses.

"You'll be okay, big guy," Darla said as she filled his bucket with grain. He sniffed at her as if he didn't believe her.

"Give him a nice armful of hay," she said as she looked back at Crew. He watched how easily she took care of the horses as if she'd done it a million times before.

It only took a minute to feed mama and the two foals, and Crew wondered what they'd do next. Darla put the wheelbarrow back then looked around with her hands on her hips.

"You're going to need a few cats," she said.

"I don't like cats," Crew told her. "I don't like having pets at all. They take too much time and I'm a busy man."

"If you want to be less busy, get some cats. I don't know why cats get such a bad rap for being independent, but they're amazing at keeping the mice out of your barn. You don't want mice sneaking into the grain and making a mess of the barn. Now that you have food in here, they'll quickly overrun it if you aren't careful. You'd do much better if you have at least three cats. You give them some food, but not too much or they'll get lazy. You also have to make sure you give them a little attention and they'll stay right here, happy and thriving, and be a true asset."

"But I won't have the horses long and then I'll have cats I have to take care of later," he argued.

"You keep telling yourself you won't have the horses long," Darla said as if she was simply humoring him.

"Maybe I can borrow some cats for now," he said thoughtfully.

"I've never heard of someone borrowing cats," Darla said with a laugh. "But I guess if you really do give up the horses, you could give the cats to your cousin. He has a large ranch. Or you could just keep them. Cats are very easy to have around."

"Ugh, taking these horses is already a pain in my ass," Crew said.

"If you think of it like that, you'll feel that way. Maybe you could try to think positive and actually enjoy it." Darla told him.

The sun was beginning to rise in the east and the darkness of night was turning to the grey of morning. It wouldn't take long for the entire area to light up. Right now, though, it felt as if they were in their own little universe.

"You always hear about kids wanting a pony for Christmas and crap like that. So, horses get abandoned all of the time because some clueless parent buys one, realizes how much work they are, and lets them go. Horses are a privilege; if you're loyal to them, they'll be loyal to you. Horses are used in therapy all over the world. They're very intuitive animals," Darla said.

"How do you know so much about horses?" Crew asked.

"I grew up with them. I even gave rodeoing a try, but I love my freedom. You're either all in with a rodeo or you might as well not waste your time."

"Ah, so that's why you always call me cowboy," he said with a laugh. "I can picture you at a rodeo, though I've never been to one."

She gaped at him as if that was the craziest thing she'd ever heard.

"How in the world have you lived so long without going to a rodeo?"

"I've always thought it was a waste of time. There are too many other things to do in life," he told her.

"Then it's my mission to take you to one. I'll find the nearest one that's coming up soon," she said.

"I'm good. I don't need to do that," he told her.

"Nope. We *have* to go. You can watch the barrel racing, which is what I did, but my favorite event is the bull riding. There's nothing hotter than a cowboy in chaps lasting for eight seconds," she told him with a wink.

"Eight seconds? That doesn't seem too impressive," he told her. And dammit, if her words hadn't hardened him again. But what in the world could this woman say that wouldn't make him hot and needy?

"Baby, when something's beneath you bucking and grunting, eight seconds is a long time to hold on," she said with a deep throated growl that had him close to dropping to his knees. He could guarantee he'd ride her longer than eight seconds. He couldn't wait to prove it.

Before he could respond to her bold statement, she moved to the stall of the beautiful stallion who was eyeing them both as if assessing whether to stomp them to death or not.

"Have you decided on a name for him yet?" Darla asked.

He moved closer to her and the horse. The stallion locked gazes with him, and Crew felt as if he'd been judged and had come up wanting.

"What do you think I should name him?" Crew asked. "Satan?"

Darla laughed. "You're not Satan, are you, boy?" she crooned. The horse shifted his head and looked at her, the demonic light in his eyes softening. He knew how the horse felt. This woman had a way of calming a male.

"He really is quite beautiful," Crew admitted. The stallion went back to eating his food, but he looked up often to keep an eye on the two of them.

"Yes, he's very handsome," Darla agreed. She reached through the bars and gave the horse a few pets on his smooth black hair. Crew was shocked the stallion allowed it. He wanted to do the same, but decided not to push it as Darla seemed to be bonding with the animal.

"He watches us as if he's law enforcement and about to place us under arrest," Crew said after another moment. The horse was definitely keeping his eye on both of them.

Darla laughed and the horse almost seemed to smile at her. The sound of her amusement was quite mesmerizing. "I think you've just come up with a name for him," she said.

"What? What name?" Crew asked.

"Sheriff," she said. "He does seem to be the boss of this barn so it's quite fitting."

Crew liked it. "I guess that's okay." Then he turned and looked at the mama horse who seemed more at ease after only a couple of days. "What about her?"

"Hmm, she's obviously a good mama," Darla began as she pulled her hand from Sheriff's stall, resting her fingers on the bar. He felt his hand itching to reach for hers, to feel the sparks that always ignited between them. It took a lot of willpower not to act.

"Why don't we call her Lucky? She's very lucky indeed to have been brought here," Darla told him after a moment.

"Isn't that pretty generic?" he asked.

"Not when it's true," she said.

"Then Lucky it is." Mama horse looked up and whinnied at them as he said it. "I guess you agree with your name." She nodded. Could the animal understand him?

Crew shook his head. What in the hell was wrong with him? He turned and looked at Darla who was beaming at him. It was her. It was always her. She made him act in ways he'd never thought of acting before.

He had to get out of the barn. Without another word, he turned and walked away. He was sure she'd follow. He just wasn't sure what he was going to do about it when she did.

Chapter Seven

Crew walked inside his house, knowing Darla wasn't far behind him. The two of them had to have a serious talk, there was no doubt about it. If they didn't do something about the chemistry between them, and damn soon, he feared he might lose his mind. It was close to happening now.

She stepped in the door just as his phone rang, the number blocked.

"Hello." He waited, not saying more.

"Hi, Crew, it's Brackish. Are you home?"

Crew laughed. "You tell me," he said.

Brackish chuckled. "Yeah, I know you're home, but it's polite to ask," Brackish told him. "Are you free?"

Crew rolled his eyes, something he never did. "Really?" he said.

"Yeah, I see your schedule's clear. I'll be there in thirty minutes." There wasn't a goodbye, the phone simply disconnected.

"What's going on?" Darla asked.

"That was Brackish. I assume he has information for me."

For a rare moment his mind wasn't focused on having sex with Darla. Tension rippled through his body.

"Did he give you any clues about what information he has?" Darla asked.

"Nope, no clues," Crew said.

"I hate waiting. I've never been good at that," Darla told him. She walked over to the coffee pot and made herself a new cup.

"Yeah, I'm usually very patient, but not in this matter," Crew said. He decided a cup of coffee was a good idea and followed Darla's example.

Now wasn't the time to talk about the two of them, so after their coffee was ready, they pulled out all of the information they had so far then sat and chatted while they waited.

Brackish knocked on his door thirty minutes later and Crew was quick to answer.

"It's good to see you," Brackish said as he walked inside with Crew. "I like your place. You could definitely use a security overhaul, but it's not critical yet."

"Can the average person break into my home, or just you?" Crew asked.

Joseph had challenged Brackish and his team to see if they could break into his fortress. They'd done it without breaking a sweat. Joseph had been horrified at how easily the men had done it. Granted, Brackish was a computer genius who could pretty much break into anything he wanted, but Joseph had taken pride in his former security system. Brackish had completely overhauled it. Now, his uncle's property was more secure than Fort Knox . . . really.

"The average criminal won't get in here, but thieves are getting smarter by the day," Brackish warned.

"I guess we'll have to look at the system then," Crew said.

"I don't want to keep you waiting," Brackish said. "It didn't take long to track down the woman you spent the night with at the hotel." He stopped as he pulled out some folders.

Both he and Darla looked over the information Brackish had found. Her name was Sandy Fountain. Darla raised her brows at that one and he shrugged. No wonder he'd been thinking about candy when he'd spoken to her. It should be a crime to name your child something like that, giving other kids plenty of opportunities to make fun of them.

Brackish had current pictures of her and details of her background.

"Does she have a child?" Crew asked.

Brackish shook his head. "She doesn't have any," he said after a moment. "Are you sure this is the only possibility?" he questioned.

Crew had spent a lot of time trying to recall any woman who could have his child, especially a three-to-six-year-old child. He hadn't trusted the note about the kid's age, wondering if they were telling the truth on that.

"I honestly don't see how it's possible. I don't have one-night stands . . . normally," he added after a pause, since he'd obviously had a one-night stand with Sandy.

"What about any other relationships in that period?" Brackish pushed.

"Do you know something?" Crew asked.

He'd had two other short relationships in that period, but he'd looked up both of those women and hadn't seen a child who could be his. One of them had a one-year-old, but there was no chance that was his. The other had no children he'd been able to find.

Brackish pulled out another folder and Crew felt his heart nearly beat out of his chest.

"These are the women I could find associated with you," Brackish said, pushing the folder over.

Crew took it, fidgeting in his seat with Darla next to him. He didn't want to open it and expose his past to this woman he was becoming more and more interested in. Would it change what she was feeling toward him? Would it change how he felt about her if her entire dating world was put on display in front of him? He honestly didn't know.

With a sigh, he opened the folder. There were a dozen women in the folder. He gaped as he looked at the names. Then he glanced up at Brackish who was making himself a cup of coffee and helping himself to a cookie on the counter.

"How in the heck did you find my middle school girlfriend? I forgot I even dated her. There definitely wasn't sex with her," Crew said. He knew of Brackish's abilities, but he was wondering if he truly had no clue what this man did. Brackish seemed able to find things that weren't possible to find.

"I can find anything," Brackish said. "Great cookie. Homemade?"

"No, I got them at the store, but I like them in a container," Darla answered. She'd brought all sorts of goodies to Crew's house when she started coming over to work on this case with him.

Crew looked at Darla as the two of them scanned the printouts on the women Crew had dated. Some he'd slept with, some he hadn't.

"What does this mean? Is there anyone on here I could have a child with?" Crew asked. His heart was thundering. This situation had been tearing him up for months. Why hadn't he come to his family sooner? He could've saved himself a lot of hell.

Brackish smiled as he pushed over one more folder. Crew was afraid of opening it. He couldn't read that smile on Brackish's face. He hadn't known the man long enough to know his expressions.

"Open the folder. It's killing me," Darla said. Crew could see her fingers itching to yank the tan folder from his hand.

He opened it to a picture of an older couple. Crew looked up with confusion. "Now, I can guarantee I haven't slept with *this* woman," he told both Brackish and Darla.

Brackish laughed hard, seeming very amused by this.

"You never know. You could be a cougar chaser," Brackish said.

Crew glared at him.

"Sorry. I had to," he told him as he polished off his third cookie. "This is Dennis and Heidi Robo." He stopped.

"Those names mean nothing to me," Crew said.

"I didn't think they would. But apparently they've been linked to a lot of scams for a lot of years. They've made a pretty decent living blackmailing people whether they have a nugget of truth or none at all. You happened to hit their radar," Brackish said.

"And?" Crew pushed.

"And . . . you don't have a long-lost child out there. If you'd come to me when you got your first note I would've found this and probably saved you a lot of sleepless nights," Brackish told him.

Crew felt a rush of emotion flow through him. Relief. Happiness. Despair. Anger. The emotions mixed and mingled, leaving him utterly exhausted.

"You're sure?" Crew asked.

"I'm one hundred percent sure," Brackish said.

Crew's eyes narrowed. "We can't let them keep doing this to people," he said, his fist slamming down on the counter.

"I fully agree. That's why the Washington police department received their very own folder listing all of their crimes with foolproof evidence. They were picked up this morning. It seems they also have committed a lot of check fraud as well. They're going to prison for a very, *very* long time," Brackish said.

"So, this is over?" Crew asked, almost unable to believe it.

"It's over," Brackish said.

"You don't look happy," Darla pointed out. They were both staring at him, wondering at his reaction.

"I don't know what I'm feeling," he said. "I've gone through a lot of emotions over the past few months, wondering if there was a child out there who needed me. The thought has been killing me. And then I knew I wasn't ready to be a dad, but at the same time, the thought of a child of mine out there and not being a part of her life has killed me. So, I guess right now I can't get my brain to switch over to the fact that I don't have a little girl needing me."

"Oh, Crew, I'm so sorry," Darla said, not caring that Brackish was there. She wrapped her arms around Crew and hugged him. He was glad for the embrace.

"You do realize you're not an old man. You could have a child the right way without any blackmail or shared custody," Brackish pointed out.

Darla let Crew go and he glared at Brackish. "Thanks for the advice," he said with sarcasm.

"No problem. I'm a man of many talents. I can hack a computer or soothe a male ego, whatever I'm called on for the day."

"I'll take your hacking abilities but pass on the personal advice," Crew said. "I know I should feel a lot more relief and maybe it'll kick in once all of this really sets in. But for now, I just feel a bit lost."

"Maybe Brackish is right. Maybe you feel as if you lost something you hadn't known you wanted," Darla said with understanding and something else in her eyes he wasn't quite sure how to read.

"Maybe," he said quietly. He wasn't sure who in the room was more shocked by those words, the two standing with him or himself. He hadn't had that urge to settle down and have kids, not with his job and all of the patients he spoke to on a regular basis, their lives ruined by bad marriages, bad parents, or even bad children. Why would he take a chance on that?

As he had that thought, he looked at Darla, a flush stealing through him. She was safe. She was the kind of woman he could trust. She wasn't into games, and she wasn't someone who'd hide her thoughts or feelings.

"I can see the two of you want to be alone," Brackish said with a chuckle. "I'll see myself out. But remember, the next time you need me, try to make it more of a challenge. This was far too easy."

Crew should thank the man, but he was completely captured by Darla at that moment. What did all of this mean for the two of them? They heard Brackish walk away, the sound of his laughter trailing behind as he left.

"What's next?" Crew asked Darla when they were alone.

"What do you want to be next?" she asked, turning the decision around on him.

"I don't want you to go," he said.

"Good. I don't like playing games, and I want to stay," she said. Heat once again surged through him.

"But what excuse shall we use to keep you here?" he finally asked, a smile returning to his lips. Darla threw back her head and laughed. It was several seconds before she met his gaze.

"Well, it can't be just because we like being together," she said, lifting a finger to her lips as if she was really thinking. "Maybe it's a good thing you got those horses, because I'm a horse whisperer, and you aren't. I better teach you how to take care of your animals."

His grin grew. "Maybe I'll keep them after all," he said, feeling lighter than he had in a while.

Her grin shifted, and he saw the teasing light in her eyes grow more intense. He waited, finding himself holding his breath for what she was going to say next.

"Then maybe we'll talk about those babies you seem to want," she told him. She winked as he felt the color in his cheeks quickly drain. She turned and left him standing speechless in his kitchen.

Now *her* laughter trailed behind as she walked from the kitchen. He should tuck tail and run as fast as he possibly could. But he found the only place he wanted to run was after her.

Crew was thinking he should simply follow his instincts, get the woman, and throw all rational thought out the window. He smiled.

Chapter Eight

Darla leaned against the fence and watched the horses frolic in the field. The older ones were still leery, but they were adjusting much better than she'd expected they would. That told her they'd been far more neglected than abused. An abused horse could take a very long time to heal, but they were worth the extra effort.

Before long Crew walked up to her. She'd felt him coming before she'd heard a sound. She'd never been so in tune with a man. Yes, she was flirty with him and bolder than normal, though she *was* a confident woman. But something really drew her to Crew.

That was why she hadn't gone home all day. The two of them had worked with the horses for a few hours after Brackish had dropped his bombshell. The glances he'd been giving her all day had singed her skin. The words she'd shot out at him were most certainly hitting their mark.

As bold as Darla was, she didn't normally make it so clear she was interested in a man. She definitely wanted to scare weak men away, but she didn't normally want to take a man to bed without being in a romantic relationship of some sort.

She didn't know how to define what she and Crew were. She couldn't say they were friends. They'd moved past that the first night they'd met and shared that toe-curling kiss. They weren't boyfriend and girlfriend; those terms horrified her. She wasn't in high school.

So, what in the heck were they? Maybe they'd be lovers soon. No, scratch the maybe, they'd *definitely* become lovers. Would it last long?

When Darla had been next to him as he looked through a folder of his previous lovers, she'd felt an emotion she couldn't remember feeling before — jealousy. She hadn't known what it was at first. She'd never been the jealous type. She didn't see a point in it. If a man didn't want to be with her, she certainly wasn't going to chase him down and demand he do it. If he was looking at other women, they could have him. But seeing Crew's past, seeing the stunning women he'd been with, had sent a surge of jealousy through her.

Darla knew who she was and knew she had a nice face and a great body. She worked hard to keep fit. She loved food, so she forced herself to love cardio as well. Maybe that's why she loved horses so much. They exercised a body far more than people realized. If she took too long between rides, she'd be walking funny for a day or two after getting in the saddle again.

"They really are quite beautiful," Crew said.

"Yes, they are, and they show such intense emotion in their eyes," Darla told him.

"Dinner's ready," he said. "I set it on the back deck so we can enjoy the warm evening and watch the horses play."

"Oh, really?" She turned and smiled at him. "Did you make a fire too?"

He chuckled. "Does it count if I simply lit the gas firepit?"

She reached over and squeezed his arm. "Oh, it certainly counts," she told him. "I happen to like being wined and dined. You just might get lucky if you included wine."

The flare in his eyes told her he was hoping she wasn't joking. She wasn't sure if she was or not. The night before she'd been ready to climb into bed with him. And she'd finally made it to his bed by throwing up her entire stomach and having him take care of her. Not too sexy.

"I get lucky every minute we're together," he said. Warmth flowed through her. Crew didn't seem to be a man prone to lines. He said what he meant when he wanted to. It was another thing she liked about him.

They walked to his impressive back deck that looked nearly as big as his house. She lived in an apartment that was smaller than his deck. She didn't mind, though; she wasn't home often. She'd much rather be out in the world, not home alone.

True to his word, the table was set, wine was chilling in a bucket, and dishes were holding food in the middle of it all. His large gas firepit was burning, warding off the cooling air. It had been a beautiful day, but the sun was beginning to set, and Washington cooled fast when the sun went down.

"What did you make?" she asked.

"I grilled burgers and have all of the fixings. I also had one of those salad kits," he told her. "It was an easy dinner. I told you I don't normally do meals. I do like to grill, though."

"Yummy. I could eat burgers every day in the summer. Well, except when I go to baseball games. Then it's all about hot dogs loaded down with every topping possible. You've cooked twice for me today. I'll have to make it up to you."

"I know a few ways you can," he said with a wiggle of his brows. Darla laughed with joy. Each day Crew grew less stiff. He'd practically had a board attached to his back the first few times she'd been around him. Now, he was flirting with her while wearing his typical slacks, but at least his shirt had been untucked and his hair might have a strand or two out of place. She considered that progress.

Crew held out her chair and she took a seat, thanking him as he handed her a hot burger on an open bun. She prepared her burger, adding double cheese and extra pickles, dished up some salad, then gratefully took the wine glass after he filled it.

"I think this is where I'd eat breakfast, lunch, and dinner," she told him as she leaned back and took a bite of her hamburger, gazing out at the horses that had trotted closer to graze on the nearby grass, looking up every so often to see that they were still there.

Darla had begun her life on a farm in eastern Oregon, and she'd loved every minute of it. Her family had owned horses and cows, and she'd never been unhappy about early morning feedings or staying up all night with a sick animal, even when she was young. Being on a farm had been all she'd wanted, and then life changed. If it hadn't been for Daisy, Darla wasn't sure she'd have survived the move to Washington.

But if they hadn't moved she never would've met her best friend, so everything in life happened for a reason. She had no regrets.

"I know you and Daisy went through school together, but I don't know a heck of a lot about you," Crew said after a bit.

"I'm an open book," Darla told him, which was mostly true. "I don't have any skeletons or baggage in my closet. There's not much to hide."

"You don't have *much*?" he asked with a grin.

"We all have to carry some secrets," she told him. "Otherwise there'd be no mystery, and how boring would that be?"

"When do I get to learn these secrets?" he asked.

"I don't know. I've never shared everything about my life with anyone other than Daisy," she admitted.

"So, you're telling me there's a chance I can squeeze it out of you," he pushed.

She laughed. "I think we'd both be better off if *I'm* the one doing the squeezing," she said, loving the instant flush in his cheeks at her blatant reply.

"You really do enjoy playing with fire, don't you?" he asked with a low growl that pleased all the parts of her body.

"Oh, most certainly," she agreed. She finished her burger and leaned back, then stretched out her arm and ran her hand quickly through the dancing flame of the firepit next to them. His eyes narrowed a bit.

"I think you're dangerous to any man's health," he said.

"I sure hope so. I wouldn't want to be in a man's life who didn't jump a bit when I walk into the room," she said. She finished her glass of wine and smiled as he refilled it.

"Do you want them to jump to attention or jump in fear?" Crew asked.

She narrowed her eyes. "Are you trying to psychoanalyze me?" she asked.

He started laughing hard, leaning back in his seat. "Maybe," he said.

It took a second, and then she was laughing too. "I almost fell for that. You're paying me back for all of the sex comments, aren't you?"

"Damn, Darla, you're so unlike most women I know. You have zero problems saying whatever's on your mind."

"Life's too short to keep things inside. I say spew it all out and let the pieces fall where they may."

"What if the pieces land wrong?" he asked.

"Then you have a whole new puzzle to figure out," she assured him.

He laughed again, and she leaned back, loving the deep throaty sound escaping him. Crew hadn't laughed a lot when she'd first met him, but the joyous sound was coming out more and more. Just like the horses, the more comfortable he was around her, the more he let his guard down. She wondered if she'd be able to eventually chip away at all of his defenses.

"Have you lived here since you were a little kid, Darla?" he asked after another minute.

"Yes, since we moved from eastern Oregon when I was five. We had horses and cows, and I was very upset when we moved away. I cried for weeks. It was the middle of the school year, but I didn't care about my friends, I cared about my animals."

"You didn't get to bring them?" he asked.

She felt the familiar pang of sadness thinking about her first horse, but she pushed it down. "No, they stayed with my uncle. I'd go back every summer and be with them, and when Daisy got older she'd come and spend a few weeks out there with me, but I had to leave them behind. I was so angry for a while. But I met Daisy on my first day of school, and we bonded instantly. I forgave my parents, saying Daisy was the sister I'd always wanted. And I'd get to go back and see my animals anyway."

"Why don't you have animals here?" he asked her.

"I haven't had time. I realize now how much time and energy it takes to have horses. Gramps would've let me have a horse on his property since my parents definitely don't have room, and it's beyond expensive to board them anywhere near Seattle. It comes down to time. When I need a fix I go to one of the ranches around here or fly to Bend for the weekend and visit my uncle."

"So, you're telling me that you want me to keep these horses that take so much time and money when you aren't willing to do the same?" he asked with his brow raised.

She laughed. "Exactly. If you have them here, I can come ride every single day. And you're saving horses. It's a win-win." She hoped her innocent smile would soften him up.

"You make it sound as if I'm getting the winning end of this deal," he said, sounding intrigued. "I've been fascinated by psychology my entire life, but being around you for a few weeks could seriously throw everything I've learned and thought was true right out the window."

"You don't sound really concerned," Daisy said with a giggle.

"Nope. For some reason, I'm not. I'm utterly fascinated," he told her.

"Maybe because you feel this thing between us as much as I do," she suggested.

"What are we going to do about it?" he asked.

She was warm, full, and uninterested in fighting the next step they were about to take. But she needed him to be the one to make the next move. She needed him to step up and take the offer she'd placed on the table. She needed him to be the man she knew he was.

"What are you going to do about it?" she asked right back.

He stood . . . and her body lit on fire.

Chapter Nine

Crew had always been in control, always. But there was something about Darla that made him want to rip off his shirt, beat his chest, and act like a Neanderthal. What in the world had this woman done to his sensibilities?

Right now he didn't care.

Without saying another word about her taunt, he approached her then shocked them both when he pulled her from the chair and swiftly threw her over his shoulder. He wasn't sure which of them was more confused or excited.

"What in the world?" Darla gasped, the air knocked from her lungs as her head hung down his back. She smacked him a few times on the butt.

He smiled as he lifted his own hand and gave her a good slap on her luscious butt that was right next to his face. He turned and gently bit her hip, making her groan before she giggled. He smacked her butt again just to show her who was in charge.

"You need cooling off," he told her.

"Wait? What?" The giggling stopped as he stepped into his large bathroom. He paused only long enough to kick off his shoes before moving inside his shower that could easily fit six people. He reached for the spicket. "Don't you dare, Crew Anderson!" she shrieked a second before the cold water rained down on them.

Her yell this time was of shock as the two of them were soaked, all of their clothing still in place. "I'm going to murder you," she said through clattering teeth as she pounded her hands against his butt.

Crew laughed, feeling a mixture of joy and so much heat that the cold water didn't affect him. He had hot water on demand, so the cold spray quickly heated as he ran his hand over her soaked behind.

He shifted her, finally placing her on her feet and looking into her eyes. They were wide. He'd finally managed to stun this woman who could turn a man's insides completely out.

"I can't believe you just did that," she said. The spray from two jets washed over them, their clothes plastered to their bodies. She might be shocked, but he could see desire burning in her gaze. He was sure it matched his own to perfection.

"You've been driving me mad, woman," he said in a low growl.

"Good," she told him.

And then he didn't want to talk anymore. He pulled her tightly against him and leaned down, kissing her the way he'd been wanting to do for days. She was a temptress who would surely lead him down a path he'd probably needed to go down for many years, and he knew there'd be no regrets.

Darla didn't hold back as he stepped forward, pushing her against the wall while his mouth devoured hers. Their tongues mated and danced, their bodies pushed at each other, and their hands roamed over their drenched clothes.

He wrenched his mouth from hers and slid his tongue down her throat, her moan echoing in his shower as he glided a hand beneath her shirt and skated it against her wet skin. He nipped at the sensitive place her neck met her shoulder and she threw her head back as she tangled her fingers in his hair. He moved lower and bit at her peaked nipple through the material of her shirt.

He'd never wanted a woman more than he wanted Darla. The clothes needed to go.

He pulled away and turned her, grabbing her arms and holding them up. With a quick tug he pulled the tee from her and tossed it aside before unfastening her bra and doing the same.

He placed her hands on the wall in front of her. She turned her head and the wanton look in her eyes was nearly his undoing. He wanted to pull off his pants and plunge deep inside of her — but not yet.

Pushing against her, he let her feel how turned on he was as he ran his hands up her slim waist and cupped her full breasts. She moaned as he squeezed her nipples and sucked on her neck. She tried to reach for him.

"Keep your hands on the wall," he demanded, reaching one hand down and smacking her butt again. Who was he? He'd never done anything like this before, never wanted to control sex. But he did now, and he was beyond turned on by it.

She listened, placing her palms flat against the shower wall. He reached into the waistband of his sweats she was still wearing, pulling them and her tiny panties down her beautiful toned legs. He ran his hands along them before lifting first one of her feet, and then the other, and tossing the last of her clothes away. She was panting as she leaned against the wall, her body trembling.

He kissed the back of her legs, then ran his mouth up the curve of her butt before standing again, enjoying her silken skin. He kissed her neck while he spread her thighs before running his hand down her back, and through the slit of her butt until he found her slick heat.

The water was cascading over them, but she was still hot and wet inside, her walls slick with desire. She quivered around his fingers as he pushed two deep inside her and pumped them.

She yelled out, her body shaking.

"You're so damn responsive," he growled, not recognizing his voice. His breath whispered over her ear before he licked the lobe and gently bit down on it. She shook, her legs seeming unsteady.

"Crew, I need . . ." She stopped, her voice barely audible.

"What do you need?" he asked as he kept pumping his fingers inside her while he licked and sucked on the smooth skin of her neck and shoulder. His body was throbbing with need, and if he'd already removed his clothes, he feared he'd plunge in right then. He needed to feel her heat clench around him.

"I'm so hot, Crew, so damn hot. I ache," she told him as she pushed her butt backward, rotating her hips in time with his plunging fingers.

"I don't know who I am with you, Darla. I want to please you, I want to own you," he said.

"You have me, Crew. I'm all yours," she panted as he added another finger and plunged deeper inside of her. She cried out, her walls squeezing him. "More, I want more. I want you," she begged.

His arousal leapt at her words. He needed this woman.

He plunged his fingers in her again, and felt her tightening as she cried out his name. He pulled out, and she groaned in disapproval. He turned her around, her face flushed, her eyes hooded. He kissed her hard as he reached up and squeezed her breasts.

Then he stepped back and pulled off his wet shirt. Her eyes caressed him, seeming quite pleased with what she saw. He kept fit and was proud of his body. He'd never been more grateful for it than right then.

He reached into the pocket of his pants and pulled out a condom. She glanced down and smiled before licking her lips. "Confident, weren't you?" she asked in a deep throaty purr.

"Hopeful," he told her. "You've been driving me mad for weeks."

"Good. I wanted to," she said. She was leaning against the wall. It seemed it was the only thing holding her up right then. He pulled off his pants and underwear, having to put some effort into the task since the soaked fabric stuck to his skin.

Her gasp at the sight of him when he sprang free made his blood boil. He pulsed with need, his erection hard, reaching for her. She reached out and ran a finger across the head and he felt pleasure from his head to his toes.

"I'm going to take us both over the edge," he promised her, the pants finally free. He stood there as they gazed at each other. He was totally drunk on this woman.

Before he could grab her, she dropped to her knees. For just a moment he was worried she'd fallen, but then she grabbed the back of his thighs as she leaned forward and ran her tongue along his wet thigh. The water was cascading over them, but it didn't seem to deter Darla at all.

She wrapped her fingers around his arousal and, without the slightest hesitation, leaned in and circled her mouth around his throbbing head. He quickly reached for the wall, fearing he was going to fall if he didn't. She made his legs weak, and his body was on fire.

She sucked him in while running her tongue over and over his head. Her fingers squeezed and moved back and forth before caressing his balls.

"Baby, please," he said, now the one begging. She sucked him harder, showing no mercy.

She moaned around him, the vibration sending a whole other level of pleasure through him as she licked and sucked and stroked. He held on to the wall with one hand and reached down into her hair with the other, holding her to him as she worked her magical tongue and lips over his sensitive arousal.

"Enough," he finally said as he felt his climax coming too close. Not like this, not their first time. He wanted to be buried deep inside her when he came. He wanted her walls clenching around him at the same time. He grasped her hair and pulled her from his body. His arousal wept with the loss of her mouth.

He lifted her, pressing her against the wall as he leaned in and devoured her lips again, his tongue stroking hers, in and out while he sucked and nibbled and sucked some more.

Then he moved down her neck and nibbled and licked. He reached her peaked nipples, and she grasped his shoulders as he sucked one beautiful strawberry bud into his mouth and ran his tongue over it. She trembled before him.

Then he dropped to his knees, and kissed her stomach.

"Crew, please, I'm going to fall," she begged.

"Then hold on," he warned. That was all the talking he had in him. He grabbed one of her legs and threw it over his shoulder, opening her wide to him, and then he ran his tongue along the seam of her heat.

She yelled as her fingers trembled against his shoulders, and her leg shook against his back. Her thighs quivered against him as he swept his tongue along her opening before sinking his tongue in and out of her. Her cries of pleasure were nearly his undoing.

He ran his tongue up to her clit and swept it over the pulsing nerves before closing his lips and sucking. She screamed. He plunged a finger inside her as he licked and sucked, and then she cried out again as she clenched him, her body shaking, her insides holding his fingers tight as she pulsed.

He slowed the motion of his tongue as he swept it across her heat, drawing every last throb of pleasure from her. He could worship this woman's body every single minute of the day and it still might not be enough.

He needed to be inside her. He found the condom at her feet, long ago slipped from his fingers. He ripped the packet open and stumbled as he slid it over his throbbing flesh. He was shocked to find his fingers shaking. This woman made him lose all semblance of control.

He took her leg from his shoulder, then stood, holding her close. He reached for her thighs and lifted her, wrapping her legs around his back as he pushed her against the wall.

He slammed deep inside of her at the same time he connected their mouths again. Their lips hummed together with their mutual cries of pleasure at finally becoming one.

He stopped as he tried to gain some control, but she wrenched her mouth from his, her eyes foggy with desire. "More," she demanded. Then she buried her head against his neck and bit into his skin.

And he lost all control.

He held her tight as he pulled out and plunged back inside of her. She bit him and his fingers dug into her butt as he pulled out and slammed back inside of her again. She was so hot, so slick, so damn responsive.

He let go of all thoughts as he pounded in and out of her. Her head fell back as her next orgasm slammed into her, her body growing so tight he could barely move. She squeezed him as he pushed inside of her again and then let out his own cry as his orgasm ripped through him, his body pulsing in time to hers.

They rode the wave together, their cries mingling as hot water cascaded over them. She finally sagged against him, and he was incredibly grateful for the wall or they'd both fall to the ground. He'd never been so sated.

"Oh, Crew, that was better than I could've ever dreamed," she sighed.

"Yeah, baby, that was incredible," he told her. He had to find the strength to climb from the shower and get them to his bed.

She moved, and her walls clenched against him, his body still buried inside of her. He was actually shocked when he felt a stirring of need rising again. He pulsed against her walls, and she snapped her head up, gazing at him in awe.

"How?" she gasped.

"I don't know. It doesn't seem I'm ever going to have enough of you," he told her.

Crew had always enjoyed sex. But when he was done, he was done. That didn't appear to be the case with Darla. Of course, it wasn't. Everything was extraordinary when it came to this woman.

"Mmm, let's go to bed," she sighed, her eyes glazed, her smile dreamy.

"Yes, let's go to bed," he told her. He reluctantly pulled from her body, his arousal still there. Then he shut off the water and held her close as he stepped from the shower and grabbed towels. They weren't going to sleep much that night . . . and maybe not for the next week.

He had this woman — and he didn't think he was ever letting her go.

Chapter Ten

Darla hadn't left Crew's house in three days. She knew she was walking funny, but assured herself she could blame that on riding the horses rather than riding the man if anyone noticed. What shocked her was she hadn't wanted to leave his side.

They'd gone to her place and she'd packed a bag of clothes. They'd decided she was staying with him for a few days. It wasn't permanent — that would be ridiculous — but it was for a few days. Of course, it had already been three days. How many more would be appropriate. Wasn't this all happening a bit fast?

Yes, it was, but she liked being with him, and Darla had always done what gave her pleasure, whether it was at work or play. They'd both had to work, but they'd driven in together and come home together. No, it wasn't her home; it was his. But they wanted to spend evenings together. For how long? Heck, she didn't know. It was now Saturday and Crew had just left to find food.

Relief filled Darla when Daisy pulled up. She needed to talk to her bestie. She'd never been unsure of herself, and she didn't enjoy the feeling right now.

Darla was in the front yard and rushed to Daisy's vehicle as she climbed out. There was a new softness in Daisy Darla had never seen before. Her once reluctant bestie was now all girlie. It was sort of odd. She was even wearing a dress, her blonde hair was cascading over her back, and a slight amount of makeup highlighted her naturally gorgeous eyes and full lips.

"I love seeing you in love," Darla said as the two women hugged each other.

"I love being in love," Daisy said with a light chuckle.

Then she leaned back and eyed Darla. "You, on the other hand, seem very confused, not at all like your normal self," Daisy pointed out.

"I know!" Darla said as she threw her hands in the air. "I feel as if I'm a fish out of water. I'm a mess."

"I want you to tell me all, no holding back," Daisy insisted.

"Isn't it odd how the shoe's on the other foot now? Wasn't I just lecturing you about living free and all of that? Now, I feel as if I'm the one who needs a lecture. But I need you to tell me to stay grounded and free at the same time," Darla said.

"This conversation will require wine," Daisy said.

Darla looked at her watch. "It's only eleven," she pointed out.

"Good point, we'd better have mimosas so it's appropriate," Daisy said. She put her arm through Darla's, then walked with her into Crew's house. "I've loved this place from the first time I saw it. Hudson's got a few more months of work on our place and then we'll be out of the rental and in our dream home. It's slightly bigger than my farm home."

"Just a tad," Darla said with a laugh. She felt more grounded the second she was with Daisy. They had a way of doing that for one another. "Isn't it like ten thousand square feet?"

"No," Daisy said with a scowl. Then she chuckled. "Okay, it's close to that, but not quite ten thousand. I tried to argue with Hudson about it, but then he totally sidetracked me when he pulled out the plans for the two-story library with a huge fireplace in it. How could I refuse when he was giving me my dream room?"

"I totally understand," Darla said. "But didn't he also put in a two-lane bowling alley and a massive game room?"

"I have to admit, that might be my other favorite room of the place." Daisy groaned. "I hate that I love the monstrosity so much! I've always been about saving the environment and this place is ridiculous."

"He's doing all energy saver options so that has to count," Darla said.

"That's true," Daisy said with a happy gleam in her eyes. "And we have massive amounts of solar panels so it's not going to consume any more energy than my old farmhouse. That place was so old that it was far more of a pollutant than the new home."

Darla laughed hard at her words. She also didn't point out that the old farmhouse was now a museum and still using that power. "I love how you're working so hard to justify your love of the new home. Enjoy it, girl. You're still a warrior for causes, and it's okay to love the home you're going to raise a family in."

Daisy sighed. "I guess so. I'm starting to talk more with Hudson about having kids. You know I never wanted children. But I love this man so much that I can't imagine the world not having his offspring. He's beautiful inside and out, and now I'm having all of these urges to procreate. I'm wondering who in the hell I even am anymore," Daisy gasped.

Darla was adding orange juice to glasses of champagne. "Should you have this?" she asked.

"I'm definitely not pregnant," Daisy insisted. "I'm only considering it for down the road."

"Good. I want to be an auntie," Darla said.

The two women walked out to the back deck and took a seat, bringing the bottles of orange juice and champagne with them for easy refills. They sat down and watched the horses playing in the field, enjoying the sound of squirrels running around the trees, and birds singing as they flew past.

"Now that we've talked about me, why don't you tell me how and why you're living with Crew Anderson when I didn't even know the two of you were in a relationship. I knew there were sparks, and I knew something was going to happen. But you went from zero to a hundred in less than a second," Daisy said, a big grin resting on her lips.

"I'm not living with him," Darla said, nearly draining her mimosa. She sighed. "I've been here for four days, and yes, we're both going to work, but we're either at work, with the horses, or in bed. And let me tell you, the heat level gets so intense the bedroom should be destroyed by now."

Daisy's grin grew. "I imagine sex with him is out of this world, because sex with Hudson is unlike anything I could've ever dreamed. Had I known there was a man out there who could do to my body what that man does, I'd have been his willing slave long ago."

Darla laughed, so glad Daisy was there. She made her feel better all the way around. "I completely understand. I've been a pain in the ass for Crew for months. I've teased him, and acted as you know I do, and he hasn't backed down. Daisy, this man is as close to perfect as it gets, and for the first time ever with a man, I'm a bit scared. I like him . . . a lot."

"And you're freaked out because it's happening so quickly?" Daisy surmised. They both finished their first glasses and Daisy refilled them.

"Yeah, seriously freaked. I know the dangers of moving too fast in a relationship. I see it all the time in my job. I see the kids born from one-night stands. I see the devastation from single moms and a few single dads. I know more than anyone that the first six months of a relationship are always hormones and love drugs. Crew knows this too. The man's a damn psychologist. And he's been put through the ringer with the kid scare and his world going out of control. I'm not worried about having an incredible love affair. I *am* worried about how I'm feeling about him."

"You told me a few months ago you'd been in lust and like before, but never love," Daisy reminded her.

"It's seriously hard to explain," Darla said.

"Take some deep breaths and do the best you can," Daisy insisted.

"I've actually only slept with two men," Darla admitted. Daisy seemed shocked. She understood why her friend would think she'd slept with a lot of men. "I know, I know, I make myself out like I'm some siren, but the reality is that men are fun to flirt with, and I like to tease them, but I don't sleep with someone unless I feel something real. I haven't felt love before, but I have to feel committed at least."

"Like feel extreme lust?" Daisy asked.

Darla laughed. The mimosa was helping to calm her frazzled nerves.

"Yes, lust is good," Darla told her. "But lust can fade. I didn't lie, I've never been in love. You know that even in school I'd date a boy for a week or two and be finished with him. I've never felt a spark that made me need to be with the guy."

"Oh," Daisy said, her eyes widening. "You're feeling the spark." It was a statement, not a question.

Darla felt a bit of panic invading her. "No, it's just sex," she finally said.

"Don't panic, and don't you dare lie to me. You were all over me for denying what I was feeling for Hudson," Daisy said.

"I'm not panicked, and you're absolutely right. That was a knee jerk reaction," Darla said, taking in a few deep breaths.

They heard a vehicle pull up to the front of the house and Darla felt her heart accelerate. She was torn between rushing out and throwing her arms around Crew, and needing to speak to her bestie.

As if Crew could read her mind, her phone dinged with a message. She picked up her phone and smiled as she held it out for Daisy to see.

I see Daisy's here. I got items for the horses, so I'll be a while unloading in the barn. Enjoy your time with your bestie. There was a kissing emoji after the message that made Darla sigh.

"Damn, you do have it bad," Daisy said.

"I know," Darla said with another sigh. "I'm disgusting myself right now."

They both laughed at that. And then Daisy whistled low beneath her breath.

"What?" Darla asked. Daisy pointed over to the barn where Hudson had just emerged. The man's shirt was off, a slight gleam of sweat on his skin as he hauled a bale of hay inside.

"Hot damn, I think all of the Anderson men are secretly models," Daisy said. "Hudson, of course, is sexier than Crew, but I'll have to admit Crew's a very close second."

Darla laughed at the words and the smile. "Let's agree they're equally sexy," Darla said. "I can't actually verify this as I haven't seen Crew without a shirt yet, but we can always have a lake day so I can assess the situation more accurately."

The two of them laughed. If only the men knew how they actually spoke about them. They had to be worse than any men's groups out there. But since they were women they got away with it — and they wouldn't have it any other way.

"How long will you stay here?" Daisy asked as they continued to watch the show of Crew moving in and out of the barn. It was better than anything on television. One of the men he'd just hired full-time to help with the horses was assisting him, but they didn't see the young college student.

"I don't know. I can't seem to make myself leave, and Crew doesn't seem to be in a hurry for me to go anytime soon."

"Sooooo, what's next?" Daisy asked. She seemed utterly relaxed.

"I have no clue. This is really odd for me since I always know what I'm doing and when I'm doing it," Darla said.

"Maybe it's good for you to simply float with the tide. You might find out more about yourself, and you might like the journey."

"Ugh, I knew giving you advice with Hudson would come back to bite me in the ass," Darla told her.

"Hey, it's payback time. I'm in love, I know exactly where I'm going and what I'm doing. That's been you you're entire life. I'm loving being on the other side of this," Daisy told her.

"I have to admit, I'd be feeling the same way if the roles were reversed," Darla told her.

"The roles were always reversed, you dork. But I have a feeling neither of us will need advice for much longer," Daisy said. "We might need to vent once in a while though."

"Daisy, don't get hopeful we're going to marry brothers. I'm falling for this guy, but I don't trust that it's more than lust. It feels like more than lust and I'm not going to fight it, however I'm very aware that something this hot can definitely burn out."

"As long as you're not fighting it, I don't see a problem with that at all," Daisy told her. "I was an idiot and you helped me. I don't really need to help you; I just need to tell you that it's all going to be okay in the end."

"I can toast to that," Darla said as she raised her glass.

The two clinked their glasses as they sat back and watched Crew work at the barn. It was a day Darla could grow very used to. She was becoming acclimated to this daily routine with Crew. Would she be willing to leave?

Chapter Eleven

Crew was breaking a sweat as he cleaned up in the barn. He'd unloaded the products he'd bought for the horses. He could've sent his newest employee, Don, but he'd found he liked taking care of the animals. There was no way he was admitting that to his uncle Joseph. The man would be far too smug about it.

He'd always scoffed when people said horses were good therapy. But he was revising his earlier thoughts on animal therapy. There was something very soothing in taking care of animals. They had minimal expectations: some food, a little attention, and care. They didn't ask for much more than that.

Crew was also a huge proponent of a hard day's work. There was something to be said about your muscles aching from working hard. He didn't do it often enough in his profession so he ran regularly and lifted weights. He wasn't a fanatic about it, but he liked to keep in shape. And he liked donuts, therefore exercise was important.

As Crew finished mucking stalls, he heard a vehicle pull up to the house. He hadn't gone inside since he'd come home, figuring Darla needed some girl time. They'd been together a lot in the past few weeks and practically inseparable for the past few days. Neither of them had put a meaning behind what was happening between them, but neither of them seemed willing to part ways, especially at night.

What was odd to Crew was that it was about more than sex, for him and for her. He knew feelings were growing. He just didn't know exactly what that meant. He grabbed a rag and stepped from the barn, wondering who'd shown up.

His brother Hudson was heading toward the house and Crew called out to him. Hudson stopped and turned, a smile on his face as he lifted his hand, waved, and jogged over to Crew.

"Are you doing a magazine shoot?" Hudson asked with a laugh. "Something for Cowboy Weekly?"

Crew rolled his eyes. "Is that even a real magazine?"

"Hell if I know. A new magazine pops up on a weekly basis, it seems."

"This is what hard work looks like. You should try it sometime," Crew told his brother as he wiped more sweat from his brow. "It's certainly warm today."

"Brother, I've been building since I started walking. Trust me, I know how to get hot and sweaty, much more than you in your air-conditioned office, sitting in a chair staring at a paper while a client spills all of their secrets to you," Hudson said.

"Yeah, yeah, I know, I'm a nerd who doesn't sweat," Crew said. Then he laughed. "Why don't you show me your mad skills and help while we chat?"

"My wife's here and told me she and Darla are having a mimosa lunch. I figured she'd need a ride home."

"Hmm, the women are day-drinking again. Should we be worried?" Crew asked, not in the least meaning the words.

"Hell no. The last time they did this Daisy and I had a fantastic night," Hudson said. "Of course, we have a great night every day we're together. I can't get enough of my fiancée."

Crew decided not to talk about his night at home after Darla and Daisy's last adventure, though he hadn't been too disappointed. It had been the first time he'd gotten her into his bed. Granted, she'd been sick and had passed out, but the point was she'd still been with him. The bonus was she hadn't left since.

"Well, they'll let us know when we're invited to join them," Hudson said as he threw off his shirt. "What do you need me to do?"

"I was just about to put fresh shavings down in the stalls," Crew said.

"Don't you have help for this sort of thing?" Hudson asked as they entered the barn.

"Sure, but I'm finding I like the work."

"Yeah, that's why I still pound nails and haul boards. I have good men who can do the job, but the minute you start thinking work's beneath you, is the minute you begin to lose yourself," Hudson told him.

He grabbed a second wheelbarrow and they began moving cedar shavings into the stalls. The horses were frolicking in the field, enjoying the sunshine and the freedom of grazing and playing. They'd still be hungry when they came in.

Hudson had discovered that Pixie had a fondness for oatmeal cookies. Darla had been horrified when he'd handed them to the horses. But then she'd made a batch of cookies just for the horses with healthier ingredients.

"Darla feeds these horses better than we feed ourselves," Crew told his brother.

"I've always found it odd that people say human food is so bad for animals. If it's that bad for them, then isn't it bad for us?" Hudson questioned.

"I was having the same thoughts. As Darla was telling me not to give the horses the cookies I bought, she was eating one. She didn't seem to understand my confusion.

"I know a lot of the stuff I put in my body is terrible for me. I try to make up for it by eating super healthy seventy percent of the time," Crew told him.

"Exactly. If I eat my fruits and veggies, then I can have a bacon cheeseburger and greasy fries every once in a while," Hudson said.

"I wish it was simply once in a while," Crew told him with a laugh.

"What are you feeding me tonight. If I'm here working, I should get fed extremely well," Hudson said.

"I guess we could do takeout. There's a great Italian place that delivers," Crew said.

"Perfect. I want extra breadsticks and a variety of pasta," Hudson told him.

"Sounds good to me. Let's make sure the women are going to be up to eating after their mimosa lunch." Crew laughed.

"I'm sure they're having a few snacks to soak up the alcohol. Maybe we shouldn't stay gone for too long." He stopped as he eyed his brother. "I don't want to pry, but what's happening between you and Darla? It seems you two are together far more than you're apart," Hudson said.

Crew thought about his answer. "The past few months have given me some definite highs and lows. I was consumed with thoughts of a daughter out there I'd missed out on, and then all of the sudden that was ripped out from under me. I guess Darla has been a constant through the worst of it. I like having her around," he finally said.

Hudson gave him an understanding look. "I can't imagine dealing with that on my own. I wish you would've come to us sooner." He stopped and held out his hand. "I'm not upset with you. We all have to come to things on our own. I just hope you know that you can always come to me or any of our family with anything. We might flick each other a lot of crap a lot of the time, but when the cards are all on the table you know we'd do anything for each other."

"I know. I'm a damn psychologist. I don't know why I didn't come to you guys. I don't know why I let it consume me for so long. I don't know why I let it mess with my head. It's still messing with it a bit. I feel as if I've lost something, which is ridiculous when I never had anything to lose in the first place."

Hudson studied him for several seconds. "Maybe you're ready to settle down. All of your siblings are now in healthy, happy relationships, and you thought for months you might be a father.

Maybe what's bothering you is the thought of that appealed to you and now it feels as if something is missing."

"I don't know. I've never had anything against kids. I don't like their messiness or the fact that you have to dramatically change your life for them, but then I see my nieces and think I want that. It's such a weird feeling for me," Crew admitted.

"I've had the same feelings," Hudson admitted. "When I first talked to Daisy about kids she was emphatic she didn't ever want to be a mother. And if that's her final decision I'll support her in it and love her just as much. But, honestly, I want to be a father. I want a little girl with Daisy's eyes and smile to ride on my shoulders. I want a son with an infectious laugh. I want kids to teach how to build, hunt, fish, and survive in a crazy world. I want it all."

"Isn't the fact that this world is crazy enough to scare you out of having kids?" Crew asked.

"It would seem that way, but no. I feel like I can protect them from anything while they're young, and teach them how to protect themselves as they get older," Hudson told him.

"I feel the same," Crew said. "We sure as hell didn't get that from our father, so it's a damn good thing our mother was a good enough mother to play the role of both parents."

"I never felt as if I was missing something growing up. We might not have had much money, but we had everything we needed. If I do have kids we'll step things back a bit and teach them the basics in life," Hudson said.

Crew laughed. "How in the hell are you going to step things back in a ten-thousand-square-foot house?" he asked.

"We'll go camping a lot in the woods without a camper," Hudson said. "And we'll limit the stupid electronic time. Hell, I go to a park where kids should be running and screaming and I see five-year-olds sitting in the grass with a dang tablet in their hands. I believe in progress, and I like the luxury of certain electronics, but I think we need to let go of them sometimes."

"Yeah, some of my favorite memories are when we were young, camping by a river, fishing and playing hide-and-go-seek. I never see kids doing that anymore when I go to parks," Crew said.

"Maybe we've been in the city too long. It might not be a bad idea to move somewhere far away from the hustle and bustle of Seattle," Hudson suggested.

"I've been looking at property in Oregon. There are some beautiful small towns where I wouldn't mind owning property. We could all go in together and at least have a place to go a few months of the year that isn't as luxurious as our places here," Crew suggested.

"Hell yes. I love that idea," Hudson said. "I'll start doing some searches. We can build cabins and have ourselves a bit of a compound, maybe spend summers there growing a garden and raising animals."

"It's odd how appealing that sounds. I would've laughed at you last year had you suggested that, but being with these horses and doing this work has changed my mind about the pleasure of simple living."

"How did Joseph talk you into this?" Hudson asked.

"You know Uncle Joseph. The man's good. He can get you to agree to something before you actually realize you've agreed," Crew said.

Hudson laughed hard. "If any of us could outsmart him, it would be you. It seems that even the psychologist in our family can't escape Joseph's meddling ways."

"I know," Crew said. "I was highly irritated with myself for a while, but then I realized he's done it to all of us, and now I actually like the dang horses."

A mewing sound came from one of the empty stalls. Hudson turned and stared at the wall before looking back at Crew. "What was that?"

"Don't say anything when we go to the house. I just brought them home. Darla's going to be excited," Crew said as he moved over to the stall with his brother. They peeked over the rail where an orange cat was lying comfortably in what could only be described as a cat castle. Her five tiny kittens were nursing. She looked up, her body relaxed, her eyes half open.

"Where did you find her?" Hudson asked.

"I went to a shelter to find some barn cats that Darla said I needed to keep mice away, and they had an event going on. They needed foster care for several animals. I ended up adopting the mother and her kittens. They obviously can't be separated for at least seven more weeks, and I have plenty of space," he told his brother.

"Do you really think Darla will let them stay down here instead of in the house?" Hudson questioned.

"This is better than the house," Crew pointed out. I practically bought out the store in cat supplies, giving them a miniature house, toys, food, and medicine. It will be weeks before the kittens can climb the wall. The mama has already jumped up to peer at me before going back to her babies, so she can come and go as she pleases.

"They are pretty damn cute," Hudson admitted.

"Yeah, when the mama cat looked at me from her small cage at the event, I was instantly screwed. Her pleading eyes drew me in. I walked around looking for some raggedy old cats, but when I passed by her again, she meowed right at me. I leaned down and reached through the holes of the cage and she instantly rubbed her head against my finger and purred. It was over and done with that easily."

"Damn, Crew, you've gotten completely soft on me," Hudson said with a laugh. "I think I like it."

"I'm so glad I'm entertaining you. While you stand there and laugh, I'm analyzing myself trying to figure out what in the hell's going on. I've never wanted to commit to anything long term, and now here I am buying kittens."

"It happens to the best of us," Hudson told him. "It always starts with, *I've met a woman*." He laughed at his own joke.

"Yeah, I miss the days I was sitting back laughing at all of the torture you, Finn, Noah, and Brandon were going through as women entered your lives. But then something shifted. I watched, noticing that it's not always easy for any of you, but you're so much happier, so much more at peace. I've advised clients for years that they must love themselves before they're going to be able to be in healthy relationships. The thing I hadn't realized until watching your journeys was how important it is to have someone by your side who knows you, loves you, and will walk next to you. I know that you're all healthy on your own. But I also realize you thrive with the women you've chosen by your sides."

"I couldn't have said it any better. I was happy on my own. I didn't know something was missing from my life. But now that Daisy's a part of me, it would be like losing myself to lose her. I know I could survive, but I wouldn't want to. I want us to be there for each other."

"I have a whole new understanding of people who lose their spouses after thirty, forty, or fifty years of marriage. I've wondered how some are so peaceful while others are a complete mess," Crew said.

"The ones who are peaceful are that way because they know they'll be together again soon. The ones who are a mess are that way not because they can't do it on their own but because they don't want to. There's a big difference between needing someone and wanting someone. I might joke and say I need Daisy, and I do. But more than that, I want her. I want her as my partner, as my equal, and as my challenger. I want her in my life. I need her because I love how she makes me feel about myself and life in general."

"What does Darla think of all of this?" Hudson asked. "You know if this thing between you fails, it's going to suck because she and Daisy are tighter than siblings."

"That's run through my mind a lot, but even if we fail romantically, I don't see us being bitter enemies. We haven't lied to one another, and we began as friends," Crew said.

"Yeah, a lot of people say that, and even believe it when things are great. But break-ups tend to bring out the beast in all of us."

Crew laughed. "I can't imagine being bitter or angry over a break-up. I've never understood it when I've listened to clients," he said.

"That's because you've never held on to someone who truly mattered," Hudson pointed out.

Those words seemed to stop Crew cold. He thought about his past relationships, and Hudson was a hundred percent correct. He'd never been upset or even disappointed when a relationship had come to its foregone conclusion.

"I don't know what to tell you. There's no way of stopping this now. I don't want her to leave," Crew said honestly.

"Is she living here?" Hudson asked.

"No, but she's been here for four nights," Crew said. "We went on a run to her place to get some clothes. It's far too early to move in together, but we get to use the animals as an excuse for her being here. She's helping me."

"Do you need an excuse?" Hudson asked.

Crew shrugged. "Kind of. It helps my rational brain process all of it. But again, we were even honest about that," he admitted.

"Damn, Darla seems like a wild and free child on the outside, but on the inside she's truly as nerdy and rational as you are," Hudson said.

The kittens finished nursing and were moving around their mother, their eyes still not quite open, their tiny bodies unsure of their movements.

"They are damn cute," Crew said. "I've never been a cat person, like never. But these little things completely own me."

"I love the awe in your voice. You seem as if your entire world has been flipped upside down," Hudson said.

"It has," Crew said. "The strangest thing about it is that I don't care."

"That's pretty awesome," Hudson said.

"It's so weird how we've all evolved. I know we change a lot as we grow up, but I've been a professional for over fifteen years. I'm not supposed to change this much in a few months at my age. I'd tell my clients to slow down and make sure they're not having a midlife crisis."

"It could be that. If you go buy a sleek sports car and find a twenty-year-old bimbo, I'll worry. But this looks like you've found an incredible woman and you're wanting to settle down. There's nothing wrong with that."

"I think we've given the women long enough to gossip," Crew said. He was missing Darla, which was crazy. But he'd already decided he wasn't going to analyze everything he was feeling or doing. He was simply going to let it be what it was. "I want to tell her about the kittens."

"You think you're going to get an extra thank you from her later, don't you?" Hudson said with a hearty laugh.

"Hell yes," Crew said. "I think she'll say thank you again and again," he smugly said.

"Damn, maybe I'll go find my own kittens," Hudson said. "Not that I need to. Daisy is quite thankful on a regular basis."

The two of them left the barn, still too hot to put on their shirts. They moved down the path and entered the front of the house. They could hear the women laughing over something on the back deck, the door open so a breeze could blow through the home.

"I have to admit, I show my thanks just as much," Crew said after they grabbed a beer from the fridge.

Hudson laughed again, making both women turn as they moved toward the door. "Oh, brother, so do I," Hudson told him.

Crew wasn't going to deny he enjoyed sex with Darla. It was honestly the best sex he'd ever had. He got as much pleasure from pleasing her as he got from being pleased. But if their relationship was only about sex, he wouldn't be consumed with thoughts of her throughout the entire day. If it was only about sex he wouldn't be trying to figure out ways to make her laugh.

Crew knew what they had was unique. He just didn't know how long it would last. He didn't want to think in those terms and set himself up for failure. And if he set himself up that way, he was also setting Darla up to fail. That was unacceptable.

"Hello boys," Darla said, glancing briefly at Hudson before she drank in Crew. His body felt the burn of her gaze as if her fingers had just trailed their way down his entire torso. They'd made love only a few hours earlier, and he had the urge to haul her back over his shoulder and cart her off to his bedroom again. The only thing stopping him was their guests.

"Hello, my sexy fiancé," Daisy said with a little giggle. His brother was wearing the same light in his eyes that Crew was sure was shining in his own.

Before either of them could say a word, Darla laughed and turned to Daisy. "Fine, I'll agree to a tie," Darla said. The girls started giggling harder and Crew and Hudson looked at each other in confusion.

"What do you agree to a tie about?" Crew asked.

"It's a girl thing," Daisy said. Then she looked at Darla. "I'll agree to a tie too."

Crew and Hudson looked at each other and shrugged, knowing the girls would only tell them what they wanted to, and they wouldn't be invited into their private jokes. That was okay with both of them.

"Want to take a walk?" Crew asked. "I have something to show you."

"A walk sounds wonderful," she said with a wink. Oh, she was killing him.

"I'm coming," Daisy said with a laugh. "I know you're trying to get alone, and I wouldn't mind some alone time myself, but torturing you is quite fun."

Daisy rose to her feet and walked to Hudson, giving him a quick kiss before wrapping her arm around his waist. "Where are we going?"

"To the barn," Crew said, laughing as he helped Darla up. She might be a little buzzed with two empty champagne bottles sitting on the table, but she was in a great mood and steady on her feet.

"Great idea. You'll love the baby horses," she told Daisy.

They made their way to the barn, and stepped inside, still laughing and talking. A mama cat jumped onto the top of the stall and the kittens instantly mewed. All talking stopped as Darla's eyes widened and she let go of Crew to run over to the stall. Mama cat had already jumped back down. Darla stared inside for several seconds before she turned, tears in her eyes, and a big smile on her face.

"Are they ours?" she asked with so much hope in her voice he'd have given her the entire farm if she asked for it right then. He really loved the tingles that shot through his body at the word *ours*.

"Yep, I adopted them today. You told me we needed barn cats here," he said, wondering at the tightness in his chest. He wanted to surprise her every single day for the rest of his life.

"Oh, Crew, they're beautiful," she said. She rushed back to him, threw her arms around his neck, then kissed him hard. He was definitely wishing they were alone now. He'd haul her to the nearest clean stall and ravish her.

But she let him go just as quickly as she'd grabbed him, then took Daisy's hand and the two women went into the stall and sat before the kittens. They petted the mama, both women seeming in total heaven.

"I think they'll be here a while," Hudson said as he and Crew leaned against the stall and looked at the pleasure on the women's faces.

"Yep, let's leave them and order food," Crew said.

He smiled all the way back to the house. He'd never felt so happy in his life — and it was all because of a bold, beautiful, crazy, confidant woman he wanted to hand the world to.

Chapter Twelve

The girls took an hour to return from the barn, both of them wearing huge grins. Crew and Hudson had been enjoying the beautiful sunset while they sipped on a beer and waited.

"We have dinner coming," Hudson said as he pulled Daisy onto his lap. "Dinner and a view. It doesn't get better." She leaned in and kissed him.

"Nope, we want to go out," Daisy told him. "We decided the day's been too fun to stop now."

"But I already ordered," Crew said.

"Then have them donate it to the fire department. They'll be thrilled. We want to go to town," Daisy said again.

Hudson laughed. "My girl is always feeding the policemen and fire department. The good news is that if anything ever happens at our home, we're going to have a slew of first responders there in seconds. She also takes them all sorts of baked goods."

Crew laughed as he lifted his phone and told the restaurant they had a change of plans and to triple the order and take it to the local fire station.

"You just became a lot sexier," Darla said as she moved to him, and copied her friend, sitting on his lap. "I'm very impressed."

He wanted to call the restaurant and tell them to cook up the entire menu and deliver to every first responder in a fifty-mile radius. He loved pleasing this woman.

"Where do you want to go for dinner?" he asked.

"We still want Italian, we just want to sit in the restaurant," Darla said. Then she smiled again. "You do realize you and I still haven't had an official first date, don't you?"

Crew was confused for a second, then he sat back and laughed. "It feels as if we've been together for a year, but you're right, I need to wine and dine you. I'm slacking."

She scowled. "A year? Are you saying I'm an old habit now?"

"Baby, you could never be an old habit," he assured her, before grabbing the back of her head and pulling her in for a deeper kiss.

"If you two don't stop that right now, this date night's getting cancelled," Hudson warned.

"Not going to happen," Daisy said as she beamed at the two of them. "Darla and I have never been out on a double date. It's about dang time."

"You two have never gone out on a double date?" Crew questioned.

"Nope. We didn't manage to find two decent men at the same time to make that happen," Darla answered.

"I guess I haven't had a double date with any of my brothers either," he said, surprised by that fact. He hadn't dated a woman he'd wanted his brothers to know more about. With Darla, it had just happened naturally.

The women rushed off to freshen up for their night out while Crew and Hudson went to take quick showers and change. It was a good thing Crew had clothes that would fit his brother because they'd ruined their other outfits out in the barn. Within a half hour they all met in the kitchen.

Damn, Darla truly did take his breath away. She was naturally beautiful and didn't need to put effort into her appearance, but with her hair curled and a shiny pink lip stain on her luscious lips, he was getting all sorts of ideas of what would happen when they made it back home.

Their drive to the restaurant took about twenty minutes with light traffic. He'd chosen his home away from the city for that reason and moved his practice to the small town. Every year the small cities surrounding Seattle grew, yet he didn't feel closed in where he was living.

They were seated right away and the girls seemed as if this was the greatest night of their life.

"Good evening, I'm Jason," the waiter said as he handed out menus. "Tim's bringing out water and bread. Can I get you something else to drink?"

"Wine. We want lots and lots of wine," Daisy said with a giggle.

"We have some excellent wines," Jason said, seeming a little besotted by the giggling women at his table. Crew could see why. Though Jason was college-aged, the girls' charm was infectious and naturally drew others to them.

"Umm, you pick a good red one then," Darla told him. "We trust you."

Crew wanted to argue with her. He'd never had a waiter pick out a wine before, but Darla was having so much fun he wasn't going to take it away from her.

"We have a variety of wines," Jason said, thrown off by the request.

"Then choose the best," Crew easily said. "Don't worry, we'll trust your selection. Bring out two different reds to start with."

"Do you want our most popular or the most expensive?" Jason asked. He was quickly regaining his composure.

"The most popular for flavor not because it's cheap," Daisy told him. "Trust me I've had a lot of boxed wine, and some of it's actually very good. But tonight, we want flavors to burst on our tongues." Crew hardened at her words. There were some things he wouldn't mind bursting on her tongue.

Jason smiled at her, probably halfway in love already. "I know exactly what to get you," he assured her. He turned just as Tim arrived with water and bread that smelled so good it made Crew's stomach rumble.

"I'm not sure we should've taken the girls out. They look like they're on a mission to cause trouble," Hudson said with a laugh. But it was clear to all of them that Daisy could do no wrong in his eyes. His brother was completely in love and whatever Daisy wanted, she'd get.

"We *are* trouble. Don't forget it," Darla said as she sent an air kiss at Crew.

Hudson chuckled. "Darla, I liked you from the minute I met you," he told her.

Crew had been curious about Darla from the way his brother had spoken about her — and though she'd blown in like a tornado, his brother had been right — she was absolutely fantastic. He'd first met her the night of the barbeque at his home a few months earlier. They'd shared one hell of a kiss that night, and then he'd let her go.

He'd been so upset over dealing with the blackmail notes and hadn't known what he was going to do about it. Finally, he'd turned to Darla. It was the best decision he'd ever made.

Their wine was delivered and Jason most definitely picked two excellent bottles. The women gushed over the flavor, telling Jason he was a perfect waiter. They ordered appetizers and enough food for ten people. Jason looked at the table, obviously wondering where he'd put all of the platters.

"Jason, let's cut that order in half," Crew said with a laugh. "But definitely bring a couple more bottles of wine."

"Sure thing," Jason said before walking away.

"I think we could've eaten all of that food," Darla said.

"We could've come close, but I like to be able to walk," Crew told her.

"True. That much pasta might make us immobile," Daisy said.

"We don't want to be immobile," Hudson said. "I like when you're bendy." He waggled his brows at his wife.

"We're going to get kicked out of here," Crew said with a laugh. "Or frighten other patrons."

"Ah, it's fun to be adventurous," Darla told him. "And even if someone manages to hear something, they'll either have a great story for later, or they'll forget all about it by the end of the night."

"I love that you don't care what people think," Crew said. "It shocks me to say that; I've always cared about people's opinions of me. But being with you makes me rethink that."

"Good. I think we can meet in the middle, because you help me see that life doesn't have to be all fun and games," Darla told him. "I'm kinda falling for you, Crew."

"Yeah, the feeling's mutual," he said.

Daisy laughed. "You two are adorable. I love it." She gave Crew a wide smile. "Okay, Crew, I don't know enough about you except what Darla tells me, and some of that can't be repeated at this table, so why don't you share some interesting facts about yourself," she said before sipping her wine.

Crew didn't want to know what couldn't be repeated at the table. Darla wouldn't talk about their sex life, right? No way. Women didn't talk about sex with other women. From the gleam in Daisy's and Darla's eyes, he was afraid he had that one wrong. He'd rather live in the dark.

"I'm an open book," he told her. He wasn't *exactly* an open book, but he hoped with his brother there, Daisy would show him some mercy.

"Where have you traveled? What have you done in life? Have you always wanted to be a psychologist? Did you choose that profession because your brothers are all crazy?" Daisy fired off.

Crew sent an SOS signal to Darla with his eyes and she reached over and patted his leg, but the look in her gaze told him she wasn't going to rescue him. He was on his own.

"I've done a decent amount of traveling," he began. "One place I haven't gone yet is Greece. I'd really like to go there."

"Oh, me too. After I watched Mama Mia, I've been determined to go. I haven't managed to do it yet," Darla exclaimed. "Maybe this year. I'm keeping my fingers crossed."

"I'll take you," Crew said before he could think twice about taking it back.

"Oh, I want to go too," Daisy said. Let's plan a trip."

"We'll talk more about it," Darla said as she patted his leg again, as if letting him know she was very aware he'd simply puked out the words before giving himself time to think. The fact that she was giving him an out irritated him. He wasn't sure why. He'd instantly regretted saying them. He should just leave it alone, and go on to answer the next question. That's not what happened though.

"Why don't you want to plan the trip now?" he asked.

She seemed shocked by his words. "I have to put in for time off and do some planning. And a vacation like that isn't cheap," Darla told him. He opened his mouth and she glared at him. "If you dare say you'll pay for it, I might punch you in the throat. I've always taken care of myself, and I'm still perfectly capable of doing that. It's a trip I've wanted to do for a while and I'll do it. But I have to do some research first," she finished, firmly putting him in his place.

Crew was stunned at how much he liked this woman. The more she spoke, the more he liked her. He'd gone from being horrified he'd invited her on the trip to determined he'd take her, all in the span of a few seconds. He had a feeling she'd be tying him in knots for as long as he was with her.

Crew decided to move on to the next question. "Yes, I definitely became a psychologist because of my crazy family," he told Daisy.

"I knew it," she said. "It's okay, I like a little crazy in my life. Normal is too boring." She leaned over and kissed Hudson, who seemed more than pleased to kiss her back.

Crew was about to go on when Darla glanced up to the front of the restaurant. She looked confused for a second, then she tensed, and her face washed out of all color. Crew, Daisy, and Hudson all turned to see what had caused that reaction.

Daisy immediately turned back to Darla and reached over the table, grabbing her arm. "It's okay, he won't get near you," Daisy promised.

Hudson tensed. "No, he won't," Crew's brother said.

"Who in the hell is that?" Crew asked, staring from the man who'd just spotted them. Darla went from scared to ticked in a matter of seconds.

The man was wearing a business suit, his slick hair pushed back, and he was walking through the restaurant as if he owned the place, coming straight toward them.

"I was with Daisy and Darla several months ago when this asshole approached saying he had a claim over Darla. I knocked him out," Hudson quickly told his brother.

"Good job," Crew said.

Crew looked over the man. He wasn't exactly small, but he wasn't overly intimidating either, not that Crew had a worry. But he could see how the women would feel alarmed. Men like him were easy to call out; they had big egos and nothing to back them. This guy looked like he enjoyed intimidating people, especially women. It probably fed his screwed-up brain.

When he was a few feet away both Crew and Hudson rose at the same time. They weren't going to sit below this man, and it appeared he was looking for trouble. As they faced him, the man's eyes narrowed, his gaze leaving Darla's for a short while to size up Crew and Hudson. A brief flash of recognition sparked in his eyes as he glanced over Hudson. Good, Crew thought, the man would know he'd been knocked out once by his brother, and it surely would happen again if he wanted any kind of trouble.

"Sir, can I help you?" a woman asked as she approached, dressed as one of the cook staff.

"No, stay back," the man called.

"Sir, people are dining. We don't want to ruin that experience," the cook said, not backing away.

"I'm just going to talk to my girlfriend," the man said. Crew felt rage flow through him. Did this idiot believe what he'd just said? Had he marked some sort of creepy territory thing on Darla? He'd seen it happen before, had counseled patients who thought they were in love and had a claim over the person they were obsessed with. Pulling them from the delusion depended on how far gone a patient was.

The man stopped at their table, his eyes on Darla. She sat back, making sure to stay as far from him as possible.

"I am in no way your girlfriend, Steve. I've told you repeatedly to leave me alone. Did the last arrest not convince you of that?" Darla snapped.

The man's face reddened with rage. Crew didn't want a fight in the restaurant, but he had a bad feeling one was on the way. If this man attempted to touch Darla in any way, Crew wouldn't tolerate it. If he said nasty words to her, Crew would have to set him straight.

Steve took a menacing step toward Darla, and Crew blocked him, holding out a hand and stopping him. Steve looked at Crew incredulously as if completely shocked someone had gotten in his way. Crew wondered how many times Steve had bulldozed his way through a situation.

"I'll kill you if you get in my way," Steve said with so much malice in his tone, Crew realized the man might try to carry out this threat. He wasn't worried, but he had no doubt this man belonged in jail. It was only a matter of time before he did something that couldn't be undone.

"You've been told multiple times to leave Darla alone. Leave now," Daisy said, a warrior look on her face that made both Crew and Hudson proud. These girls would die for one another, a rare thing indeed.

"I don't know what you're thinking, Steve, but you have no right to speak to me, and you certainly don't have the right to frighten all of these people trying to have a nice evening out. I wanted nothing to do with you within five minutes of meeting you. Go away and never talk to me again," Darla said. Both she and Daisy stood, glaring at the man.

It was four against one. Crew wouldn't discount either Darla or Daisy. They might be small, but they were warriors.

"You heard the ladies," Crew said. Hudson just stood there waiting, being a second to his brother. He didn't need to add fuel to the fire.

Steve's attention was suddenly focused on Crew, assessing him. Crew gave him a mocking smile and waited to see what the man would do next. He could pretty much predict it. Steve turned back to Darla, giving her a hateful glance. The saying *if looks could kill* had come about for a specific reason.

"Who in the hell is this guy, Darla? Are you cheating on me?" Steve gasped as if he couldn't conceive of that happening.

Darla's eyes widened in shock as if she couldn't believe what this man was saying. Crew knew how she felt. He'd met with clients who had no idea how a man had become so obsessed with them. And it was clear this Steve was obsessed with Darla.

"Number one, I don't belong to you, never have, and never will," she began, her shoulders stiff, her eyes on fire. "Number two, you need to get the hell out of here. If you approach me again I'll have you thrown in jail. This is clearly harassment."

The determination in her eyes truly impressed Crew. The fact that she was getting her say was the only reason Crew hadn't pounded this guy yet. He wanted her to know she was strong enough to defend herself. He was there as backup in case this idiot thought about grabbing her in public.

"You little bitch. Do you have any idea who I am?" he sneered. "You can't do a thing to me, but trust me I can do whatever I want to you. And I will. You're mine, and nobody's going to convince me otherwise." His fists were clenched, and Crew decided he'd had enough.

"You've spoken too long. It's time to go," Crew told the man. "Now!" The pure steel in his voice made other men cower. This loser in front of him was too stupid to realize the danger he was in.

"Who's going to make me?" Steve mocked.

"I love dealing with assholes with more ego than brains," Crew said. "Let's go."

The man tensed, and Crew knew he was about to throw a punch. It was almost laughable. Without much effort, Crew grabbed the man, quickly flipping him around and wrenching one arm up his back, while he grabbed the other, making it impossible for Steve to move in any direction other than the one Crew chose.

"Need help?" Hudson asked, sounding bored. Crew rolled his eyes. Like he'd need help with some idiot like this. He knew better than to turn his back on a crazy person, but he certainly didn't have to worry about him when he was in front of him. "Good. I'm hungry." Hudson looked at the girls. "Ladies," he said, holding out his hand, indicating for them to sit. Their eyes flashed between Hudson and Crew, who was holding Steve. Then Darla shrugged and sat.

"Sounds good to me. I'm hungry too," Darla said.

"You're all going to pay for this," Steve sputtered, spit flying from his mouth as he tried to break the grip Crew had on him.

"Yep, tell it to your lawyer," Crew said as he began pushing the man to the front of the restaurant.

"I don't need lawyers. I have other people who will help me take care of you," Steve snapped.

Crew didn't doubt the man was telling the truth. A patron opened the door for Crew and he marched Steve outside, not stopping until he was twenty feet from the restaurant. He cranked the man's arm up a bit higher on his back, making Steve cry out in pain. He leaned in and whispered to him in his most menacing voice.

"I have people too, Steve. And I guarantee my people are far deadlier than yours. Don't come near Darla again, or you'll meet them," Crew promised the man. He cursed at Crew, but Crew felt the shudder of fear pass through his body.

Crew was done with the man. He'd made his point. He pushed him hard and Steve fell from his arms and hit the sidewalk, turning to glare at Crew. "This isn't the last you'll see of me," he promised as he shakily got back to his feet.

"I'm counting on it," Crew said, making sure the man saw the deadly determination in his eyes. Crew was normally a mellow man, but he'd put in his years in the military and had training. He preferred a mellow existence but would fight for what was important.

Steve decided smartly to not say anything else. He walked to a sleek Mercedes SUV with blacked out windows, climbed in the driver's side, started it, and whipped out into traffic nearly crashing into another vehicle that laid on its horn. Steve held his hand out the window and flipped the person off. He was a real class act, that was for sure.

When his taillights were long gone, Crew walked back to the restaurant. He knew this man was trouble, but how much trouble? He'd have to ask Brackish to look into him. Some guys were all talk, some weren't. Crew hadn't decided about Steve.

When he walked back in the restaurant, conversation stopped as all of the diners looked his way. Their gazes went from weary to happy in a matter of seconds.

"That was bad ass," some kid said as he stood from his table where it appeared he was dining with his parents. "I so want to learn that arm move."

"Then join the military," Crew told him with a smile.

"I'm a senior in high school," the kid said. "Maybe I will if I can look like you after training." The kid was tall and lanky, but Crew had no doubt a few years in the military would beef him up quite nicely.

"Good luck," he told him, meaning it.

A few more people thanked him for defusing the situation as he made his way to his table. Darla looked up at him with a bit of hero-worship on her face and his chest puffed out a bit more than it already was.

"That guy just won't go away. I like to handle things myself, but he scares me a little," Darla said as she rose and threw her arms around him. "First, your brother knocks him down a few months ago, and now you're here to rescue me. I might get used to this," she told him. She leaned in and kissed him. Warmth flooded him.

There were a few whistles and clapping behind them, and Darla pulled back with a laugh. She turned and took a bow. "Thank you all for coming to the show. It's not a great dinner without a show," she said, making several people laugh.

A woman approached them, her smile wide, her eyes sparkling. "You look real familiar," she said as she looked between Hudson and Crew.

"We're just out for dinner," Crew quickly said.

Her eyes narrowed as if she was thinking, and he knew the second comprehension clicked in her eyes. "You're those Anderson boys who were all over the news when it was discovered you were long lost heirs, aren't you?"

Hudson laughed as he held out a hand. "We sure are," he said. "But we had our five seconds of fame already. Now we're just normal stiffs like the rest of the world. Is this your place?"

She seemed immediately charmed by Hudson. Crew's brother had a way of doing that with people. Both he and Brandon were incredibly good at charming the daylights out of both the young and old.

"Yes, it is. How did you know?" she asked.

"Well, the apron you're wearing gives it away," Hudson told her. She looked down and laughed, as if she'd forgotten she was wearing it. In big, bold letters, it stated, I'M THE BOSS. BACK OFF . . . OR FEEL THE BURN. There was a burned dish below the words.

"This was a gift from one of my cooks who said I was so sweet and mellow I needed something to show I was the boss."

Both Crew and Hudson laughed hard at her words. "I have a feeling sweet and mellow isn't used to describe you," Crew said. She didn't take offense.

"Well, I really appreciate you getting Steve out of here. He's been in before and he's a real pig. He likes to disrupt, and he thinks everyone should bow to him. He's a damn politician's kid and he pretty much has free rein wherever he goes. I can't stand him."

"A politician's kid. Lovely," Crew said.

Darla gasped. "I had no idea. I went out with the man one time and the date lasted about thirty minutes before I made a quick exit. He *was* a total pig," Darla said, agreeing with the woman.

"I can see that. I can't imagine anyone wants a second date with that man." She shook her head. "But let's forget all about him. I'm sending out a special treat. Finish your dinner and enjoy your evening. Don't let that man ruin it." She didn't let them respond before she disappeared into the kitchen.

Jason quickly appeared. "You're in for a real treat. She doesn't send things out too often," he told them. "Can I get you more wine?"

Four resounding yesses made Jason laugh as he walked away. Everything went back to normal and Steve was forgotten within minutes.

Crew had learned long ago that the best thing to do in a tense situation was to not focus on the bad. He definitely wanted to get more information on Steve, but he wanted to finish his first official date night with Darla on a positive note. He'd have time to dig into Steve later. Hell, once he put Brackish on it, it would probably be done in minutes. That man was a damn genius.

Their wine was delivered, and Crew filled all of their glasses. "To fantastic and entertaining double dates," Crew said, making the other three laugh.

"To many more," Daisy said.

"Well, many more dates, maybe a few less psychos," Hudson said.

"Here, here," Darla agreed.

They clinked glasses.

Chapter Thirteen

Crew and Darla got into a routine. It was so odd for him, and though he was questioning what was happening between the two of them, he was grateful to have her in his life. He knew he wasn't in love in such a short time, but he liked her, he liked her a lot. And he wanted to protect her.

She'd stayed with him for nearly two weeks before she told him she had to go home. He'd questioned her on what came next, and she'd wrapped her arms around him, kissed him sweetly, and in her spunky way had told him they were officially dating.

He'd grinned like a loon. It was so odd. They were in a relationship. She'd stayed at her place for a couple nights and his home had never seemed so empty. It was odd. He'd always put restrictions on his relationships. He'd never wanted them defined. He'd made it clear they had to have lives of their own.

With Darla it was different. He wanted to claim her as his. He wanted to sleep next to her every night. He just wanted to be with her. On the third night away from him, she'd come back, her face pale. She'd told him she wanted to stay for a while. He hadn't pushed her to find out what was bothering her, but he wanted her there so he wasn't complaining.

She'd been with him for a week since her return. Her mood had lightened, and they'd settled into a routine. But he had questions. What was scaring her? What could he do to stop it?

Brackish had come back with a lot of information on Steve. The man's full name was Steve Landon Oscar, Jr. He was forty-three years old and had no record. Hudson had told him the man had been hauled away by the cops a few months ago, so he found that rather odd. Had his family cleared him?

It was true that his father was a California state senator. Had his family wanted him to move away? Had he caused too much trouble down there? Brackish assured Crew he'd find out more information, but Crew had a feeling the team was working on something else at the moment. Brackish's personal problems weren't any of Crew's business.

Darla was playing with the kittens in the barn. Their eyes had opened, and she loved spending hours with them crawling on their tiny legs all over her lap. The mama cat loved her. She'd named her Spice and the cat responded with excitement whenever Darla entered the barn. She'd suggested they move the kittens into the house, but she'd agreed they had a palace in the barn. They had a litter box for now, but as soon as the little things could move around, he was eliminating that. He hated the smell and sight of it.

Daisy walked in beside him and Crew gave her a smile. "Is my brother with you?" he asked.

"No, I'm picking up Darla for lunch. I've been worried about her," Daisy said.

"Me too. What in the hell is going on with this Steve guy? Has she told you more than she's told me?" he asked. If anyone could help him, it was her best friend.

"I don't think Steve would have the balls to confront her while she's with you, but he seriously creeps me out. Darla's so determined to handle things on her own, that she won't say anything unless it gets really bad. I've seen her stand up to a person twice her size and have them back down just from the determination in her eyes. I've always felt safe around Darla, like she's my protector," Daisy said.

"Why do you think he's obsessed with her?" Crew asked.

"I'm not sure. She went on one very short date, realized he wasn't even close to the kind of man she could spend any time with, and then he harassed her. She told me months ago it had stopped. She'd blocked him, then she decided to unblock him to make sure he'd given up. Within days, he began messaging her again. She didn't block him again, but she didn't respond and didn't have send receipts on so he couldn't see if his messages were going through. It's been months since she's seen him, and his messaging hasn't stopped that entire time. I'd have thought he'd have moved on by now," Daisy said, clearly worried.

"What are some of the messages?" Crew asked, feeling a need to scoop Darla up right then and wrap his arms around her. That man wouldn't get near her.

"It's odd — sometimes they're mild messages about how much he loves her smile, the curve of her waist, the sound of her voice. Then the messages get meaner as the day goes on. He asks where she's at, tells her she's his and he won't tolerate being ignored, and asks her if she's whoring around. He's seriously like Dr. Jekyll and Mr. Hyde."

Crew felt his adrenaline pumping. What in the hell was wrong with people that they thought it was okay to act this way? He'd been trying to figure that out for years. He still didn't have the answers he was seeking.

"Is it daily?" Crew asked.

"Yes, it's daily. She just admitted that to me. She was brushing it off, but that scene at the restaurant seemed to send him into a new realm. He sent pictures last week of him with another woman, who was tied up, telling her this was what he was going to do to her."

"What?" Crew exclaimed before forcing his voice to calm. "She turned him in, right?" he thundered.

"Yes, she feared he'd raped the woman. But the cops showed up and said the woman was a willing accomplice, and Steve managed to once again not get into trouble. She told me about it and I told her she couldn't be alone anymore, at least now. That's when she called you. I was hoping she'd talk to you about it, but if she hasn't, don't push her. Just be there for her."

"I don't think I can let her leave here again," Crew said, scared for this woman he cared so much about.

"Don't become her captor, just help her out and be there for her. This guy will do something that will land him in jail. I don't understand the power and influence politicians have. Shouldn't they be more transparent than the rest of us, not using their power to get their friends and family out of jail? It horrifies me, and it seriously scares the crud out of me. The things they get away with should frighten every American," Daisy finished with a shudder.

"I don't know how I can't talk about this with her," he admitted.

"I'm trusting you, Crew, because I think you honestly have Darla's best interest at heart. Please don't betray that trust. If Darla thinks she can't talk to me, she might not talk to anyone. She thinks this will all blow over. I'm not so sure," Daisy told him.

It was harder for Crew to sit and do nothing. She was asking the impossible from him. But, he reminded himself, he wasn't doing nothing, he had Brackish on this guy, and if he even attempted to come near Darla again, they could make him disappear.

The real question, however, was how far outside the law was Crew willing to go? Was there anything he wouldn't do to protect those he cared about?

"Fine, I'll handle it," Crew said after a while.

Daisy's eyes narrowed. "What do you mean by 'handle it'?" she asked.

"I assure you I'll watch out for her and if he even looks as if he's moving to harm her, I know a lot of people, and he won't be able to touch anyone ever again," Crew said.

Daisy laughed, not seeming upset by his words. "Don't do something you'll regret. That man isn't worth a life in prison," she told him.

"I'm not talking murder. But a few broken bones might wake him up," Crew said.

"I'm sure people have accidents all of the time," Daisy said with a wink. He was shocked. Daisy was such a kind person and they were talking about vigilante justice as if they were discussing rainbows. It was just another day and another topic. Crew laughed with Daisy.

"I'm really glad my brother met you," he told her. "You're good for him and you fit perfectly in our family."

She reached over and hugged him. "I'm very glad to be a part of your family too. I love Hudson with all of my heart and I've never felt so happy or free. I love you and your brother, too, because you *are* family. But beyond that, I've learned what good men you are."

Crew wondered at how easy it was for some people to speak so freely of love. He didn't often use the word love. When he did, it was always meant. He didn't even use the word to describe food or movies. The word love was thrown around so casually he felt it really didn't have much meaning anymore. People said they loved pizza, popcorn, a movie, a stranger, or even a piece of furniture. He liked all of those things, but he didn't *love* them.

He loved his brothers. He loved his family. He loved life. He liked everything else.

Darla heard their laughter and called out. "I thought I heard you, Daisy. Get your butt in here. The kittens are wide awake and playful."

"Yea. We'll play for a bit before lunch."

Daisy gave Crew one last look. "Behave," she said with a wiggle of her finger. Then she laughed as she walked away from him.

Women. They truly were a pain in the ass. But he'd learned long ago that none of the men in the world, including him, could live without them. For one, it was basic biology. They needed women to bring life into the world. But the main point was that women brought something to life that other men couldn't. They brought warmth and laughter, softness and nurturing. He wasn't so caveman that he didn't think men could bring some of the same. He just appreciated that men and women were different.

Even in the military he'd seen some of the baddest of the bad women who could kick a man's ass with no problem. He'd seen men who were weak and fizzled out. But at the end of the day yin and yang was real and he wanted to appreciate the difference in the male and female species.

He laughed to himself as he left the barn. Why his mind went to some of the places it went he'd never know. But he'd accepted that about himself long ago. He'd continue to worry about Darla, but he'd also enjoy their time and not obsess on problems at the same time.

Life was too good to live in fear.

Chapter Fourteen

After a long day at work, Crew walked into his house to the scent of basil, tomato sauce, and garlic. His stomach grumbled, and he realized he'd forgotten to eat lunch. He'd had a busy day with two clients at his office and a trip to the state prison. He loved doing work at the prison, loved trying to solve the puzzle of severely damaged minds.

He turned a corner and saw Darla at the stove, a large spoon in her hand as she tasted a red sauce. She sighed, not realizing he was there. He stood and watched her for a moment as she set the spoon down, then picked up a bottle of spice and shook it over the pot. Her hips were swaying to a sweet country song as she moved over to the sink, humming the words, *five . . . more . . . minutes*. He'd never been a big country music fan, but the deep timbre of Scotty McCreery's voice had gotten to him.

Darla stopped, spotted him, then took his breath away when she smiled, the expression reaching her eyes and making his heart skip a beat. He loved coming home to her.

"It looks like you've been home a while," he told her.

"I got off early and decided to make you my famous spaghetti. I warned you I'm not a great cook, but the five dishes I do make, I make to perfection," she said. She moved over to the fridge and pulled out a half-empty bottle of wine. He spotted the glass on the counter that was nearly empty. She took another glass down, filled it, then refilled her own before sliding the other to him.

"Mmm," he said with a wicked smile as he leaned over the kitchen island. "Good. I like my woman barefoot and serving me."

She gaped at him for a moment, and he saw murder in her eyes. Then she saw the sparkle in his own and she laughed with him. Walking around the island, she wrapped her hands behind his head and kissed him, all laughter instantly draining away. Just as he was about to throw her over his shoulder again, she nipped his bottom lip hard enough to make him gasp, then quickly danced away with a laugh.

"That's for the sexist comment," she told him, putting an extra sway in her hips as she moved back to the stove. His eyes were on her ass, just where she knew they'd be.

"Little minx," he said as he lifted his glass. "Do you need help?" He could sit at the counter all night and watch her. She was poetry in motion, and he never knew what would come out of her mouth from one minute to the next.

"Nope. You'd just ruin it. You're a worse cook than I am, and that's really saying something," she told him.

"What else do you have cooking? The house smells like a fine Italian restaurant," he said as he looked at the counter full of bowls and dishes of food. It appeared as if a small tornado had come in and hit only the counters and sink.

"We're having spaghetti, garlic cheese bread, stuffed mushrooms, and Italian salad. My mom had this amazing hand-written recipe book passed down from her great-grandmother. She had it typed up and included pictures, since I hate recipe books without pictures, and then reproduced it for the family. There's not a ton of recipes in it, but they are the only ones I ever took time to learn how to cook. Obviously, I didn't get to meet my great-great-grandmother, but I like having a piece of her with me. Mom even had family pictures added to the back."

Darla grabbed the spiral bound cookbook and handed it to him. The front cover had a picture of an Italian bakery with an older woman sitting in a rocking chair, holding something in her hands.

"Is this your great-great-grandmother?" Crew asked.

"Yep, it's Grandma Madiana. I've heard so much about her, it's almost like I know her. This was her bakery in Portofino, Italy. Back when she lived in the coastal fishing town it wasn't a tourist destination. Now it has a famous resort for very wealthy jet-setters. But even with tourists, the town looks like a postcard."

"I went to Italy a few years ago and heard about the town. We never made it there. It curves around the cove of a natural harbor, right?" he asked.

She pulled a tray of mushrooms and garlic cheese toast from the oven, the scent of cheese, herbs, and seafood making his head a little fuzzy. He was hungry and, if the aroma was any indication, this might be the best meal he'd ever eaten.

"Yes, when my family lived in Italy it was a small fishing town. Now it's full of upscale shops, decadent restaurants and cafes, and luxurious hotels and spas. But I still have some distant family there and they tell me they know all of the local places the tourists rarely manage to find, so I hope to visit one day," Darla said.

"Was your great-great-grandmother fully Italian?" he asked.

"Yep," she said. "And then she did the unthinkable and married an American," Darla said with mock horror.

"They had six children and lived out their days in Italy, not feeling a need to travel much. Of course, when you live in a paradise like Portofino, why would you?" Darla asked. She kept working as they talked and Crew looked through the cookbook at the pictures in the back.

"I'm all about progress, but there are times I wish I would've been born a hundred years ago," he told her.

"I agree," Darla said. She poured the spaghetti sauce over her noodles and mixed it all together. Each time she did something new, it sent incredible smells into the air. He wanted to reach out and grab one of the bubbling mushrooms that were close to him, but feared he might get his hand slapped if he took something too soon. She'd put so much work into the dinner, he didn't want to ruin it.

"Grandma's home was still just a fishing village when she was a girl. In that picture she is looking out over the water as she waits for her husband to get back with dinner. Her brother took him under his wing and my great-great grandpa became quite the fisherman. Grandma ran her bakery, and he earned a small living fishing. But they never went without food," Darla said with a laugh.

"Is the only access by sea?" Crew asked.

Darla set the last dish on the kitchen island and Crew was practically drooling. "Dish up," she told him, and he didn't hesitate.

He began piling food on his plate, making Darla laugh. "You'd think you'd never eaten before," she told him.

"I forgot lunch and only had toast this morning. It was a busy day," he said as he sprinkled fresh parmesan on top of his spaghetti. He dug in and took a bite, flavors exploding on his tongue. "Damn, best spaghetti I've ever had," he said after he swallowed. He kept on digging in while Darla scooped food on her own plate.

"Sorry," he muttered when he realized he hadn't waited for her. Where in the hell were his manners?

"The best compliment to the chef is an appreciative diner," she told him. "I'd be offended if you weren't scarfing it down right now." She began eating as well so he continued. "Back to Portofino," she said after a minute. He'd nearly forgotten about their conversation in his desire to fill his belly. He finally slowed down, wanting to savor each and every bite.

"You can get to Portofino by road, but the road is winding and nerve-wracking I've been told. It's a much smoother ride by boat. It's a really isolated location. This is one of the reasons it draws the rich and famous who want a break. The pictures of the town show a sapphire sea and boldly colorful homes. If you add in the lush green foliage and rising hills, you have a picturesque town."

"How come you haven't gone yet?" he asked.

"I don't know. I get so busy with life, and I haven't been able to justify the expense of international travel. I absolutely can't ride for nine or ten hours in coach and the cost of first-class is outrageous. So, I keep telling myself I'll go someday," Darla said.

"You do realize I have access to a private jet, right?" he told her with a grin.

"Hmm," she said with a chuckle. "I might consider that if we haven't gotten sick of each other by this time next year," she told him.

"I can guarantee I won't get sick of you," he told her. He looked up and met her gaze. She was still smiling, but when she saw the seriousness of his expression her grin slowly faded. She looked at him as if seeing him for the first time, and he saw some unknown emotion flash in her eyes that gave him hope this would lead to so much more than it already was. Did he want to let all his defenses down and fully let her in? He just might.

She reached over and kissed him, a soft kiss, then pulled back. "You better get seconds, Crew. I've been cooking for two hours. I *never* do that," she said, trying to lighten the mood.

"Don't worry, I'll eat until I burst," he assured her.

"Do you want to know the coolest thing about Portofino?" she asked.

"Of course, I do," he said as he bit into a stuffed mushroom that once again sent his senses into overdrive. He finished chewing then added, "I bet it's pirates. I bet pirates built the town."

She laughed. "I haven't heard any pirate legends, but I'm sure they were there," Darla told him. "Nope, the coolest thing is that Portofino was a Roman colony originally named Portus Delphini, supposedly because of dolphins in the harbor. It was a strategic point for centuries. But the coolest fact of all is that it was placed under the republic of Genova in 1229." She stopped and he looked at her quizzically.

"Um, okay, I guess, but why is that the coolest fact?" he asked as he searched his mind for possibilities.

"Because my favorite princess movie of all time is *The Princess Diaries*, and she's the princess of Genovia. When I found out there was a place called Genova that my family is from I was quite pleased."

He looked at her and waited, but she simply went back to her food. He was seriously confused.

"You're excited that your family comes from a place in Italy that's one letter off from your favorite fictional movie?" he asked just to clarify.

"Yep, very excited," she told him.

"Maybe I should make an appointment for you on my couch," he said with a straight face.

Her head whipped up as she glared at him. "Just for that, you're going to watch *The Princess Diaries* with me tonight," she said.

"I'm sorry," he told her, holding his hands in the air. "I was just kidding. I think it's an incredible and unique fact. Please, for the love of all that's holy, don't make me watch that movie."

"Too late. I haven't seen it in years. And, do you know what the best part of all is?" she asked. He was no longer fooled by her sweet, innocent smile. She was truly a devil in disguise.

"What's that?" he asked as he reached for the wine bottle and filled his glass to the top. He was going to need a lot more if he had to watch princess movies.

"There's a part two," she said with evil glee. "They have a script eighteen years later for a part three, but it hasn't been made yet."

Crew groaned, then guzzled half of his glass of wine. Darla got up and grabbed another bottle, opening it while he ate more food. Maybe if he ate really, *really* slow she'd forget about her princess movie. He could always hope and dream.

Chapter Fifteen

Crew's hopes and dreams were quickly squashed. He spent thirty minutes cleaning the huge mess she'd made in the kitchen. He could've done it in half the time but he was hoping she'd turn her movie on, and he'd only have to suffer for about forty-five minutes. Nope. She'd pulled up the movie on Disney Plus, paused it, and waited for him.

If he hadn't wanted to hold her in his arms so much, he would've found some excuse to get out of watching it. It wasn't so bad once she was curled up against him, a blanket shielding them from the world as the movie began playing.

It was terrible, absolutely terrible. He liked the grandmother played by Julie Andrews, but other than that it was a teenage girl's dream and a grown man's nightmare. However, Darla's sighs of joy as Mia — the princess played by Anne Hathaway — found herself made the movie adventure worth it.

The more she snuggled into him, the more he tolerated the movie. His body had heated up and he was ready to take her to his bed. No matter how often the two of them made love, it was never enough. He had a hunger for this woman that was never going away.

Unfortunately the hunger had to wait. Darla went straight from the credits of *The Princess Diaries* to *The Princess Diaries 2*. His torture wouldn't be complete until Princess Mia got her happily ever after.

When the second movie ended, Crew felt his IQ had dropped a few points. "Do you want to watch another of my favorite princess movies?" she asked.

That was it, Crew had most certainly suffered enough.

"Woman, you're torturing me on purpose," he growled.

She laughed, and that's when he knew he'd been suckered. "I didn't think you'd get through the first movie, let alone two. I really have power over you," she told him, laughing so hard she could barely get the words out.

"You're going to pay for this," he told her. "I was being that nice because you made me a spectacular dinner. Now I know you're just a sneaky little vixen," he said as he flipped them over on the couch and pinned her.

"I got you to watch two princess movies. That makes me the most brilliant woman in the universe," she said. "I might even post it on my social media page."

"Don't you dare. I'll find some dirt on you and do the same," he promised. The thought of his brothers knowing he'd been suckered into cheesy chick flicks was terrifying. He'd never live it down.

"Oh, come on, Crew, you've found your sensitive side," she said, still laughing. "The truth is men really do love chick flicks. They just don't want to admit it, so they act as if it's torture to watch them."

Crew knew of one sure way to end this dispute. He closed the space between them and lowered his head, claiming her mouth as his own, kissing her with a savageness that spoke of too much time passing since their last kiss. Whether five minutes or five hours, his hunger for her couldn't be sated.

As soon as their mouths connected, Darla's laughter turned to passion. She melted against him as his lips molded perfectly to hers and he dipped inside to explore the sweetness of her mouth. It didn't take much convincing to have her tongue dancing with his, making his body ignite as he pressed his arousal against her.

He sucked up the sweet sounds of hunger escaping her mouth as he pushed harder against her. The way her hands reached around him and tangled in his hair only made him greedier for her. They fit perfectly together, her plump breasts pressed against his solid chest, the sweet V of her thighs a perfect home to bury himself.

In every other relationship he'd been disciplined, in control, doing what was best for him and his partner. But not with Darla. No matter how hard he tried to maintain a semblance of calm, the second they touched he lost control, becoming a man he barely recognized. He instantly wanted to stake his claim, pound his chest, and own this woman.

Discipline flew out the window when he was in Darla's arms, and the longer the two of them were together, the more he hoped he'd never find that control again. She made him a new man, a better man, a happier man.

He didn't care that she pushed him past the point of no return on a daily basis and took away all semblance of restraint it had taken him years to develop. That was the beauty of it. He liked to be messy and uncomfortable around this woman. He liked letting it all go.

Crew's hand lifted as he moved his lips over her jaw. He drew light circles on her collarbone with his tongue and fingers, causing her flesh to quiver beneath him. She was so damn responsive, so very much his. His lips ran over her pulse that hammered beneath her silky skin. She moaned, the sound circling him.

She was so vulnerable with him. Part of him wanted to claim her again and again, and part of him wanted to stand at her door and defend her from the cruelties of the world. He wanted to own her and defend her, be her white knight and her captor. He wanted to be her everything.

He leaned back and looked at her. It took a moment before she realized he'd stopped. He watched in fascination as her eyes slowly opened and gazed at him, lust burning in them.

"Don't stop now, cowboy," she slurred, drunk on his kisses. He bent down and kissed her nose, making a sweet smile spread across her swollen lips. She moved her hands down from his neck and trailed her fingers over his arms.

"I get lost in you, Darla. What you do to me should be illegal," he told her.

"Oh, Crew, I second that. When you kiss me, I'm taken to another world. When you make love to me, it's heavenly," she told him.

"Do you ever not say what's on your mind?" he asked her with a gentle smile.

"I like honesty. I don't always want to share every hope, desire, and thought in my head, but if I do want to say something, I don't normally hold back," she told him.

"I love that about you the most," he said. He leaned down and softly brushed his lips against hers again. It was impossible to look into her flushed face and not kiss her. "I'm not going to ever let you go," he finished.

She smiled a serene, happy smile. "You won't get a choice if I want to be free," she said, stunning him.

"What?" he asked. He hadn't meant to blurt out those words, but her reply wasn't what he expected at all.

"I'm here because I want to be here, Crew, not because I feel pressured or because I don't want to let you down. I'm here because being away from you feels like a part of me is missing. I hope that feeling lasts, but sometimes it doesn't. Sometimes the world gets in the way, and sometimes beautiful passion fades and turns into loathing. I don't want that to happen with us, but I can't promise it won't. If it does, I'll walk away," she told him.

What she was saying was totally rational; it was the conversation he previously would have with a woman before they slept together. But with Darla, each word was like a stab to his heart.

"I guess I'll have to make sure you don't ever want to go," he said, deciding he didn't want to discuss it anymore.

He leapt from the couch and scooped her into his arms. "No more princess movies for you. Tomorrow we watch *Rocky*." She laughed as he carried her to the bedroom. "And do you know what the best part is?" he taunted as he stepped inside what he now considered *their* bedroom.

"What?" she asked.

"There are *six* Rocky movies. Payback will be very satisfying." Her eyes widened in horror.

"That's not even sort of fair," she gasped as he grabbed her shirt and pulled it over her head.

"Haven't you been told that life's not fair?" he asked, stopping the discussion by pulling her against him and kissing her again.

There was no more talk of movies that night, just a lot of moans and sounds of appreciation. They might have vastly different tastes in movies, but their bodies sang together when they were wrapped in each other's arms.

He wasn't going to ever let her go — and he'd make sure she didn't ask to be set free.

Chapter Sixteen

Darla froze as a man chased her. She tried to run, but her feet wouldn't move. "You're mine, Darla, all mine," he said, his face in shadows. She knew she had to run, knew she had to get away. She tried moving and still couldn't. She opened her mouth and let out a cry.

The sound jerked her awake.

Crew was holding her and looked down with concern before he laughed.

"Really? You fell asleep again?" he asked. "That's three times now. Are you going to get through even one of these movies?"

It took a moment for Darla to realize she'd been dreaming. True to his word, Crew had insisted they were watching all of the Rocky movies. She liked them, she did, but there were some really slow parts, and if she heard the name Adrian yelled out one more time she might have to punch someone.

"You didn't say I had to stay awake through all of the movies," she told him. She cuddled in closer to him, enjoying the scent of his skin as she kissed his neck.

"Don't think you can distract me with that tempting mouth of yours," he warned. But she laughed. She could hear the huskiness in his voice. It didn't matter how many times they made love, it was never enough.

She was tired. She hadn't slept well the past few days. There was too much going on in her life. But, she always felt grounded again when she was with Crew.

"Every Rocky movie is exactly the same," she complained.

"No way! How can a woman who loves the rodeo not like Rocky?" he asked, completely confounded.

"I like live sports. I'm not a huge fan of watching them on television," she said. "If I can't get to a live game for a long time, I'll cave and watch one on the screen. But the rodeo and live sports are so exhilarating with the crowds around you. You can practically taste the fear, desire, and excitement in the air. Plus, there's always fried food and good liquor," she added.

"I don't know how you manage to have such a fantastic body with your love of fried foods," he said.

"It's all about self-control. If I go crazy at events and then work out hard, I can stay in shape. If there was an event every day I'd weigh five hundred pounds." She stopped and laughed. "I could probably live with that." A shudder went through her. No, scratch that, she couldn't handle being too tired to move, and anytime she gained weight she felt it in her joints. She hated that feeling.

"So, what are your plans tomorrow?" he asked. She enjoyed the domestic bliss of being with him, enjoyed chatting about their days.

"I have a full caseload this week," she said.

He wrapped her a little tighter.

"You can quit anytime you want," he said. "I know you don't know what's going to come next, but I hate to see you so miserable with your job."

"I go through this sometimes. It doesn't mean I want to give up . . . not yet. I just don't know if I'm hurting things more than I'm helping."

"I don't think it's possible for you to hurt anything. You're amazing, and I'm sure the people you've helped along the way appreciate you more than words can say," he told her.

"You have to say that so you can get lucky," she told him.

"Well, I am a psychologist so I have to stroke your ego," he told her.

"You're such a brat," she said as she moved quickly, straddling him in an instant and pinning his arms to his sides. She had no doubt he could break the hold, but he was allowing her to take control. It was another thing she loved about the man.

"I might be slightly stubborn, but you're the queen of battiness," he told her, his voice growing huskier as he pushed up his hips, letting her feel the effect she was having on him.

"I like being queen," she said as she leaned down and kissed the side of his neck, pressing her breasts against him, making both of them ache.

"I'll give you any title you please," he said as he freed his arms and wrapped them around her, his hands cupping her butt and squeezing as he pulled her more fully against him.

"That's because you're a very smart man. Are you trying to follow in your brothers' footsteps, enjoying the benefit of having a good woman around?"

"I think it's because you burst into my life like a tornado and I can either jump in and ride the wind, or you'll destroy me," he said with a chuckle.

She leaned back and glared at him. "Are you seriously comparing me to a natural disaster?"

"Damn straight I am, and I don't even regret it," he said.

"You'll regret it when Tornado Darla touches down," she warned.

"I guess I'll have to try to make it to the eye of the storm," he said. Then he grasped the back of her neck and kissed her again, stopping their conversation for a moment. She got lost in his embrace, feeling safe and cared for.

He pulled back and looked in her eyes, his blue ones absolutely mesmerizing. "I don't know what it is about you, but I am your willing puppet," he told her. She was shocked by the words. Admitting the power she held over their relationship was a huge thing for any man, especially Crew Anderson. He was a psychologist who knew what his words meant. She was so overwhelmed, she chuckled a little and made a joke.

"I think you want me around for my ass and boobs," she said. She was expecting a joke back.

"The ass is wonderful," he told her. "And the rest of you is too good to be true. But it's the smile, the humor, the loyalty you show to others. It's the total package that has me willing to do anything you want," he said.

"Crew, I worry sometimes that you're too good to be true," she admitted.

He held her close. "I have the same worries, Darla. I was never interested in a relationship this intense, but now that I'm in it, I can't picture my existence without you there."

She didn't know what that meant for either of them. So she leaned forward and kissed him. They'd figure it out. They had plenty of time. For now, there was one thing she was very sure of, and she was going to make sure he knew how she felt about him with every kiss of her lips and touch of her fingers. She could let go in his arms and be free.

Chapter Seventeen

Crew had turned into a regular sex fiend. If he and Darla weren't eating, it seemed they were in bed together. She sure as hell didn't have any complaints, so why should he think anything was wrong?

He wanted to talk to her about their next steps, but he'd begin to talk, then clothes were ripping away and he was pushing her into the mattress, the table, or against a wall, burying himself deep inside of her.

The woman was both sin and salvation. Shouldn't he at least attempt to make what they had more real? He felt like he should but he was afraid he'd screw everything up if he did. So, instead of talking, he gave her orgasm after orgasm and hoped that was enough.

"Crew, now!" Darla demanded. They'd made love the night before, and he'd woke up hungry for more. Her bare ass had been pressed against his very hard groin, so he'd simply lifted her leg and thrust inside of her.

Heaven. She was always pure heaven.

Crew yelled as he thrust deep inside of her one more time and then felt his release.

"Oh, I want to wake up like this every single day," Darla said with a happy moan, her core still pulsing around him.

Crew froze. He'd buried himself deep inside of her without a second thought. He'd barely been awake when he'd done it, but he'd woken up real fast as her body had squeezed him.

"What's wrong?" she asked, feeling him tense behind her.

"I forgot a condom," he said. He should be more horrified than he was. He'd never forgotten a condom in his life.

The tension in Darla's body eased as she giggled. "I thought something was *really* wrong. You stiffened like you'd just seen a ghost," she said.

"Darla," he groaned, "that was foolish."

"Don't worry. I trust you," she told him. "I'm not worried you're going to give me some dastardly disease."

"What about a baby?" he asked. Even speaking those words should've filled him with the worst kind of dread. But with Darla it didn't. He was more concerned with how she'd feel.

"I'm on birth control. Even so, I swore I'd never trust a man enough to have condomless sex. The birth control is more so I don't have periods. I hate those things," she said.

"Wait? What? I've been using condoms every time," he told her.

"It's good for you and far less messy for me," she told him with a giggle.

He laughed as he pulled from her and flipped her onto her back. "You truly are a terror, you do realize that, right?" he said before he leaned down and kissed her.

"Yep, I know I am," she assured him. "But at least I keep you on your toes."

"That's more than true," he said.

"Yep, I need a shower. You left me quite the mess," she told him as she laughed.

"What?" He was confused once again.

"Um, darling, I love the feel of your pleasure, but now that pleasure is all over me," she said. "And all over the bed."

Crew wasn't sure why, but he found his cheeks heating. He'd never had sex without a condom before, and it wasn't something he'd even thought about. His embarrassment must've been obvious because Darla started laughing harder.

"Oh my gosh, I can't believe I just embarrassed you. I can't wait to tell Daisy."

He looked at her with terror. "Please, if you have any feelings for me at all, you will not share this with Daisy when it's sure to get back to my brother," he gasped.

"Um, I hate to tell you this but I don't think Daisy and Hudson use condoms either. They *are* engaged, so your brother probably realizes how messy sex is," she said with another laugh.

"Do women really have these conversations?" he asked.

Darla looked highly amused. "Of course we do. Otherwise how in the heck would we know what's good and what's not? Don't tell me you haven't had some locker room chats," she said.

"No. I don't think men are nearly as crude as women. That's a total misconception. We might say something here or there, but we don't talk about our sex lives — like, not ever," he told her.

"Hmm, interesting," she said. "Well, we do, and we like it."

"I could hold out," he threatened, and she threw her head back and laughed so hard tears rolled from her eyes. Her bare breasts bounced in her mirth and he felt himself growing solid again.

"Oh, that's such an empty threat, darling," she said as she reached down and proved her point by wrapping her fingers around his erection that instantly danced in her palm. He glared at her. And just to prove he was strong, he pulled away.

He rose from the bed and looked down at her with triumph. "I'm going to take a shower," he said.

She laughed again. "You go ahead and show me," she said in between giggles. "You prove your point." As she said that she kicked the rest of the blanket from her naked body and dragged one foot up along her thigh while stretching her arms out. "Mmm, I feel good. I had two orgasms. How about you?"

He almost jumped right back in bed. But like a fool he turned and stomped into the bathroom, his body throbbing, his head screaming at him. Darla's laughter followed him until he turned on the jet of the shower. He quickly turned it to cool and climbed inside.

Crew wasn't feeling a heck of a lot better when he stepped from the shower and grabbed a towel, roughly drying himself. He knew Darla was laughing at him because his stubbornness was only making him suffer, but a man had to have principles, dang it. He was proving a point. He'd already forgotten what the point was.

And he was hungry . . . in more ways than one.

Crew made it to the bottom of the stairs when his phone rang. He smiled when he saw who it was on the caller ID. He held the phone a little ways from his ear before answering, knowing if he didn't he just might lose his eardrums. That's what happened when his uncle spoke.

"Good morning, Uncle Joseph. I hope your day's going well," Crew said. He rounded the corner, surprised not to see Darla. She'd most likely gone into the other bathroom upstairs to shower. Damn, now he had an image of her all wet and soapy, suds running down her ample breasts, making a trail across her stomach, and slithering to that sweet spot between her thighs. He internally groaned.

"Are you listening to me, boy?" Joseph thundered. While he'd been fantasizing he'd allowed the phone to rest against his ear and he winced. Ouch.

"Of course I am," Crew quickly responded. He didn't want to be having fantasies about Darla while he was on the phone with his uncle. He had to stay sharp when Joseph was speaking. Crew wasn't convinced Joseph couldn't read minds. The man knew far too much to not have psychic abilities.

"How's Aunt Katherine feeling?" Crew asked, knowing the best way to get heat off himself was for his uncle to talk about his wife. Joseph loved her with such an intense passion it made people around him want to fall in love so they could feel even a smidgeon of the same emotion.

"She's doing really well," Joseph said. There was a long pause and Crew laughed.

"How are *you* feeling?" Crew finally asked. He'd been debating whether he wanted to ask or not. The entire family had a thread going with Joseph's medical updates. They knew Joseph was milking his gunshot for all it was worth.

Of course, it had been terrifying, but after they knew Joseph was out of danger, they apparently hadn't given the ornery old man enough attention. So Joseph, who didn't do frail so well, was trying to guilt them all.

"I can't say I'm a hundred percent, but I'm feeling a little better as each day passes," Joseph said, even managing to turn down the volume of his voice slightly. It would only take seconds for his act to fade, though, because Joseph talked loud. It was just who he was.

"I'm glad to hear that," Crew told him. He was listening for any sounds from upstairs, hoping Darla would join him soon. He was hungry and she'd mentioned she wanted to go out, so he wasn't sure if he should start cooking or wait. She loved having diner breakfast food, saying it always tasted better than making eggs at home. He had to agree. He wasn't sure what those diners did to the food, but it always came out to perfection, especially if a person had a hangover, which he didn't at the moment.

"How are you doing, Crew, and what's happening with Darla?" Joseph asked. Crew had known his uncle wouldn't be able to last long without trying to pry into his personal life. Crew would just have to see how long he could make the man suffer by ignoring the second part of his question.

"I can't complain. We've been having a lot of sunshine, and as much as I didn't want to have the horses, I have to admit they aren't too bad." He wasn't going to tell Joseph how much he actually liked the animals. Joseph's ego was already the size of Texas, they didn't need to water it, and watch it grow bigger.

"I knew you'd love the horses. You have too big of a home to have it all empty," Joseph said. "How many stalls do you have?"

Crew laughed. "Nope. I'm not telling you. I like these four horses just fine, but I don't need more."

"That's nonsense, my boy. If you have the space you might as well use it," Joseph told him. "Horses are good for the soul. Kids like them too," he added slyly.

"Well, that's good. Then my nieces can play with them when they visit," Crew assured his uncle.

"Did you know that your mama really loved horses when she was young?" Joseph asked, stunning Crew. He hadn't been expecting that.

"No, I didn't know. She never mentioned it."

"Yep, some of the information Brackish was able to find had a picture of her on a horse. She'd written on the back that it was a neighbor's horse, but she hoped she'd have one someday. I know your aunt Katherine is putting all of the pictures together so she can make albums for each of you guys. Your mother was a beauty from the day she was born to the day she left this world."

Crew felt a tightness in his throat.

"I wish she was still here so I could give her a horse. Had any of us known, we would've each bought her one," Crew told him.

Joseph chuckled. "She knew that, boy. She wanted you guys to live your own lives, not try to take care of her. She certainly loved horses when she was young, but then she found other loves as she got older. That happens to us all," Joseph assured him.

"That sounds just like Mom," Crew said. His mother had been the rock of their family. They all missed her every day. Their lives moved on, but they each felt as if something was missing. That feeling would never go away.

"I know the fact that your mother didn't let you know about our family sooner has been the hardest on you, Crew, but understand she did what she did out of love and pride. We'll never know the fear she lived with after all of the nasty things your father said to her about our family. But we do know that she wanted you to have this family when she was gone. I'm here to talk about it anytime you need to," Joseph told him.

Crew felt a myriad of emotion at Joseph's words. It had been difficult for him to reject the lies he'd been told his entire life. No, he wouldn't blame his mother. He fully blamed his father for scaring her so badly she hadn't known who she could trust. It was odd how people could be controlled by fear.

"I learned long ago that if you scare people enough with a lie, knowing the truth wouldn't eliminate the fear. I don't like all of the choices that were made for my brothers and me when we were young, but I do understand why my mother made the decisions she did," Crew told Joseph. "What I don't understand is why I know that to be true, but still feel resentment. You'd think with my profession, I'd be able to understand it all a lot better."

"Just as they say a doctor can't operate on himself, a psychologist can't get inside his own head," Joseph told him. "You and your brothers have all overcome immeasurable odds. And now, you're exactly where you want to be and should be. That's what you should focus on," Joseph told him.

"I'm not a hundred percent sure I'm where I want to be, but I feel I get closer all of the time," Crew said with honesty.

"That's all any of us can do," Joseph assured him. Before he could say something, Joseph continued. "Now, back to Darla. What's happening with that fine young lady? Have you made her an honest woman yet?"

Crew smiled again. He knew he wouldn't be able to put Joseph off too long. The man enjoyed meddling far too much. Crew didn't like the idea of anyone meddling in his life, but he also wasn't scared when it came to Darla. He liked the woman, liked her a lot, and he wasn't too worried about the future . . . well, maybe a little, but it wasn't like a weight pulling him under.

"Darla and I are . . . well, we're fine," Crew said. He knew he could keep teasing his uncle, but he feared that would only cause the conversation to go on for hours.

"What do you mean, you're fine?" Joseph thundered, making Crew chuckle. "Fine isn't a good word to describe a great relationship."

"We like being together," Crew tried again.

"I don't know how you keep the woman around with an attitude like that. You sound as if she's no more important than a kitchen appliance," Joseph said with a sound of disgust.

"She's most definitely better to have around than all of the appliances in the house," Crew said. He might be poking the bear a bit, but he couldn't seem to help himself. Joseph growled again, and Crew wondered if he'd poked him a little too hard and had forgotten to step back. He also looked around to make sure Darla hadn't walked in. If she heard him making a comment like that he was likely to get his butt kicked — and he'd deserve it.

"Crew Anderson, your mama raised you better than that," Joseph told him.

"I'm just picking on you, Uncle," Crew assured him. "But honestly, I don't know what you're looking for."

"Does she know how important she is to you?" Joseph asked.

"How do you know she is?" Crew responded, again looking around. She was important to him, more than important.

"If I thought you meant that I'd march on over there and smack you upside the head," Joseph said. "I like Darla. She's a good woman and you're lucky to have her."

"I have to agree with you on that," Crew said.

"Well, does she know how you feel about her?" Joseph asked. Crew was going to respond with a solid yes, but then he realized they hadn't really talked about how they were feeling. They knew they wanted to be together, but they hadn't delved further than that.

"She knows I respect her. She knows I want her to be here," Crew finally said.

"That's not good enough, Crew. You need a big gesture. You need to make yourself vulnerable, and you need to make sure she knows you want her with you," Joseph lectured.

"How in the world am I supposed to do that?" Crew asked. Before Joseph could tell him, he continued. "I've never been with a woman I wanted to stay with for long. I've never been with a woman, for that matter, that I've thought about from the time I wake up until the time I fall asleep. Hell, for that matter, Darla appears in my dreams too. I know this could all be because it's exciting and still pretty new, and I've had a lot of stress lately, but I truly do like this woman."

Joseph sighed. Crew had obviously been forgiven for his earlier insurrection. What confused Crew was that he'd gone from teasing Joseph to wanting to hear his advice.

"Those words are music to my soul, Crew," Joseph said. "You're lucky to have me because I can help you out with this one."

Crew chuckled again. "And how are you going to do that?" Crew asked.

"You need to find something that shows her how you feel, and that you listen to her, that you understand her and *respect* her. Make it good," Joseph insisted.

Crew leaned back against the counter as he watched the entrance to the kitchen. He didn't want Darla to walk in now and hear this part of the conversation. What would she think about it? He wasn't sure.

"She wants to go to Italy," Crew finally said. "But she said there was no way she'd let me take her."

"Well, that's just nonsense. There's no reason for you not to take her," Joseph said. "You pick the date — sooner, rather than later —

and I'll have the jet gassed up and ready to go for as long as you want."

As soon as Joseph said that, Crew felt a thrill shoot through him. "She told me about a place her grandmother was born and raised. She had a bakery there. She's always wanted to visit."

"Well then, you must take her. Do you need help planning the trip?" Joseph asked excitedly.

"No, I think I can handle it," Crew said, excited to do just that. Darla was either going to love him or beat him over the head for not listening to her. But he *was* listening. He wanted to give her something she truly wanted. She'd just have to get over the fact that he was paying for it. He had a hell of a lot of money, it was simply a part of who he was. She could love him in spite of that and accept that he could literally whisk her around the world and back, or she'd never be happy with him.

"Then my work here is done," Joseph said.

"Your work?" Crew asked, as Darla stepped into the kitchen, looking fresh-faced, her hair still damp from her shower. She was stunning.

"If it wasn't for me none of you clueless children would've managed to find true love and eternal happiness. Someday you all owe me a huge celebration of thanks. The Andersons will go on for generations to come because of me." He paused. "Well, I guess George and Richard get some of the credit too," he added quietly.

"You're such a humble man, Uncle," Crew said with a laugh.

"I know. But once in a while a horn must be tooted," Joseph told him as if he'd taken Crew's words seriously.

"It was good to talk to you. I'll come by soon," Crew promised.

"You'd better. I like company," Joseph told him.

They hung up the phone.

"Well, that was good timing. I just got off the phone with Daisy," Darla said, her cheeks glowing. She was such a positive woman. Of course she had bad moments, as they all did, but she didn't let the negative impact how she lived her life.

"How's Daisy doing?" Crew asked.

"Wonderful. She and Hudson are taking a long weekend together. They've been working so much they haven't gotten away in a while."

"That sounds like an amazing idea," Crew said.

"I always find it hard to take time off of work. I feel as if I'm letting the kids down when I do," she admitted, shocking him.

"You have to refresh to stay mentally healthy when you're dealing with cases involving kids," he told her.

"I know. I've been less satisfied lately," she said. "I'm thinking about a change. I see too many lost cases with the kids getting tossed around as if they're no more important than garbage. There has to be a better way for me to help them than being a social worker. Sometimes I feel like my hands are tied more than at an orgy at a BDSM club."

Crew choked on his coffee and she rolled her eyes at him. "Like they don't use binds at those clubs," she said.

"Do you go often?" he asked, slightly horrified.

"Of course I don't go, it was just a saying."

"I wouldn't mind some binding at home," he told her with a wink. He'd recovered quickly, *and* he'd managed to pull her from the dark place she was heading to.

"You're not going to distract me with sex when you had your chance earlier," Darla warned, a twinkle back in her eyes. "Now you have to wait until tonight."

Crew felt the taunt and challenge of her words, and his muscles tensed with the need to take her right there against the counter. He began taking a step toward her. The triumph in her eyes told him that's exactly what she'd been taunting him for. She wanted to make him cave. She'd nearly accomplished her goal.

"Good try. But if you want it, just ask," he said as he leaned back and made sure she could see what she was missing.

"Nope. Not going to happen. I'm starving," she told him. He internally groaned. They were playing chicken and she'd totally won . . . again. "I want to go to that diner by the freeway. I love the owner and the food is greasy and excellent."

"I love that place. Let's go," he said as he grabbed his keys then held out his hand.

He had a feeling he was going to regret his decision not to take her then and there against the counter. How much was pride really worth in the long run?

Chapter Eighteen

Darla both loved and hated home calls. When they were good homes, she adored going to them, meeting the other children in the house, and seeing how people lived. It truly fascinated her. What might be comfort and protection for one person was utter chaos for another.

Darla was by no means a control freak or a perfectionist, but she did like a clean home and a bit of quiet. She loved an evening sitting outside by a fire with a glass of wine and the hushed sounds of frogs croaking and bats flying.

People had varying definitions of clean. The home she was going to that afternoon wasn't a place she enjoyed visiting. She was calling on the parents of a five-year-old little girl who'd been taken from them twice.

Their house always smelled like animal urine, the sink was messy and full, and the floors looked as if they hadn't seen a broom or vacuum in at least a year. How could anyone live that way? She understood people got busy. Heck, she got so busy she'd sometimes walk in the house and pass through a cobweb, but once her feet began sticking to the floor, she knew it was time to take a day off to clean.

If Darla knew people were coming to her house, she went all out with organizing. Her counters were normally cluttered. Sometimes she'd let a month pass before she opened her mail, which got her into trouble once or twice. But she made sure there weren't dishes in the sink at the end of the day or pieces of garbage lying around.

Since she'd been with Crew, she'd had to adjust even more. When you shared a place with a person you had to learn their habits, and the older a person got, the harder it was to change.

Darla pulled up to the rundown home at the end of a street. It wasn't the most kid-friendly neighborhood in her opinion, but since there were a lot of kids running around, she might be too judgmental. Maybe it really was time for her to get out. She was questioning whether she should've brought a cop with her or not. She shook her head. That was nonsense. She'd never experienced anything untoward with these parents. She just didn't particularly like them.

Darla grabbed her bag, exited her car, and walked the overgrown path to the front door of the house. Everything in her was screaming turn around and leave. But she knew better than that. She had a job to do, and that sometimes meant she was in uncomfortable situations. She'd figure it out.

She knocked on the door.

A voice inside the house yelled out, and Darla had to bite down the urge to leave. If the man yelling was violent, it was her duty to report him. She wasn't a weak, simpering female. She could handle herself if things turned iffy. She'd taken some self-defense classes. Granted, it had been a while ago, but she'd done a weekend course with Daisy.

It had been kind of funny when they'd walked out of the class, feeling as if they were superheroes. Neither of them had ever had to test their skills though. Maybe it was time for a refresher course. Darla knew Crew's brother, Finn, taught them. As a matter of fact, that's how he'd met his wife. She'd attended his class and taken him down to the ground. She loved hearing him tell the story because he still looked at her with adoration when he told how his tiny little wife was able to take him down. It was quite impressive.

The door suddenly flung open, and despite her convictions, Darla took a couple of steps back when the furious man in front of her snarled. He was wearing a stained white tank top, ripped jeans, and no shoes. His hair was a mess, he looked as if he hadn't shaved in four or five days, and his eyes were bloodshot. This wasn't the same man who'd been in the office two weeks earlier. This was a person on drugs.

"What in the hell do you want?" he barked.

"I'm sorry, Mr. Dame. I have an appointment to speak with you and your wife today about bringing Misty home," Darla said. She took another step back but maintained eye contact with the man.

"We didn't have no appointment today. This is a trick visit, ain't it? This is just you and that office trying to sneak up on us to check in and see if we're suitable." He took a menacing step toward her, and Darla felt her heart thunder. Her fight or flight mode was definitely kicking in hard core.

"I'm sorry about the misunderstanding, Mr. Dame, but there is an appointment. I don't do surprise visits," Darla told him in a calm voice as if everything was perfectly okay in the world.

"I don't believe you," he snapped. He took another step closer to her. "You took my little girl away. It's all your fault. And now my wife is being a real bitch and blamin' me," he screamed.

He clearly wasn't in his right mind. This visit wasn't going to happen.

"I'm sorry you feel that way, Mr. Dame. I can see this isn't a good time. I'm just going to leave," Darla told him. She backed a few more steps away from him. She didn't want him to see the fear. She knew men like him thrived on instilling fear in others. She knew he preyed on weakness, so she couldn't present herself as smaller than him, though she certainly was.

"You ain't going nowhere. I want my daughter. Where do you have her?" he thundered as he stepped closer. She really needed to carry mace with her. This situation was getting out of control the more they stood facing each other.

"Chris, you get in here. Leave Darla alone," Janet Dame said from the doorway. Her eye was black and her lip was swollen. Darla really needed to get to the safety of her car and call this in. It had the potential of getting really bad really fast.

"Shut the hell up!" he yelled, turning his attention away from Darla. "You've done enough today. Go set your fat ass down!"

Janet was definitely a defeated woman. She didn't walk away, but she hung her head as tears fell from her eyes. Darla took that moment to make her break for it. She needed her phone, which was in her car. She didn't care if he could see her fear now, she just needed to escape.

She nearly made it to her vehicle when a hand snaked out and grabbed her hair. With her forward motion, it completely knocked her off balance as her feet went forward and her head went back. There was no stopping hitting the ground. He tugged hard as she began falling, and she landed with a hard thump that took her breath away.

She looked up to find the man towering over her, a sneer on his face. "Where in the hell do you think you're going? I told you I want my daughter here, now!" he said, his voice growing louder with each word he spoke.

"I'm going to call now, Mr. Dame," Darla said, tears in her voice as she tried catching her breath. She knew for sure she had a bruise on her hip and a scrape on her leg and elbow. She didn't like being below him in such a vulnerable position. She quickly scrambled to her feet, facing him again, not attempting to pick up the bag she'd brought with her.

He reached out so quickly she didn't have a chance to defend herself as he grabbed her arms and shook her hard enough to rattle her brain.

"You get me my daughter or I'm going to kill you," he said.

Darla didn't doubt he'd do just that. "Okay, I have to call," she said, tears choking her as she struggled against him.

"Hey, what's going on?" a man yelled as he jogged up to them. "Chris, what in the hell are you doing?" he asked.

"You stay out of this, Earl. This is the woman who took my daughter away. She needs to pay," Chris said.

"Let her go. You're already in a crapload of trouble, Chris. Let her go," the man said.

"You mind your own business," Chris said, his fingers clamping even tighter on her arms.

"I've called the police," a woman shouted from across the street. "You unhand her now or you're going to be in jail for a very long time."

"You meddling bi—" His words were cut off when Earl decked him. His fingers finally let her go. Darla quickly scrambled to the other side of her car as she assessed the situation.

"Don't you talk to my wife that way," Earl said as he kicked Chris, who was now on the ground groaning, his nose bleeding.

"I wouldn't have to if she stayed in her house where she belongs," Chris said.

"She doesn't like how you've been treating Janet or your daughter. The whole neighborhood is sick of your crap," Earl said. Chris tried rising and Earl kicked him in the ribs, making him curl up on himself.

Darla took in her first real breath when she heard sirens. The police were near. Two cars screeched to a stop in front of the house and officers jumped out. They quickly approached and assessed the situation. Darla had a feeling they'd been there before.

"Ma'am, are you okay?" one of the officers asked.

"Yes, Mr. Dame was attacking me, but then his neighbor here, Earl, came out and helped me," she said. "I'm Darla, I work for children services and this was a home visit."

The cop nodded at her. "I hope this means little Misty won't be coming back here. Her mama sure loves her but she won't keep Chris out of the house. As much as I want to say he'll be going to jail for a long time after this, he won't. He'll be in there a max of twenty-four hours."

"Is it going to take killing someone for him to get locked up?" Darla asked, horrified this man would be released with how his violence was escalating.

"Unfortunately, with our laws, pretty much," the officer said. "I don't like it, but my hands are tied."

"His wife is really beat up. That should lock him up for at least a week," Darla said hopefully. Maybe that would be enough time for her to be strong enough to leave him.

"I doubt it," the officer said. "She probably won't press charges." He obviously knew this family well.

She gave her statement then pulled Janet aside, gave her a card, and told her to call her if she wanted out. She didn't try to pressure her, just let her know there were options.

She left the Dame's house feeling defeated. One more family that wouldn't get the help they needed. She ached a little, but she decided right then and there she wasn't telling Crew about it. He'd come and nearly kill Chris. She certainly didn't want that to happen or he'd be the one locked up. The system really was messed up.

Darla stopped at a store and cleaned up a little before she went back to her office. As much as she disliked encounters like that one, and that had been the worst she'd had yet, she really hated sitting in a tiny cubicle where she felt as if she couldn't breathe.

She returned to the office to file her paperwork before calling it a day and found a bouquet of roses on her desk.

She smiled — big.

Crew didn't know the hell she'd been through that day, but he'd still managed to cheer her up. It was her first flowers from him. She just might be able to turn him into a romantic after all.

She opened the card and frowned. There was only one word. How odd.

Soon

Chapter Nineteen

Darla was sitting at a café with Crew sipping on a nice salted caramel coffee and munching on a blueberry scone. It was heaven, pure heaven. The air was cooler even though it was August in Washington. A thunderstorm was blowing in, a welcome relief from the constant heat.

"Darla, I'm worried about you," Crew told her. "And before you tell me everything's just fine, don't. You're going through the motions and you still wear a smile on your face, but there's pain in your eyes that I don't like."

"Are you psychoanalyzing me?" she asked with a false laugh.

"This has nothing to do with my profession. I think I've gotten to know you quite well. Something happened this week, and you've closed in on yourself. Tell me what's wrong," he demanded.

Tears welled in her eyes. She was in so much pain.

She attempted to smile but failed. "You're right; I'm burned out. My job's killing me. I feel so damn helpless, and I'm at a crossroads over what I'm going to do," Darla told him after a minute.

"You've been burned out for a while. Why not do something else?" Crew asked as he reached out and held her hand.

"I've been thinking about that. I hate how the state fails these children over and over again. Everyone talks about parental rights, but what about the rights of the innocent children? It drives me crazy. They put these kids into good, solid, stable foster homes, and then the parents jump through a few minor hoops and they're ripped right back out again," Darla told him, slamming her fist down on the table, making her coffee slosh over the side of her cup.

Crew was thoughtful for a moment before he spoke. "I guess they go back home because deep down most of us want to see children in their family home," Crew said.

"Of course it's ideal to be with mom and dad, or grandparents like in Daisy's case, but some humans just shouldn't have children. I'm not saying kids are perfect. There are certainly little jerks out there, but what makes them that way? It should be first and foremost what the *kids* need, not what the parents need. The parents have had a lifetime to figure out who they are. The kids haven't. So why don't we focus more on the kids instead of the parents?"

"This last case really got to you, didn't it?" Crew asked.

Daisy didn't mention she'd been attacked by a parent. She feared it would send him over the edge.

"Yeah, it really did." Darla's eyes filled with tears. "I could use some rum in this coffee." She added a laugh that had no amusement in it.

"Tell me about it. You've barely spoken of it," Crew told her.

Darla sighed. "Baily's three years old."

"What happened?" Crew gently asked, pushing her again.

"The parents were meth users and walked away from the hospital after giving birth. They simply abandoned her there. She was born with a cleft lip and palate, and she was in the NICU for three months. Patsy and Jeff were her foster parents. They visited her every single day, getting to hold her as soon as she was stable enough to come out of her bed, then they took her home. They immediately fell in love with her, taking her for her surgeries, and loving on her with all of their hearts." Darla choked up, grabbed a napkin, wiped her nose, then continued.

"They have three other children, and I visit once a month. There is no difference in how they, or the children, treat Baily. She's a part of their family. She's the children's sister, and the parents' daughter. They all love her immeasurably. They began fighting to adopt her the moment she was brought home."

"So, what happened?" Crew asked.

"The biological parents didn't even attempt to see her for a solid two years, but after the first year they stalled the adoption by taking the mandatory state classes. They did just enough to keep the judge from signing off on the adoption." Darla choked up again. Crew reached for her.

"The bottom line is the birthparents managed to get her back a few days ago. I had to rip Baily from the arms of her real mother. Patsy fell to the floor weeping in pain as she said goodbye to her little girl. Her big sister, who's only six years old, grabbed my leg, her crystal blue eyes pleading at me as tears fell down her face. She begged me not to take Baily away. Her oldest brother, only fourteen and such a beautiful young man, stood in front of me, his arms crossed, a glare of hurt shooting at me from his eyes. He told me what I was doing was wrong. He told me Baily was their family and she needed them. The entire time Baily felt the tension in the room and was sobbing, reaching for her mama. It was the most awful moment of my life."

"Oh, Darla, I had no idea," Crew said with a gasp.

"I stepped from the house and her oldest brother ran from the door. The officer with me just stood there. He hated what was happening as well. He knew Baily should stay with them. He knew taking her away was wrong. Then Jacob spoke." Tears were falling down her cheeks.

"What did he say?" Crew asked. He appeared a little choked up himself, but she was so lost in her story she couldn't even see Crew at the moment.

"He stood there, showing the man he'd be some day," Darla said. "He said: *She's our sister, Ms. Winters. We need her here, and she needs us. Please don't take her away. We protect her, we love her. She's our sister. They didn't want her, they didn't appreciate her, they didn't protect her. Please don't take her. Please don't take her. I'll do anything you ask. I'll do whatever it takes. You can't take her away. She needs us and we need her.* He fell to the ground in front of me and sobbed. This young man, this child on the verge of manhood was begging me." She sobbed as she paused, taking a moment to compose herself.

Crew didn't say anything, he just waited for her to go on.

"I looked at the cop and there was accusation in his eyes. We both knew this was wrong. We *knew* it. But I also knew if I walked away, someone else would come in. Our hands were tied. As a social worker, I have no right to defy the system. It was so wrong on so many levels. Baily was reaching for her brother, begging for me to let her down. She wanted to protect him. Even this sweet little three-year-old girl was glaring at me, accusing me."

"Oh, hell, Darla," Crew said. "I don't have words."

"I told him I was sorry, that I was so very sorry. And then I buckled Baily into the car seat in my vehicle. He rose from the ground, his shoulders firm. If he needed to hit me, I was going to let him. I deserved it. I was a monster."

"No, you weren't," Crew told her.

"Yes, yes I was. I know my hands were tied, but it still wasn't enough. He finally wiped his tears away, his shoulders back, so tall and proud. *You bring her back, Ms. Winters. You bring her back,* he told me. He didn't move, just stood there as I nodded at him, my throat too closed to say anything more. I drove around the block, then pulled over and sobbed."

"Where's Baily now?" Crew asked.

"It's been three days. She's with those people who gave birth to her. There's already been one call from the neighbors about loud fighting from their home. They'll kill her, Crew. I know they'll kill her, and there's absolutely nothing I can do to stop it."

She shook with sobs now. She felt so utterly helpless. She'd betrayed this family, betrayed this little girl, and there were people higher up than her who were tying her hands. She'd never felt so helpless in her life.

"No, they won't. Let's get her back to her family," Crew said.

"How?" she asked, anger filling her.

Crew smile. She finally looked into his eyes. He seemed so confident it gave her a bit of hope.

"*My* hands aren't tied," he told her. Then he paused. "I think you need to put in for two weeks of time off, and then you really need to reconsider your job. There's so much more you can do. You have a passion for fighting for those without a voice. If you stay in this job it'll kill you."

She opened her mouth to argue, then shut it again. "You're right," she said. "I'm not this weak, pathetic person. I can't let the system bring me down."

"No, you can't. Let's get Baily home. And then let's figure out how to help others."

Darla realized right then and there she was in love with this man. And for the first time in her life, she was truly scared of having her heart broken.

Crew *did* help her. She wasn't exactly sure how, but he helped her, and Baily was safely returned to her rightful parents. She'd been working within the system, and he'd worked outside of it. He'd gotten more done in twenty-four hours than she'd managed to do in years.

What did that mean? What was she going to do about it? Was a new chapter in her life about to be opened? Something big was happening, and she didn't want to run away from it.

Chapter Twenty

Darla stood at the steps of the most luxurious jet she'd ever seen. She gazed from it to Crew and back again at the jet. "What in the world are you doing, Crew?" she asked with suspicion.

"We're taking a trip and I'm not allowing you to say no," Crew told her.

"Where?"

"It's a surprise," he insisted. "Just get on the jet or I'll carry you on. With the narrow opening, it might get tricky, so it's probably best you willingly go aboard," he said with a grin.

"Crew, my life's a mess right now. I quit my job, and I don't know what I'm going to do next. I can't just fly off somewhere," she insisted.

"Your life's a mess right now which means you *absolutely* need to go on vacation and figure it all out. There will be beaches. And there's no better way to find your path in life than on a beach," he insisted.

"But . . . what about Daisy? What about finding a new job?" she said. She wanted to get on the jet, wanted to fly off into the sunset, but it seemed wrong somehow, as if she were slacking.

"Darla, you can argue on the jet. We have a long flight, and I'm not taking no for an answer," he said, his arms crossed.

"Fine!" she snapped. "But what about clothes? I can't go somewhere and stay naked for days."

Crew's eyes flashed at those words. "I wouldn't mind you staying naked for the entire trip," he told her with a wink. She rolled her eyes. "However, don't worry. Daisy packed for you."

Darla's eyes widened. "That traitor. She didn't say a word to me. I'm going to have some words for her."

Crew laughed. "Her exact words were: *Great job, Crew. You're a genius. Don't let her talk you out of this. She needs it.*"

"She knows where I'm going?" Darla asked, not used to people taking control of her life. She didn't like that much. But she completely trusted Crew.

"Yep, she knows, and she approves. I wouldn't be surprised if she finds her way there. Now, the pilots are waiting so let's board and then you can continue yelling at me," he said as he pushed on her back. She found herself moving up the stairs.

"I am not yelling," she said with her voice raised, making him laugh and the flight attendant at the top of the stairs look down as her lips twitched. "I'm not," Darla emphasized, her voice slightly quieter.

"Good morning. I'm Lily. Look around then come sit down and I'll have drinks and snacks for you before takeoff. What would you like?" the sweet redhead asked. She didn't look older than twenty. Not a bad job for such a young lady. Maybe Darla could become a flight attendant and fly around the world for free.

"I'll have coffee with cream please," Crew said.

"Coffee for me too," Darla told her. "What creamers do you have?" The attendant listed them. "I'll take caramel and a splash of white mocha."

"Perfect." Lily disappeared.

Darla was stunned into a rare silence as Crew showed her the luxurious jet owned by Joseph Anderson, who, of course, was a part of this collaboration to get Darla to take a vacation. She couldn't remember the last time she'd had one. By the time they sat back down, their coffee cups waiting, she didn't know what to say.

"I was a bit shocked the first time I climbed onboard this thing," Crew said. "But damn, I like using it now. Joseph has three jets, three of them. I've built a good world for myself, but the kind of money the Anderson family has is staggering."

"You'd think they'd be a lot flashier with that kind of wealth," Darla said. "I know they have jets and houses that make me want to weep, but they also wear Levi's and build houses for Habitat for Humanity. They do good things."

"I think that's why they have the wealth they have. It's good karma and they give back a lot. They give it the way they want to give it, to local and international programs. They know how to improve their local communities a lot better than the damn government does."

"I agree with you," Darla said. "If everyone helped locally the world would be a better place. How in the heck does some autocrat in DC know what a family in Seattle, Washington needs?"

"They believe they can fly in once or twice a year and know exactly what people need. It drives me crazy. But Joseph does his part and the rest of us do too," Crew said.

"The cost of this jet could help a lot of people," Darla pointed out.

"Trust me, I've heard that before, but this jet does help a lot of people," Crew told her. "The many hours of labor it took to build it provided jobs. The constant upkeep of it still provides jobs. And this jet is used to bring supplies to families who need them. The Andersons give a lot, and they enjoy the fruits of their labor as well. I think that's a good thing," Crew said.

"You do realize you talk about them as if you aren't one of them," she said.

He laughed. "Yeah, I know. It's still hard for me to realize I'm a part of the Anderson empire."

"Does Joseph treat you differently than the others since you came so much later?" she asked.

"No, not at all. He treats us as if he's known us our entire lives. That's who Joseph is. Whether you're family or married to family, you're in his circle and he's going to be good to you," Crew said.

"I liked Joseph from the moment I met him," Darla said.

"Good morning, Mr. Anderson and Ms. Winters. Go ahead and buckle up. The skies look friendly this morning so we should have a smooth ride. We have about an eleven-hour flight with one quick refuel in New York. You have Lily with you today to bring you whatever you need. Sit back, relax, and enjoy the friendly skies," the pilot said with a chuckle.

"He must've worked for an airline before," Crew said with his own laugh.

"Eleven hours?" Darla gasped as the jet began to taxi. "Where in the heck are we going?"

Crew grinned big. "Now that I have you trapped, I can tell you," he said. "We're off to Italy."

Darla gaped at him as the jet stopped for a moment and then began again, quickly picking up speed. She was unable to talk, opening her mouth and closing it again. They lifted into the air as she stared at Crew, who looked quite pleased with himself.

"I told you that you weren't allowed to jet me off to a foreign land," she finally said.

"And you're discovering that I'm not easily ordered about," he said back.

"Italy," she sighed in wonder. She should be furious with the man, but after the last few weeks she'd had with Baily being taken away and rescued, and a father attacking her, and then that stupid man stalking her, she didn't mind being nearly five thousand miles from home. "I should be mad, but I really want to go," she finally admitted.

The grin Crew gave her was enough to melt her inside and out. "I did a lot of research after we talked about your great-great-grandmother. Portofino has everything you could wish for in a small coastal town. We're going to visit a few other places in Italy too, but unlike Genova or even Milano, Portofino has incredible charm. It's nestled in the very core of Liguria, one of Italy's smallest regions."

"I think you might've researched it more than I have," Darla told him. "I'm afraid I won't like it, though, since it won't be the same place my grams grew up in."

"No, everything changes," Crew told her. "The town went from a quaint fishing village to a playground for the rich and famous, but you have family there and I contacted them with a little help from Brackish. They're going to show us why it's such a fantastic place."

Darla felt tears sting her eyes. She reached out and cupped Crew's face. "Do you realize I might never let you go?" she whispered.

"I'm counting on it," he told her. He leaned over and kissed her, a sweet, satisfying kiss that made her head a little bit light.

"Aren't we supposed to be anguished and afraid we're making a mistake?" she asked him. He looked confused.

"I don't understand," he finally said after a long silence.

"Well, I read a lot, and the hero and heroine are always anguished. It's what makes a good story," she said.

Crew blinked at her in confusion for several more moments, and then he leaned back and laughed. When his eyes met hers again, they were full of mirth. "We can write our own romance story," he said. "And I say that ours is full of light, laughter, and adventure."

She grinned right back at him. "I fully agree with you."

Lily came out and took their breakfast order.

"Portofino is on the Mediterranean coastline known as the Italian Riviera. Over the years it transformed from a fishing village to an exclusive holiday destination for those who like both luxury and simplicity," Darla said.

"I don't see how you have luxury and a simple life," Crew pointed out.

"Look at the Andersons. They have both. They do crazy, amazing things like jet off to a private island with all of their family and take over. But they also come together and build homes for the poor. They are happy in jeans or Armani suits. I think we can have a balance of luxury and simple," Darla said.

"I know. I was just seeing how you felt about it," Crew told her.

"You're such a brat," she said.

He kissed her again. "Let's finish our breakfast and explore the bedroom some more," he suggested with a waggle of his brows.

"That sounds just about perfect to me," she said with a giggle, feeling freer than she had in too long to remember.

Yep, she was definitely falling in love with Crew Anderson, and she just might know what she was going to do about it.

Chapter Twenty-One

Darla and Crew landed in Genova about two in the morning and were immediately whisked to a beautiful hotel overlooking the Genova Beach. The harbor city of Genova had been a very important city for thousands of years.

"It's so hard for me to imagine these cities have literally been around for thousands of years," Darla told him as they settled into their room and she immediately went out to the balcony to see and hear the soothing motion and lights on the water.

"I know what you mean," Crew told her as he stood behind her, his arms easily wrapping her in a warm embrace. His fingers rested just beneath her breasts and she relished the tingle his touch always evoked. "America is simply a baby. It feels as if it's been there forever, but we didn't become a country until 1776."

"Even if you consider the early settlements, it's still only hundreds of years old. I know there were many cities before the Revolutionary War, but most of America was unsettled and pure. There were no huge cites, no skyscrapers, just vast amounts of unsettled land. It was almost tragic to destroy it," she told him.

"Progress always causes changes, and some of those changes are really bad in my opinion. I'd be a happy man to never see a skyscraper again," he told her.

"I'm surprised to hear you say that," she said. She was so tired. She'd been too excited about their trip to sleep on the luxurious bed in the beautiful jet. But now that she was in Italy she didn't want to sleep a single minute. She wanted to experience it all.

"We can discuss America another time. We're here now and I think rich Italian history is much more interesting," he told her. "I was reading that Genova was used by both the Romans and the Etruscans as a harbor, and the city retains architectural elements from both cultures."

"I've never taken time to develop a fascination for architecture even though my best friend is all about preserving the past," she admitted. After coming to Italy, she might have to change her mind and study how people designed buildings that would literally stand for thousands of years. It was awe-inspiring.

"I know more than I should with Noah being an architect, and a brilliant one at that," Crew told her. "From the time he was little he wanted to create great works of art that would stand the test of time. He has traveled to Italy and Rome a lot. He probably spent half a year here. I'm thinking we need to spend a few months every year for at least the next ten years."

His words sent a pleasant shiver down her spine. Would they stand the test of time? Would they still be together to come back to the land her family was from? She believed they would.

"Which part of Genova are we in?" she asked. It had been dark out as their car took them to their hotel.

"We're in Nervi, which is about seven kilometers west of Genova's center. This was once a fishing village on its own, but long ago became a part of Genova. It isn't the most central area, but I chose it because of the quiet beauty even though we'll only be here for a day."

"I might never leave this country now that you've gotten me here," she warned him as she turned in his arms and looked up at his beautiful face showcased by the full moon. She could see the stars reflecting in his eyes and it made her feel as if they were all alone on the planet, just the two of them in this little slice of paradise.

"I think I'd be quite happy to leave the hustle and bustle of city life and settle into paradise," Crew told her as he lifted her in his arms and carried her to their bed. With the gentle breeze blowing in from the open French doors, he made love to her so sweetly she had tears streaming down her face then held her as she fell asleep.

Darla woke a few hours later to the sun rising in the sky. She didn't need sleep, she needed to explore this incredible country Crew had whisked her off to. The two of them showered and dressed, then walked hand in hand to the patio of their hotel. They sipped coffee and ate pastries before exploring Genova.

They took a walk along the Passeggiata Anita Garibaldi which meandered along the cliffs above the Mediterranean Sea. It was spectacular. They had lunch at a small café and laughed as they watched children splashing in the water. Crew carried her bags as she moved in and out of shops, both old and new, searching for perfect gifts to take back to her loved ones. She even found blown glass treasures for the four children who'd changed her life, setting her on a new path.

She wasn't sure what that path would yet be, but because of them she knew she could no longer do social work within the confines and rules of the state of Washington. She'd still help children, but she'd do it in a way that impacted their lives in a more positive manner.

The next day their car transported them to the train station. "I love being a tourist. It's wonderful," Darla told him as he hauled two heavy bags behind him. She had two smaller ones. He'd taken hers, and she'd taken his. She'd gotten the better end of that deal, but Crew didn't seem to mind one little bit.

"I haven't played tourist very often, but I have a feeling I'll be doing it a lot more now that you're in my life," he said with a smile that could've melted butter. "Our train ride is only about forty minutes then another car will pick us up for the last leg of our journey."

They rode the train through incredibly untouched land, Darla's eyes glued to the window as she gazed at everything around her. The trip was too short and she was disappointed when it ended. They arrived in Santa Margherita early in the morning. It was a less known destination town, but still had a lot to offer tourists. They didn't get to visit long, though. Maybe they'd come back.

Once they were in the car, the drive was astonishing. The entire coastal area was nestled into a natural hillside arch that hugged the entire town. It was a short ride, and again ended too soon. They stepped out of the car onto Portofino soil at ten in the morning.

"Oh, Crew, the pictures never do a place justice," she told him. They were staying at the Belmond Hotel Splendido, which she could be certain was the nicest place she'd ever stayed. Elegance and refined, it stood among lush woodlands overlooking the calm sea. The hotel extended over the sea, a jeweled hideaway from the busy tourist center.

Their suite had a balcony where Darla could sit for hours fully content to sip on coffee or tea and watch the activity in the harbor, but she wanted to explore. So instead of resting, she took Crew's hand and they went to the heart of the city.

They got their exercise as they walked along the steep, stone-paved streets, the town's glory revealing itself in the multicolored homes and businesses. The delightful aroma of freshly made pastries and strong Italian espresso filled the air.

"I'm going to get very fat here," she warned Crew as they stopped at a gorgeous café for an espresso and her favorite dessert, tiramisu. "I'm also never going to be able to eat tiramisu in America again. This is so moist, delicate, and flavorful. Maybe my cousins will be kind enough to give me a recipe from my great-great-grandmother. That wasn't in the book I have. I think they were trying to save my hips," she said with a laugh.

"I bet you can sweet talk them," he told her. He was eating as much as she was, but vacation calories didn't count. There was no way to enjoy their time if they worried about calories. She wanted to be a glutton for the entire trip.

They walked from one end of town to the other, enjoying the views high in the hills. It felt good to burn off breakfast calories so she could have an incredible lunch. They were meeting her cousins at noon at a central restaurant with outside dining that overlooked the sea.

"Darla," a woman called in a sing-song voice that made Darla think of a princess in a Disney movie. She turned to find two stunning women, both with dark hair and eyes that were nearly black. Their smiles grew as they made eye contact with her. "Yes, it is you . . . finally!" The two women rushed forward and enveloped Darla in a group hug.

When they pulled back, Darla was grinning as big as they were. "I'm so glad to finally see you in person," Darla told them. She turned to Crew who was looking very pleased he'd brought her there. She owed him a lot. Why had she attempted to stop him?

"Crew, these are my cousins, Carina and Bella," Darla said.

"It's a pleasure to meet you, ladies," Crew said. "Thanks for helping me kidnap Darla."

The two young women giggled as their cheeks flushed. Yep, Crew had that effect on women of all ages. They were barely out of their teens.

"My grandmother, your aunt Alessa, loves matchmaking. The moment your man wanted to whisk you off to Italy to meet your family she told us he was a match made in heaven and that the two of you would have a beautiful life together with many young kids to drive you crazy," Bella said.

"Many kids?" Darla said in mock horror. "I'm thinking one, maybe two tops, but not even that for a few more years."

"Just don't say that to your aunt Alessa or she'll lay the famous Italian guilt on you for not continuing your family line properly," Bella said with a laugh.

"I don't know if I should meet this aunt then. I'm certainly the furthest thing from a proper Italian woman there is," Darla warned.

"Ah, it's in your blood, Darla," Bella said. "And trust me, I know my grandmother, she'll love both you and Crew."

"I have a fondness for spitfire Italian grandmothers," Crew admitted.

"Have you met a lot of them?" Darla asked.

The four of them sat at the table and ordered their food. Darla had authentic Italian pizza and wondered if she'd ever be able to have Americanized Italian food again. Hopefully her taste buds would forget the exquisite flavors of Italy when she returned to American soil.

"Only a few, and they've had an impact," Crew said with a laugh.

"Only a few, huh?" Carina said. Darla already knew she'd have a lasting relationship with her cousins. They were bright, funny, and confident, and she wished she'd gotten to know them when they were younger.

"A few is more than most men can handle," Crew said.

Carina and Bella laughed at his words. "That's what Grandmama is always saying," Bella said. "She's told us many times she doesn't understand how the Italian line continues because we women are enough to drive any man mad." Bella winked at Crew. "But the secret is men can't resist us and keep coming back for more."

Crew burst out laughing, and Darla fell even more in love with him. He'd changed from the man she'd met only a few months earlier, though it felt as if they'd known each other for a lifetime. Maybe that's how love worked. Maybe once you met your soulmate, you both knew it and you were back with your feet planted on solid ground.

The four of them finished their lunch then the girls took them on an adventure as they walked to their home up the hill.

Darla was instantly in love when Aunt Alessa looked up from her rocking chair and grinned. "Ah, sweet Darla, you have finally come home," she said in a deep, raspy voice.

"I guess so," Darla said. "It truly feels like home."

"That's because your heart belongs here no matter where you go in the world," Alessa said with a smile. Then she looked Crew over and nodded her approval to Darla.

"It's a pleasure to meet you, Ms. Alessa," he told her. She'd insisted when he'd spoken to her on the phone that he wasn't to call her by her last name. He'd been raised to respect women and had to add the Ms. before her name, though. She grinned at him as if she was pleased with their compromise.

"Come, come, let us sit and talk," Alessa said as she took Darla's hand in one of hers and Crew's in the other. They moved to her patio.

"I'll get tea and pastries, Grandmama" Bella said.

"I don't know if I can eat another bite," Darla said. Her stomach was seriously close to bursting.

"That's nonsense. You're Italian. You can eat more," Aunt Alessa said.

Bella and Carina disappeared into the house.

"Are you trying to fatten us up before we're sacrificed?" Crew asked with a laugh.

"Of course," Aunt Alessa said without missing a beat. "We lure you here with beautiful views and mesmerizing scents and then throw you from the cliffs at midnight to please Poseidon. She said this with such seriousness it made it even funnier.

"Then I guess I better eat up. If that's what it takes to maintain this piece of paradise, I'm a willing sacrifice," Crew said.

"I truly like you, my boy," Alessa said.

"And I you," Crew told her.

"You knew my great-great-grandmother," Alessa said, eager to hear about the woman in the pictures.

"Yes, she was my aunt," Alessa said. "To be honest, she was my favorite, but we won't let the other relatives hear that." She laughed again, the sparkle in her eyes so much younger than the weathered skin of her face. Even at her age, she was beautiful.

"We've had a lot of people come to Portofino, and when I was younger, I enjoyed charming dazzling men. Now, I just feed them," Aunt Alessa said as if reading Crew's mind.

He blushed and Darla was fascinated by it. "I bet you've made grown men cry," he said.

"No, I always left them with a smile," Alessa told him with a wink. She and Darla laughed out loud when his flushed cheeks turned beet red.

"Enough of that, Grandmama. You're embarrassing our guest," Bella said as she set down a tray with wine, cheese, crackers, and miniature cakes.

"I thought you were bringing tea," Darla said.

"Nah, we changed to wine. No one in the world can make wine like the Italians," Carina said as she poured glasses for each of them.

"I agree, and spending the afternoon with your grandmother means I'll need several bottles of wine. She quite enjoys flustering me," Crew admitted.

"It takes a strong man to admit a woman can get to him. I like you, Crew," Alessa said.

He sipped his wine while they all continued chatting.

"Now tell me about my great-great-grandmother," Darla said. "I've dreamed about her, wondered what her life was like, who she was, and what made one of her children move to America."

"Ah, I have many stories to tell you," Aunt Alessa said. "Your grandmother was a wonderful woman, and she encouraged all of her children to fly far from the nest and explore the world. She told them their wings would always take them where they were meant to go, but those same wings would bring them back home. She always said home is where your heart is, not where your feet are planted."

"Wow, she sounds like an incredible woman. I wish I could've known her," Darla said.

"You do know her because she's a part of you. And as long as we continue telling her stories she's with us, just as my grandmother is," Aunt Alessa said.

They continued talking, Crew and Darla both mesmerized by the stories Aunt Alessa, Carina, and Bella shared. They didn't leave until long after sunset.

Darla and Crew spent the next several days in Portofino, taking advantage of the spa in their hotel, eating beautiful sunset meals, and spending time on the beaches soaking up the sun and splashing in the water.

Darla's favorite haven was about twenty minutes from the center of the small town. They'd managed to find a secluded downhill path that led to one of the most intimate, tranquil beaches Darla had ever seen. She'd never imagined a place like this existed.

The water was vibrant greens and blues, ebbing and flowing over colorful pebbles that peeked at them from just beneath the surface. They spent enough time in that place that Darla knew heaven was real, and it existed right there on earth.

Chapter Twenty-Two

Their last day in Portofino came too quickly. They spent time with Bella, Carina, and Aunt Alessa daily, but Darla was reluctant to leave them. The girls promised to come visit them in the States, and they promised to come to Portofino at least once a year. Still, Darla felt sad as she looked out over the water from their hotel suite's balcony.

"We will come back," Crew assured her.

"People say that all of the time, and then life happens, time passes, and they never go back to where they found so much peace and happiness."

He turned her around and held her, the moon a little dimmer on this night, but still bright enough to see the truth in his eyes. "I promise to bring you back as often as you please," he told her.

"I love you, Crew," she said before she even thought of stopping the words.

The warmth of his expression told her she'd said it at the perfect moment. She'd never said that to a man before. She didn't want to take it back.

"I'm going to show you what you mean to me," he told her.

She sighed as in a smooth, graceful movement he pulled her tight to him, his hands grasping her behind her back, sliding over her hips and letting her feel how aroused he was. He was both gentle and urgent, sending a slew of heat rushing through her.

He gazed into her eyes as those beautiful hands gripped her tighter and lifted her, urging her to wrap her legs around him. She felt safe in his arms, knowing he'd take care of her, knowing how much pleasure they'd bring one another. There was no better place she wanted to be — and no better way to pull her from sadness than to be in his arms.

After what seemed an eternity, his lips met hers gently as they skimmed over her mouth, his tongue wetting her lips before pushing inside to twist with hers. She sighed into his mouth as he carried her away from the balcony.

Darla felt as if she was floating as he carried her to their bed, never breaking their kiss, never loosening the grip he had on her butt until he laid her down, standing above her, gazing at her as if she was a precious jewel he knew he'd keep forever.

"Come here," she uttered, her voice husky and sure. There was no longer any doubt the two of them would have a lifetime together. They'd make it through anything, even the rough stuff in the middle would work itself out over time.

He joined her on the bed, pressing between her thighs, his arousal throbbing against her core, making her want to tear the clothes from their bodies so he could sink inside of her. He leaned down and kissed her once more, sipping from her lips as if he was breaking a long fast . . . slow and steady, setting her body on fire.

He leaned to the left and raised his hand, his palm brushing over her breast, his fingers dancing across her aching nipple. She squirmed against him, needing their clothing gone.

He broke away from her lips and kissed her jaw as he slid his hand down her stomach so it could crawl beneath her shirt and run up her hot skin. He easily slid his hand beneath her silky bra, and she moaned as his fingers squeezed her nipple. She was so hot, her hips arched against him. This man could make her orgasm without ever touching her core. She was so in-tune with him, so in-tune with her own body when she was in his arms.

"Clothes . . . gone," she whispered in a husky voice.

"Hmm, is someone impatient?" he taunted. She leaned forward and placed her lips against his shoulder then bit down. He chuckled a rich, deep, needy chuckle that went straight to her core.

"Very impatient," she said. "Now, Crew. Quit with the teasing," she said in practically a sob.

He leaned back and in seconds whipped off her shirt and bra, her nipples hardening even more as the breeze from the open patio blew over them. She groaned and arched her back, needing his mouth on the aching buds.

She reached for him, grabbing the back of his neck and leading him where she wanted him. He allowed it, and then she couldn't think as his mouth fastened around one of her nipples and he sucked it deep within his mouth. She cried out as he sucked, nibbled, and licked the swollen bud while his fingers danced over her other breast, squeezing and rubbing. She was about to explode.

"More," she begged.

He shifted to her other side, and took that nipple in his mouth, giving it attention as the ocean breeze swept over her other wet one, driving her mad. Heat and moisture built in her core. She ached all over; she wanted him deep, deep inside of her.

He let go of her nipple and leaned back. She gazed at him through half-opened eyes, her body on fire, her energy sluggish. She was his willing puppet, and she knew no matter how much they made love, it would always be this way. She'd found her soulmate.

"Please, Crew. I want you deep inside of me," she told him, loving the fire that blazed in his incredible eyes.

He tugged her pants free, leaving her naked and wanton before him. She opened her legs, inviting him in. Lust deepened his dark eyes and she ached for his touch.

Before he moved he stripped his clothes away, the sound of ripping material hanging in the air as he tossed his shirt aside. He was so damn beautiful. It didn't matter how many times she saw him naked, she'd never get enough.

As if he couldn't stand the distance between them either, he pressed back against her, his mouth taking hers with urgency. She opened to him, their tongues dancing. His hands slid across her hot skin and she wiggled against him, wanting to ride that wave with him all the way to paradise.

But he wasn't done with his torture. He whispered his lips across her jaw, then down the slope of her neck, taking his time licking and sucking her heated skin, swiping across her nipples, before lowering himself, and making his way down her belly. He moved into her open thighs, ran his finger across her heat, then moaned.

"So wet, you're always so wet," he said with a groan before closing his mouth over her clit and sucking. She screamed out his name, not caring if the sound carried all the way across the sea.

Her back arched off of the bed, whimpers escaping her as he swept his tongue across her clit, over and over, before sucking the swollen flesh inside his mouth once more. Her head thrashed on the bed as she gripped the sheets, her pleasure hanging on an edge he knew exactly how to control.

"Please, Crew, please," she cried out as he swept his tongue across her flesh again before retreating. He kept bringing her so close, but not quite enough to finish. She needed to find that beautiful ending.

With one last suck, she knew he was done torturing her, done making her body heat to volcanic levels, and she came with a cry of his name, her body shaking, her skin tingling from her toes to her head. The pulses lasted and lasted, rushing through her in wave after wave of pleasure. He slowed his magical tongue, drawing out every single ounce of pleasure she had inside her.

He held her while she floated back down to the bed, even her soul satisfied. He gave and he gave and she didn't want to hold a single thing back from him. "I'm yours, I'm all yours," she said, her voice satisfied, her body warm and tingly.

"Yes, Darla, you're mine," he told her, a possessive light in his eyes as he moved over her. "All mine." She'd never wanted a man to say that to her, but with Crew it was right. It was exactly what she wanted and needed to hear. She knew he was hers, too, but belonging to this man was even better than knowing he belonged to her.

She'd always been so stubborn, independent, and self-reliant she'd never imagined meeting a man capable of making her fully let go. But she knew she'd met that man the second she'd met Crew. It was incredibly freeing.

"Make love to me," she said.

There wasn't even a second of hesitation before he moved into the V of her thighs, right where he belonged. She wrapped her arms and legs around him, immeasurably at peace yet feeling her pleasure build again. She wondered if she'd always have dueling feelings with this man she could never get enough of.

"I love you, too, Darla," he said as he pushed deep inside her.

She groaned out his name as his moan of pleasure floated off into the night. He buried himself deep, making them one. He rested for only a moment, throbbing against her tingling walls, before he moved slowly, just a few inches at a time. She squeezed him tighter, wanting speed, wanting force.

"More," she growled, her fingernails digging into his back. "Give me everything."

She'd given it all to him. She wanted the same from him.

He growled her name before his lips slammed against hers in a fierce kiss. He held nothing back as he began moving faster and harder, gripping her hip and angling her to accept his full length and girth. She cried out his name over and over again.

She was on fire and flying. She clung to him, feeling sweet relief push up her, and then let go, wrenching her mouth from his as she threw her head back and called out his name, her walls squeezing him as she exploded, a burst of lights flashing before her eyes.

Her name echoed off his lips as he let go, his release buried deep inside her as they pulsed together. When they finally landed back on solid ground, the only sounds in the room were their ragged breaths and water lapping against the shore.

No words were needed that night. They knew who they were, and they knew where they were going. Now they just had to enjoy the journey . . . together.

Chapter Twenty-Three

When Crew and Darla made it back to Genova but kept going, he turned to her with a smile on his lips. She'd been so sad to leave the night before, however their out-of-this-world lovemaking cured that. She'd been in a fog ever since and barely managed to enjoy the stunning landscape. But when they passed through Genova, she wasn't sure what they were doing.

"I have a surprise for you," he told her.

"Another surprise?" she asked with a giggle. "You can't keep doing this, or I'll be unbearable with my demands," she warned.

"I'll give you whatever you want," he said. "So that means I can keep on surprising you."

"Then what will I do for you?" she asked.

"All you have to do is be with me. That's the greatest gift I can imagine," he told her. What shocked her was she believed his words. He truly wanted to give her the world with no expectations in return. That only made her want to give him so much more.

"We're heading to Venice for a few days."

"Venice? Really?" she asked with a delighted gasp. "I've seen all of the pictures. It's lovely. Is it true that it's slowly eroding?" What a tragic thought.

"Yes, but people are smart, and they're finding ways of slowing it down. It's stood for twelve hundred years. The buildings that stand today are up to eight hundred years old."

"That's incredible. We think of hundred-year-old houses as old," Darla told him. They sipped coffee as they were driven through the countryside of Italy on their way to the other coastline.

"To make the islands of the Venetian lagoon fit for habitation, the earliest settlers had to drain areas of the lagoon, dig canals, and shore up the banks with stakes. They placed wooden platforms on top of the stakes then stone on top of those. That's what the buildings of Venice are built on."

"I don't see how it doesn't sink into the sea," Darla told him. "That seems inevitable."

"Well, if it ever does, it will be a place for mermaids just like Atlantis," he told her.

"I want Atlantis to be real," she said.

"Maybe it is. You never know," he assured her.

"Did you know there's a place you can go in the Bahamas and feel like you're in Atlantis?" she asked.

"No, I didn't," he told her. "We'll have to go."

She sighed. "Yes, but it won't be the real place," she said with a pout.

He laughed. "I love how disappointed you are at that. We might have to spend the rest of our years searching for the real Atlantis."

"You know, if you keep encouraging my delusions you might have to give up your doctor's license," she teased.

"I'd give up anything for you."

"I'd never ask you to," she told him. "When you love someone you don't ask them to let go of something that makes them happy and helps them identify themselves."

He grinned. "So if I become an alcoholic, you won't ask me to give it up?" he teased.

"Nope, I'll just spike your drinks with that stuff that makes you puke at the smell of it," she said.

He laughed again. She loved the sound of his merriment. It made her laugh as well.

"You didn't get to hear the best part of our trip," he said as he pulled her a little closer to his side in the back of the vehicle.

"I thought the best part is that I get to be here with you," she told him and meant it.

"That's good, but what if I told you that your best friend is there waiting for you?" he asked.

Joy filled her. She leaned over and kissed him, really kissed him, enough that they were both hot and bothered when she finally pulled away.

"Okay, you're right. It doesn't get better than being there with you *and* my best friend. Now I really want to hurry." She leaned forward. "You can go as fast as you want," she said to the driver who grinned ear to ear.

"Yes, ma'am," he said as he pressed a little harder on the accelerator.

The rest of their trip was spent looking out at the country as they sipped wine, nibbled on snacks, and talked about different areas of the world they wanted to see.

"We're here," the driver told them as he held open Darla's door.

She was smiling so much she knew her cheeks would ache for days by the time they returned to Seattle. She didn't care. She'd take all of the extra wrinkles as well.

She stepped out onto the Piazza San Marco, the city's main public square that contained St Mark's Basilica and the Doge's Palace. People were buzzing around them as Darla tried to drink it all in.

"Did you know Napoleon called this place the world's most beautiful drawing room?" she asked, her tone hushed, her eyes trying to see everything at once.

"I can see why," Crew said as he stood next to her, his arm around her.

"I'll take the bags to your hotel if you want to explore," their driver said.

"Thank you," Crew told him, and they were alone under the watchful eye of the Basilica San Marco as the warm afternoon air floated around them while a stringed quartet played enchanting music.

"Darla," a voice called. Crew let her go just in time for Daisy to launch herself at her best friend.

"I'm now officially in love with Crew and demand you marry him," Daisy said as the two women hugged while jumping up and down.

"This is as good a place as any," Darla said with a wink as she looked over Daisy's shoulder at Crew. A little shiver traveled down her spine when she saw that, instead of looking horrified at Daisy's words and Darla's reply, he seemed intrigued. Whoa, that hadn't been expected.

"I take it you like this trip," Darla said with a laugh.

"We got here last night and have a darling house right on the water. It has a balcony for watching the boats driving by. The food . . . oh the food, Darla, is so sinful you could die. We went out earlier and I had orgasmic tiramisu. I'll never eat Italian desserts in America again," Daisy said, talking so quickly, her words were stumbling from her mouth.

"I had the exact same thought when I had that same dessert in Palomino," Darla told her.

"Well, I'll take you to the place here and you can compare," Daisy said. "I don't think I ever want to leave. I can't believe I never came here before."

"They fight for the preservation of their own buildings. You didn't need to come here to fight for them," Darla told her.

"Maybe I just need more pleasure trips," Daisy said.

"I've told you that for years," Darla said. "Where are we off to now?"

"I totally befriended our driver, and he said we have to eat in Giudecca. He told me it's a hidden gem from the usual tourist stops," Daisy said.

"Daisy can charm a rat," Hudson said with a smile. "This poor man was spilling the secrets to this city within five minutes of meeting her. He's probably going to get into trouble."

"I don't think he'll mind with that amazing tip you gave him," Daisy said. "I love what a good man you are." She took a moment to kiss her fiancé, before turning back to Darla. "He told me all of the places are good, but if we wanted a true taste of Italy we needed to avoid the hotspots that all of the tourists hit. So, we're going to La Palanca for a late lunch."

The four of them were off in seconds as they moved through the city, soaking up the atmosphere, the laughter and joy from others, and the charm of the centuries-old buildings. They made their way through the back streets, gazing into shop windows where Venetians crafted items to sell while they avoided the hustle and bustle of the main thoroughfares of Venice.

They had an amazing lunch, then walked and walked so they could try something new for dinner. The girls never stopped talking as they took in this beautiful place together, still holding the hands of the men they'd chosen to love.

"Matteo, our driver, told me about a great bookstore here," Daisy said as they continued making their way through Venice.

"That's a must stop," Darla said. "I can't imagine the treasures we might find."

"I'm even interested in that one," Crew said with a laugh. "I'm not complaining about the shoe stores and dress shops the two of you have insisted on going into, but a bookstore might be my stopping place while you continue on."

"Don't worry, Crew, we'll spend plenty of time in there," Darla said as they continued moving forward to the Castello Sestiere and found The Libreria Acqua Alta, an incredibly quirky bookshop. It was filled from floor to ceiling with books on every topic imaginable.

Darla's favorite parts of the entire store was a gondola full of books and a backdoor that led straight onto the canal. She moved in that direction, then gasped.

"Daisy, come here," she called. Daisy had a few books in her arms that she handed to Hudson then rushed over to Darla. They made their way out to the courtyard where they walked up a staircase made of books and found their own private view of a few of the canals of Venice.

"This is unbelievable," Darla said, amazed at the beauty and privilege of standing right where she was.

"Yes, it is," Crew said as he came to stand behind her. "I'm glad I'm seeing it for the first time with you though. You bring the magic to life."

She turned, her cheeks flushed. "You might want to be careful, Crew. They say this is a city for lovers. You might never be rid of me."

"Then I'm going to do everything they recommend, because I'm never letting you go." He leaned down and kissed her, and she was truly in paradise.

"Okay, okay, you two. You are here with your brother and future sister-in-law," Hudson said with a laugh.

"Oh you . . . leave them alone and kiss me," Daisy said. And that's exactly what Hudson did.

They left the bookstore and explored other gems of Venice some people never got to see. They went to the San Giorgio Maggiore on a small island east of the Giudecca, another island opposite of the main hub of Venice. When they reached the top, they got a view many never get to witness.

Standing at the top of a tower across from the mainland, they could see everything: St Mark's Square, the Grand Canal, the Doge's Palace, the Campanile, and the entire skyline, making the women feel they were in a real-life fairy tale.

They explored the six sestieri, the subdivisions of Venice. Darla's second favorite thing about Venice was the hidden gems she found in the many art galleries, especially the Gallerie dell'Accademia. There was so much inspiration in Italy that, of course, the artwork would be breathtaking and humbling all at once.

They couldn't end their trip without a gondola ride and Darla really felt like a princess as she went beneath the Bridge of Sighs where Crew leaned into her and gave her a kiss. She knew it was cheesy, but she didn't care. She wanted to be romanced, loved, and treasured. She wanted this time in Italy with Crew to never end.

But eventually all great things did come to an end. It wasn't about the last page most of the time, it was about the journey to get there.

Chapter Twenty-Four

When Darla and Crew came back to the States, she stayed at his house so much it was ridiculous to keep her place, so they moved in together. No great declaration of love, it just happened.

There was a smidgeon of fear in giving up her remaining freedom, but not enough to stop her from doing it. She was in love with him, and she knew it wasn't going to end. They'd work through anything that might come up.

If — and it was a very small if — they didn't manage to make it through a crisis, she could rebuild her life somewhere else. The thought of that was so horrifying she didn't want to think about it. She was in love with Crew, and there was no doubt in her mind he loved her too. That meant they'd only move forward, no steps back.

She carried the bags into the kitchen, smiling when she found him having his morning cup of coffee. She wondered if that feeling of awe was ever going to go away. When she looked at him, she knew the world was spinning in the right direction. She knew she was where she belonged.

"Good morning, beautiful," he said. "What do you have there?"

"Your outfit for the day," she told him as she placed the bags next to him. He didn't jump to open them, just looked at her with suspicion.

"Why do I need an outfit that you just bought?" he asked.

She laughed as she moved over to the coffee pot and filled a cup, sighing with pleasure at the creamy smoothness.

"I've had these bags for over a week. It's been killing me. I'm not the most patient person," she told him.

"I refuse to wear a speedo," he warned. She laughed harder.

"I wouldn't need nearly as many bags for that," she said. "But the idea's intriguing."

He rolled his eyes as he picked up the first one. He pulled out a pair of Wranglers and a cowboy shirt. He grinned as he met her gaze. "Really?" he asked.

"If you're going to be a cowboy, you have to look the part," she said. She was too impatient to wait. She pulled out the hat from the next sack and set it on his head. "Yummy. You look good enough to eat."

He snaked his arm around her waist and pulled her close. "I can't believe I'm going to put on these clothes just to see you smile." He kissed her and she felt her heart beat out of control.

"I love you because you'll put on these clothes to make me smile," she said.

"Yes, I will."

"We're going to the rodeo. I've been so excited and it's the end of the circuit so this is our last chance."

"We are, are we?" He seemed so at ease it made her giddy.

"We most certainly are. I need a corndog, cotton candy, and a good look at cowboy butts," she said.

He growled as he pulled her in tighter. "The only butt you need to be checking out is mine," he warned.

"Darlin, a true cowgirl appreciates a nice butt in a pair of Wranglers. Don't worry, the ladies will be checking your tushy out too," she said with a wink as she danced away from him. "I wanted to get you boots too, but you really have to try those on since they'll last forever. I lucked out on the hat. I grabbed one of your baseball caps and took a chance."

"I don't need to be getting in a brawl with a bunch of cowboys when they're looking where they shouldn't," he said. The twinkle in his eyes told her he was going to enjoy the day.

"Hurry up, I want to get going. We have a three-hour drive," she said. "We're off to Pendleton, Oregon."

"Did you get a room?" he asked.

"Of course I did. We can't enjoy the rodeo without a lot of beer, so there won't be any driving after."

"I don't trust the look in your eye right now," he told her.

She laughed again, feeling on top of the world. "Well, I didn't exactly get a room, but I have our night all planned out."

"I refuse to leave this house until you tell me where we're staying." He crossed his arms.

"We're camping. But I did manage to get a cabin so it's not too bad."

"Is there a shower and bathroom in this cabin?" he asked.

"Nope. But they're super close by."

He shocked her again when he got up. "It will be like the old days, but I get a bed this time. I used to camp with my mom and brothers all the time, but we'd sleep on the hard ground. A rodeo and campfire sounds pretty heavenly."

He grabbed his bags and headed from the room while she threw the last few things she needed into the cooler and took it to her SUV. She had blankets, pillows, extra clothes, and lots of road food. It was going to be a great day.

Their trip was fantastic. They listened to music, munched on beef jerky and candy, and blasted their way toward Pendleton. Darla loved Crew more with each moment they spent together.

When they arrived at their campground she could hear the sounds of the rodeo next to them and her heart thundered. She loved everything about a good rodeo and Pendleton had an excellent one.

After they got everything into the cabin, they walked hand-in-hand to the entrance of the fairground, people all around them.

"The sounds, smells, and sights of a rodeo mean something different to every person who steps through the gates," Darla told him as he pulled out his wallet to pay for admission.

"I bet," he said. "It's like a county fair."

"No, it's nothing like a fair. It's all about pride and winning and skill," she said. She felt pretty great in her snug Wranglers, worn cowboy boots, and ten-year-old tan hat. Crew looked so delicious in his jeans and blue fitted shirt that she wanted to jump him right then and there.

"Being at a rodeo is like attending a great symphony. If you stop and take it all in, you can hear the music beating within you," she said. Clanging metal, hooves stomping dirt, laughter, and cheers surrounded them.

"I guess it could be compared to a symphony," he said as he grabbed her hand. She loved how he pulled her close, knowing it was his way of keeping her safe in the large crowd of people.

There was suddenly a stillness in the air, and Darla grinned ear-to-ear. "Hurry up. We don't want to miss the opening," she said as she tugged on him and raced to the stands. Neither of them spoke as they found a seat and looked around the arena. Everyone was standing in the full stands as a rider entered the arena, a flag billowing behind her as her horse galloped in a circle. The National Anthem began, and Darla would swear every person sang along, the moment nearly magical. *Oh, say can you see by the dawn's early light, what so proudly we hailed at the twilight's last gleaming, whose broad stripes and bright stars thru the perilous fight . . . Oh say does that star-spangled banner yet wave, O'er the land of the free and the home of the brave . . .*

It didn't matter how many times Darla heard that song, or how many times she'd sung it, it still touched her, especially when surrounded by people who were just as mesmerized as she was.

At the last words, applause erupted in the arena. It was time to rodeo.

"Right now the bronc riders behind the chutes are talking about the draws they got, they're talking about the road, hearts that have been broken, and bodies that have been beaten. And they do it all with a smile because they love what they do," Darla told him.

"Okay, so far, so good," Crew said. "You might convince me to become a rodeo fan."

She cheered as the first evening event began. They'd already had the daytime events, and those were great, but once the night hit, it was magic.

Crew managed to get Darla corn dogs, popcorn, nachos, elephant ears, and cotton candy. He laughed at her as she continued stuffing food in her mouth. When she was home she ate a lot healthier, but at rodeo, she wanted to taste it all. She washed it down with spiked cider and grew quite tipsy before the bull riding began.

The crowd gasped as a cowboy was bucked and thrown against the fence. But the clowns managed to get the angry bull away, and the cowboy stood and waved to the crowd, though he was limping as he walked off the field.

By the time their night ended, Darla was tipsy, smiling, and happier than she'd been in a very long time —and that was really something for a normally happy person. But bringing Crew into a new world, and him liking it, made her happier than she'd been.

"I love you," she told him as they made their way back to their cabin.

"I adore you," he replied, his arm tightening around her.

The rodeo wasn't over though. She kept that hat on him while they had their own rodeo later. And she was one heck of a cowgirl because he couldn't buck her off.

Crew promised the next day on their ride home he'd take her to at least two rodeos a year. He assured her he'd get her front row seats in Vegas. She knew right then and there she was going to marry the man.

But the real world was waiting when they got back home. She had to figure out what she was going to do with her life now that it had changed so much. Crew went to work, and she searched her computer.

On her third week since she'd quit, she was having a bit of a pity party. Crew had come home for lunch then rushed off for a meeting. He still wasn't home so Darla walked to the barn. The kittens were big enough they were running all over the place. The horses tolerated the little munchkins, maybe even liked them a little, but she was sure they'd rather they were anywhere other than in the stalls with them. They were pretty hoity toity little things.

The horses were thriving. Both the male and female horse were still a little wary, but it wouldn't be long before they'd be riding them. The foals were completely acclimated. They loved attention and as soon as she came into the barn they whinnied at her to give them treats.

They were out in the fields at the moment, so she went straight to the kittens. They spotted her in an instant and began climbing her legs.

"I can't imagine anyone not loving kittens," she told the furry little things. "Have you found any mice yet?" She laughed to herself at what anyone would think if she was found talking to the tiny things.

She stayed in the barn for about an hour, then walked back to the house. Crew still wasn't home. She should've gone with him, but she needed to figure out what she was going to do. She was too restless to stay unemployed for long.

Should she go to law school? She was a little old for that — an irritating thought. A person was never too old to pursue what they wanted in life. If she wanted to get a law degree when she was eighty, she could.

But even as a lawyer her hands would be tied. She needed to have a talk with her bestie about the situation. Daisy had been a justice warrior for a very long time. Darla wanted to tell herself there was absolutely nothing she could do, she was just one person. But a stronger part of herself knew one person could make a difference. If she only saved one child, she was doing her part in the scheme of things. If every good person saved the life of another person there'd be a lot less senseless murder in the world.

After wandering the house for a while longer, looking at her computer, then walking away from it, she was almost giddy when she heard her doorbell ring. A legitimate distraction was exactly what she needed.

She threw open the door and froze. Before she could say a word, something came at her . . . and the world went dark.

Chapter Twenty-Five

Crew whistled as he opened the front door. "Darla, I have something for you," he called. There was no answer.

He moved into the kitchen and set down the huge bouquet he'd bought along with the box of chocolate-covered strawberries. He went to the coffee pot and poured a cup, then moved to the stairs and called her name again. No answer.

He smiled. Her computer was on the counter so there was really only one place she could be. He walked out the back door and made his way to the barn.

"Someone isn't searching for her new career like she said she was going to do. You could've come to town with me," Crew said as he walked through the barn doors. The kittens immediately attacked his legs . . . and he became concerned. Darla wasn't there.

He pulled out his phone and dialed her number, but it rang out until it went to voicemail. He sent a quick text. *Where are you hiding?* He waited. There was no response. What in the world was going on?

He finally noticed how quiet everything was. It was so still around him, and he didn't like the unsettled feeling washing over him. "It's no big deal. Don't be paranoid. I'm sure she went for a walk to clear her head," he said to himself. But his heart was racing, and he felt as if something was wrong.

He moved quickly back to the house and walked into their bedroom. Nothing was out of place. He went back to the kitchen and found her purse. Her car was in the garage, but Daisy could've picked her up. Maybe they'd been in a hurry.

He pulled out his phone again and dialed Daisy. She answered on the second ring. "Hi, Crew," she said in her sweet voice.

"Is Darla with you?" he asked, trying to keep the panic from his voice.

There was a pause. "No, but I talked to her earlier and she was fine. I haven't seen her today," she said. "Where are you?"

"I'm home and her car's here, so is her purse, she's not answering her phone, and I can't find her," he told Daisy.

"I don't like this," Daisy said. Her concern sent his own panic up several notches. What in the hell was going on?

Daisy was still on the phone with him when he stepped into the entryway to his house. His throat closed. He'd come in through the backdoor and hadn't noticed the front. The door was wide open, but more concerning were the drops of blood on the tile floor. He dropped down and felt that the blood was tacky as if it was pretty fresh. How long had he been gone? He had to think. It had been about three hours. Dammit!

What was going on? Was this Darla's blood? Had she been injured? Had someone taken her to the hospital? Had an ambulance been called? No. That was impossible. If that had happened, someone would've called him. His throat tightened. Had she been attacked?

"Crew!" Daisy's voice startled him out of his panic.

"Sorry. What?" he mumbled. He was on his knees on the floor, trying to figure out what to do.

"I've been trying to talk to you for the past minute. What in the hell is happening?" Daisy demanded. He could hear the sound of a car running.

"I don't know," he said. "Darla is just gone. I . . . the front door's open. There's, um, there's some drops of blood," he finished, his voice choked.

"I'm driving there now. Call nine one one. I'll call Hudson. He can call everyone else."

He kneeled there, not sure what to do. He didn't say anything.

"Dammit, Crew. Snap the hell out of this. Darla needs help," Daisy said, tears clearly present in her voice.

Her tone and words finally snapped him out of his paralysis. This was her best friend, and she was panicking but still moving forward. He owed it to Darla to do the same.

"You're right. I'll call nine one one. Get here fast," he told her.

"Trust me, I will." The phone went dead.

His fingers trembled as he dialed the emergency line. He explained what he'd found and they said they'd send officers his way. He hung up the phone, not knowing what to do next.

But then he did. He dialed Uncle Joseph. If anyone could get quick results, it would be his uncle. He'd keep a level head.

The next twenty minutes might as well have been three hours, it seemed to take so long. Daisy pulled in at the same time as a county sheriff. She screeched to a halt, nearly swiping the side of the sheriff's car. The men jumped from their vehicles, their hands on their weapons which, thankfully, were still resting in their holders.

"It's okay, I'm supposed to be here," Daisy said, tears streaming down her cheeks. "I'm not a bad guy. I just need you to find my best friend."

The police didn't seem fully convinced, but since Daisy ran to Crew and flung herself into his arms, they seemed to decide she might be welcome. They knew Crew.

"Have you talked to her? I've dialed her phone a dozen times in the last twenty minutes," she said. "She never doesn't answer me unless she's in a meeting. And she's not working right now, so there's no excuse for her not to answer." Daisy was talking a mile a minute, but he totally understood.

"Mr. Anderson, are you the one who called nine one one?" one of the officers asked as he stepped up.

"Yes, Chuck, my girlfriend's missing. She won't answer her phone. The front door was open, and there's blood on the entryway floor. I don't know anything else," he said.

"Have you gone through the house? Is anything disturbed or missing?" Officer Chuck asked.

Before he could answer there was a loud noise. They all turned to see a chopper drawing near. "What the hell?" Chuck asked.

Crew would've smiled if his lips would moved in that direction. "That's my uncle Joseph. Apparently, he didn't want to take the time to drive," Crew said.

There was a large open area in front of the house, and the chopper slowly lowered. It was only seconds before the door flung open and Joseph Anderson stepped out.

"Do you have any news yet?" Joseph asked. The chopper shut down and the area went eerily quiet again.

"No, nothing," Crew said. "I'm scared. I don't know what's happening."

"It has to be that piece of shit guy who's been stalking her," Daisy said. "It has to be. There's no other explanation."

Crew's blood ran cold. "There's no way he'd be that stupid. We know who he is," Crew told them.

"He's a psychopath who thinks he's untouchable. I think he'd be that stupid," Daisy said.

Another vehicle pulled up and Sheriff McCormack, a longtime friend of the family, stepped from the cruiser. He was out of his district, but it didn't matter. The officers in all of the surrounding cities of Seattle liked and respected the man.

"Any news yet?" McCormack asked.

"Nothing. But maybe a lead," Joseph said. "Some man's been stalking Darla for a while according to her best friend.

"Do you have his information?" McCormack asked.

"Yes. I have it on my phone, just in case," Daisy said as she pulled it up.

"I'll run him," McCormack said.

Another SUV pulled up, and five large men stepped from their vehicle, their very presence enough to make the first two responding officers take a step back, their hands immediately going to their guns.

Crew had to admit he was thrilled these men were on his side. They didn't necessarily look mean, they just looked capable — very, very capable. They were big, they were organized, and they seemed to see everything in a glance.

"Thank you for coming, Eyes. Darla's missing," Joseph said as he shook the hand of the first man in the V-shaped formation of men.

"Of course, Joseph," Eyes said. "How long's she been gone?"

"I don't know. I was gone for three hours, but the blood in the entryway of the house is still tacky so I think if she was taken, it was within the last hour," Crew told him.

"That's a good deduction," another of the men said.

"That's what I thought, Sleep," Joseph said. "But we all know how important the next few hours are."

"Yes, we do," Sleep said.

"We'll get her back, don't you worry about it," one of the men said. He was the largest of the group, his eyes deadly, his skin a nice light chocolate, his mouth in a firm line. Crew nearly smiled again. The man looked scary as hell, but he'd seen how he'd also become a big brother to his little cousin Jasmine, who idolized Smoke. He'd seen what a teddy bear he turned into when Jasmine was there.

"Thanks, Smoke. Having you guys here makes me think that just might happen," Crew said.

"I'm going to do my own digging on this guy," Brackish said. His computer skills might make or break the situation.

"Thanks, Brackish. You've really helped me a lot these past few months."

"I'm glad to do it," Brackish said. He left the group to set up his computer in the house and get to work.

The other men organized a search party for the nearby property, going out in a grid pattern to leave no stone unturned. Thirty minutes later, there was still no sign of her.

By the time they were done with their search, there were at least fifty people at his house, including his siblings and their wives. Several people went into the kitchen and put food and drinks together, while others splintered off into groups to try to figure out the best solution to finding Darla.

Brackish walked into the room full of people with a smile on his face. It only took about three seconds for all conversations to stop as they looked his way.

"I've got the bastard," Brackish said.

"Who is it?"

"Where?"

"Did you find Darla?"

"Let's go!"

The questions and shouts all came at once and Brackish simply held up his hand and the voices quieted once more.

"Please," Crew said as he looked at Brackish.

Brackish moved over to him and handed him a piece of paper. Both fury and panic filled Crew. Daisy was at his side in an instant as she looked down at the paper. Her eyes widened and then a mixture of confusion, fear, and anger to match his flashed through her gaze.

"Let's go," Brackish said. He then turned to Joseph. "We're going to need a few things."

Joseph nodded. "Whatever it takes," he said.

Crew's brothers surrounded him, and he knew Joseph's words were more than true. They'd get to Darla, and they'd truly do whatever it took.

Chapter Twenty-Six

Darla was dreaming. She knew she was dreaming, but she didn't want to wake from the dream. She was on a beach in her tiny bikini, red and fitted, and she could see Crew off in the distance splashing in the water, laughing before he dove back into the water. She could hear the waves slapping the shore.

It was a good dream.

Her head hurt really bad, and she knew she needed to get up and get some aspirin, but she couldn't seem to make herself wake up. It was too good there in her dream, even with her head pounding and her body aching. The longer she hung between sleep and consciousness the more aches and pains she felt.

"Wakey, wakey," a voice called to her from the sky.

What was that? She shook her head. She didn't want to wake up, didn't want to go to that voice. She looked at the water and her brow furled when Crew didn't emerge from the water. What was wrong? Was he hurt? She had to get to him. She jumped from her chair and her dream faded as she found herself sitting up in bed, her head pounding, her wrists on fire, and her body aching.

"Crew," she automatically called.

"Don't say that name," a man screamed.

Darla whipped her head around, then true fear filled her. "Steve?" she whispered. "What's happening?" She hated how shaky her voice was.

The raw anger in his expression evaporated as she said his name. He seemed . . . relaxed. He was sitting there in a chair, wearing a pair of khaki shorts and a button-down tropical shirt, and his eyes were bright as if there was nothing at all wrong with that picture.

"How did you sleep?" he asked.

She gazed blankly at him. Was the man insane? "I don't understand. Where am I?" she asked.

"We're on an island. Our own private island. I knew we needed to get away from Crew. He was brainwashing you. So, we're here. It's beautiful. You'll really like it," he said.

He rose from the chair and came closer to her. She shrank back, his eyes narrowed again, and he slapped her so fast she hadn't seen it coming.

"I've done all of this for you, so don't look at me like I'm a monster," he growled. Darla saw stars for a second as she tried to clear the pounding in her head.

"I'm sorry," she said. At this point she'd say anything to get the pain to stop.

"I know you are. I'm sorry I had to hit you. Don't make me do that again," he told her, his voice instantly pleasant again. What kind of psycho was he? What was she dealing with?

She looked around the room. She was on a huge bed, covers over her. She felt sick when she realized she was only wearing a slip of a nightgown that barely covered her. She wanted to grab the blankets and pull them up to her chin, but she didn't want to make Steve angry again.

The room was light and airy, looking like any other vacation place in the world. How was Crew going to find her? Were they even in the US?

"How long was I sleeping?" she asked. Maybe if she knew how long she'd been out, she'd have an idea of where they were.

"Twelve hours," he said. She had to stifle a groan. They could be anywhere.

"Can I have some aspirin? My head's pounding," she told him, keeping her voice as meek as possible.

"Of course. I have some ready. I'm sorry I had to knock you out, but it was the only way to get you to come with me. I knew once I got you away from Washington you'd realize your mistake in ignoring me. Those damn Andersons are good at massive mind control. But it's okay now. We're here and we can continue our relationship."

She so badly wanted to tell him he was a psychotic nut job, but she knew better than that. She couldn't rile this man. He handed her the aspirin and she took it. She had no idea if there were drugs in the water he was giving her, but she had to take the chance. She needed to get her wits about her in order to come up with a plan.

"What did you give me so I'd sleep?" she asked. She didn't say so you could keep me knocked out and do whatever you wanted. Her body ached, but she didn't feel like she'd been raped, so there were small miracles. She prayed she'd be able to save herself before that happened. If she was friendly with him, maybe he'd take his time trying to woo her. She could only hope.

"It was a shot," he said nonchalantly. It won't hurt you. You looked tired. I'm sure the rest has done you good," he said. The man actually thought he'd been doing her a favor. Bile rose in her throat.

"Thank you. I did need some rest," she said, hearing the false note in her tone. From the smile he sent her, he didn't hear the same thing.

"You'll love this place. I'm not sure how long we'll stay, but I'm thinking we could have a wedding right here," he said as he moved away from her and walked over to the open patio doors. She wanted to rush him and push him over.

But she wasn't sure if they were on the ground floor or higher. She wasn't sure if she'd hurt him or just piss him off, and she had no idea where they were. She didn't even know if he had goons around to help him control her. She needed information.

"Where are we?" she asked again.

"I told you, a private island," he said.

"Which private island. I feel so disoriented. It would help me to get my bearings," she said.

"We just arrived a couple of hours ago. It's a nice little tropical place. The where doesn't matter. We had to take a jet to a nearby airport and then boat in. It's not easy to get to . . . or to leave."

She wasn't sure if he was saying that as a good thing, or warning her that there was no escape. She smiled at him.

"I do like getaways, but I'm not much into cooking. Is there staff here?" she asked. She prayed there was someone who'd help her.

"Yes, we have servants," he said with a wave of his hands. "They don't speak English though, which is what I wanted. I like to be able to say and do what I want without worrying about people eavesdropping." Those words held a definite warning. She felt close to tears again.

"Why did you bring me here, Steve?"

He glared at her a second before he regained his composure. Then he spoke in a warning tone.

"I've told you, you're mine," he said very clearly. "I know you'll understand that soon enough. You just need some time to accept the inevitable. It will happen."

"This isn't the best way to romance me," she finally said very carefully.

"Do you realize the amount of planning this took?" he snapped at her as he stalked closer. It took a lot of willpower not to flinch from him again, but she sat there as if it was just the two of them having a normal conversation. "I did all of this for you."

She didn't tell him that consent was a pretty damn good indication of whether someone wanted something done for them. It would go right over his damn head. She'd have to swim from the island. She would if she had to. She'd rather face sharks than be violated by this man.

"Look, Darla, we've been connected from the first moment we met. I don't know why you ran away. I can only assume it's because of that damn best friend of yours who brought you to that man. They are both gone now so we can focus on us. If they continue to be a distraction . . . well, they'll have to be taken care of," he told her.

A shiver ran through her.

"No, they aren't a problem," Darla quickly said. She wasn't sure how much power this man had, but she absolutely didn't want him going after Daisy or Crew.

"Is Daisy okay?" she asked, not daring to ask a single thing about Crew.

Steve waived his hand in the air again as if that was a ridiculous question. "I haven't needed to do anything about her . . . yet."

Darla suddenly felt her head grow a little fuzzy. The pain had diminished to more of an annoyance, but she was having a difficult time keeping her eyes open.

"What did you give me?" she asked.

He smiled through a blurry gaze. Then he moved to her and ran his hand over her face and through her hair. She tried to lift her hand to push him away, but she was so weak. It had come on that suddenly.

He leaned down and brushed his lips against hers, and she had to fight not to gag. Please, no, please, please no.

"It's okay, Darla. I have to get things ready so I need you to sleep a little longer. We need to be intimate. Once we are, you'll stop fighting me so much. You'll see how good we are together. You just rest up for a while and I'll get everything ready. You'll see how good we are together, you'll see this is meant to be."

She blacked out just as he pushed his tongue into her mouth.

"Wake up, darling, wake up."

There'd been no dreams this time. When Darla opened her eyes, it was dark outside. The moon was shining through the open patio doors, but the room was cast in shadows. As she pushed the sleep away, she noticed several candles burning, but that was all.

A hand ran over her stomach and she jerked as she tried to scoot away, terror filling her. She tugged on her arms, but they were tied above her head. She was completely at this man's mercy.

"That's my girl. Do you like the room? I wanted to make our first time special. I even got red candles and red roses for love," he said. He leaned down and kissed her neck. Her skin crawled and she felt bile well up higher in her throat. She coughed as she fought back vomiting.

He pulled back and loomed over her, anger flashing in his eyes. "What's the matter with you?" he snapped. He slapped her, not as hard as last time but hard enough to make her cheek sting. "I've done all of this for *you*. Why don't you appreciate it?"

He was over her, his body pressing into hers. He had a shirt on, and she prayed he was wearing pants, but she only had a thin nighty covering her body. She had zero protection.

"This is too fast, Steve. I'm not ready," she said, not able to stop the tears from falling down her cheeks.

His anger evaporated as he looked at her, his gaze suddenly one of adoration. He brushed back the hair from her temple, leaned down, and kissed her again. She didn't kiss him back, but she didn't protest either. She wasn't sure what she was going to do.

"I know, you're a real good girl, and I know this isn't what you normally do, but baby, it will connect us. It's going to happen anyway, and I think it's a good idea to just do it now so you aren't so scared of it. The first time always hurts a little, but I'll be gentle with you," he said.

He thought she was a virgin? Oh, holy hell, was he going to be even more enraged? This night couldn't get any worse. She wasn't sure what she could do to get out of it. She knew it was smarter to talk nice to him, to appease him.

"Please, let's just talk. I'm very hungry. I don't have any energy," she told him. "I might get sick. Those drugs really hurt my stomach. I wouldn't be able to enjoy anything, and I'm scared," she said, making her voice as weak as humanly possible. She was so damn afraid, it wasn't too difficult to do.

He seemed indecisive, as if he really wanted to do things that pleased her but he really wanted to have sex with her too. She pushed a little harder.

"I feel dizzy, Steve. I really should eat some crackers or something," she told him.

She had to fight her nausea again when he shifted to the side and ran his hand down the center of her body, his fingers skimming over everything.

"Okay," he finally said. When he met her gaze again, his eyes were full of lust. She fought the revulsion as she gave him a thankful smile.

"Thank you, Steve," she said. "I really should use the bathroom too. I should also shower." She was doing anything to stall him.

"I gave you a sponge bath. You're nice and clean," he told her. "I wish you would've been awake. You'd have enjoyed it. I really did," he told her. She pushed back the tears wanting to fall at the invasion of her body.

She must've shown something on her face because he chuckled. "Don't worry, my sweet Darla, I didn't go too far. I want you to feel everything as we make love, not be asleep. After we've done it a few times, it's okay if you aren't conscious. I mean, a man's needs are so much more intense than a woman's, and it's a wife's job to please her man, but the first few times need to be special," he said as if he were being perfectly reasonable.

"Yes, Steve," she said. "Can I have those crackers and use the bathroom?" she asked. She needed a few minutes alone to clear her head.

"Of course," he said. "I want you comfortable. But I don't want you out of bed, so I got one of those bedpans," he said.

Her eyes widened in horror. She shook her head. "I can't do that," she told him.

"It's okay, darling. I won't be grossed out. I like that sort of thing anyway. I'll take good care of you. Besides, I don't like hospitals, so when you have our baby, I'll be delivering it. You have to get used to me caring for you."

Who in the hell was this man? How had he gotten through life without someone realizing how crazy he was? He was a senator's son, for goodness sake. Had no one thought to lock him up? Why hadn't she talked more to Crew about him? She'd thought she was so strong, thought she could handle him. She'd truly thought he'd go away.

He stood from the bed to get her crackers and she allowed a tear to fall. Well, she couldn't stop it was more like it. She was trapped and there was nothing she could do about it. This man was going to do terrible things to her and she'd be a shell of the person she'd been. Even if he didn't kill her, he would kill her soul.

More tears fell. She tried to take herself to another place, tried to leave her mind. Maybe if she wasn't mentally there, she'd somehow survive.

Please come, Crew, please come, she thought as she looked out the open windows. She didn't know how it was possible, but she still sent the message out into the universe.

Chapter Twenty-Seven

Crew shouldn't have been surprised at how efficiently and how quickly the Special Ops team moved once they were on a task. He'd been going out of his mind with worry from the second he'd spotted that blood, but as he'd told Steve back then, he had friends — he'd never been so grateful he hadn't been bluffing.

"That man never should've gotten his hands on Darla. I swore to her nothing would happen," Crew said.

He was in same jet he and Darla had taken to Italy just a short time before. That trip had been full of magic and the two of them had known they were meant to be together. He'd told her he loved her, but he still hadn't proposed. What if it was too late? What if he actually lost her?

"It's hard to know how psycho some people are," Eyes said as he patted Crew's shoulder.

Brackish had found the private jet and the flight pattern Steve had taken within ten minutes of entering Crew's house. Steve was psychotic. He didn't think he was doing anything wrong and didn't think he needed to hide his activities. Crew wasn't sure if that was a very, very bad thing, or a stroke of luck for the good guys.

"Tell me the plan again," Crew said. They'd allowed him to come, pretty much because he'd refused to stay behind while someone else went after his woman. He knew if they wanted him bound and gagged and left in his own closet, they could make it happen, but they told him she'd want to see his face when she was found. They warned him it might not be pretty. He refused to think that way.

"You understand that four out of five of us are Elite Special Forces trained. And the other is this guy who's the world's foremost computer genius, who also happens to be pretty damn deadly. We move without anyone seeing us," Eyes said. "We're incredibly loyal to Joseph, not because he created this group and hired us, but because we've been lucky enough to see the man he is. We're going to get your girl."

"But how?" Crew asked. He was a doctor, he tried telling himself, but that wasn't getting through. Right now he was a scared man, afraid of losing the woman who'd brought color into his black and white world.

Brackish pulled out a map. Crew should have confidence just by his appearance and the way he spoke, but this was different. This was a matter of life and death. Crew knew Darla, and knew she wouldn't go down without a fight. If Steve realized she wasn't his willing submissive, he might decide she was more trouble than she was worth.

"We're landing right here in about thirty minutes," Brackish said as he pointed to a place on the map. "From this place it's ten minutes to the marina. The rest is all arranged."

Crew wanted to know details, but he didn't want to push these men. They had a job to do and if they were catering to him they weren't focused on what really mattered.

Eyes reached out and touched his shoulder.

"Look, I know this is difficult. If it were my woman out there needing help, I'd be going out of my mind. But, it's your woman, and a damn fine one at that. You have to have faith in us. And, more importantly, you have to show more self-control than you've ever shown in your life. If one of us says jump, you jump immediately. If one of us says get down, you drop. Half a second can be the difference in you living or dying. You have to stay in control, and you have to listen. We let you come because we think Darla will need you. Don't let us regret that."

Crew wanted to punch Eyes in the face. That was irrational. He knew the man was only doing his job. He wanted to tell him that nothing was going to stop him from getting to Darla, but he knew he had to let these men do their job.

"I understand. It won't be easy, but I'll do whatever it takes," Crew said.

"Twenty minutes until we land. Let's gear up," Smoke said as he stepped from the back of the plane. "Crew, put this on." He tossed some black gear at Crew.

Crew was left alone as the five men went to the back of the jet. The plane was nearly on the ground when they came back out, and if Crew hadn't seen their faces, he'd have no clue who they were. They were covered from head to toe in black with different straps and attachments all over their clothing.

The men had the jet door unlocked and open before the aircraft came to a complete stop. They were on the ground before the jet's turbine engines quit spinning. They moved in a symmetrical order to their contact who was waiting.

"Eyes?" the man asked, as he approached, giving a wary eye to the six large men standing before him in full-on tactical gear.

"Yes, do you have new information for us?" Eyes asked.

The man was shaky as he stood there.

"No new information. My cousin was the driver who picked up this Steve you've described. He had a woman he called his wife with him. My cousin was concerned because she was passed out. Steve said she drank too much and was sleeping it off, but I've never seen a drunk person who didn't move a single finger. My cousin didn't like it, but this man has clout and we don't so there really was nothing we could do about it."

"I understand," Eyes said.

Crew wanted to pick the man up by his neck and shake him. His cousin had seen Darla, seen she needed help, and they'd done nothing. The only thing keeping him from attacking the man was his promise to Eyes on the jet.

"Did you get the transport ready?" Eyes asked. The men had been discussing hating to have to rely on other people, but this was a small place and there wasn't time to secure other means of travel.

"There's a slight problem with transport," the man said as if he was terrified to tell them anything was wrong. Crew's entire body tensed. As if Smoke knew he was about to blow he laid a hand on Crew's shoulder and squeezed. "Wait it out," Smoke whispered.

"The only plane big enough to take all six of you is broken down," the man said, sweat beading on his brow. "But my cousin does have a six-seater that can take four of you with gear. It's the only one you can jump from. We can also take a boat, but that takes three hours, two and a half if the water's clear. It seems pretty clear tonight."

"We'll quadruple the amount quoted to you if he can get that plane in the air in twenty minutes," Eyes said. He looked at Brackish who nodded. "If you can also take these two men by boat and cut that time down to two hours, we'll give a twenty percent bonus. Time matters and we need to get there before this woman's hurt."

The man's eyes widened, before he composed himself. Crew let out a breath of relief when he knew the man was going to make it happen.

"Okay." He snapped his fingers, and two men came out of the hangar. "You take these four men in the jet." He pointed to another man. "And you, take these two men over to the marina. Take the Belle Shark and get to the island in two hours. You'll get a significant bonus if you do. If you're late, you're fired."

The men nodded. Money spoke and they were quite pleased with being offered more.

Eyes pulled the team out of earshot as activity burst around them. "Sleep, Smoke, Green, and I are going on the plane. We'll jump as planned on the island. Brackish, you'll take Crew by boat. By the time we get there and settled you'll be there."

"Don't wait for us," Crew said. "Save her."

"We will," Eyes said. "But get your ass there. She will want to see your face, not our scary ones."

Crew couldn't even smile. He was so damn terrified.

The men split and Crew rushed to a vehicle where they took a harrowing ride to the harbor. The boat they were taking was turned on and ready to go, the captain waiving them over. Bonuses really did talk in this country. Crew wanted to be on that plane, wanted to be closer to her, but he knew those men jumping in were her best chance for a rescue.

"We'll get her," Brackish assured him as they sat down in the boat and the captain turned it then put the throttle to the floor as he began speeding over the calm ocean. Crew hoped it stayed that way.

"This baby has three 300 HP engines. We might start flying higher than the plane," Crew said. He liked boats with power, and this one had it. He sat back and tried to see ahead in the dark. The moon was shining, but all he could see was blackness. He closed his eyes and sent all of the love and courage he could to Darla.

"I'm coming, baby," he whispered. "I'm coming."

***

"We'll be over the island in forty minutes," the pilot said to Eyes as they loaded into the plane. His voice was nervous. Who wouldn't be when faced with their team? They expected that reaction.

"Perfect," Eyes told him. Then he lifted his radio. "Brackish, radio check."

"Comms good. Over," came the reply.

The next thirty-five minutes weren't filled with chatter. The men knew what they had to do, and they weren't worried about going over it again and again. If the situation changed on the ground, they'd deal with it then.

"We're five minutes from the jump," the pilot called. "Get ready."

"Got it," Eyes said. "Brackish, we're five minutes from the drop. See you on the ground, brother. Out." Eyes put his radio away as "Copy," came over the speaker.

Aside from the constant revolutions of the engine there was silence for the next five minutes as the men checked their parachute packs and made sure all straps were still secure. They got into place.

The pilot confirmed the island and the house the locals knew well enough as it came into sight. He was instructed to continue on the same flight path for at least fifteen minutes before turning back home, and to not come back over the island on his return. Eyes didn't want anything to look suspicious to the kidnapper. A circling plane might trigger him.

"Go time," Eyes said as he slid the side door open. The cool night air rushed into the plane, momentarily shifting his balance.

The team threw themselves from the plane one by one. Wind rushed across their covered faces as they descended. They had their heads pointed down, arms tucked to their sides, their speed increasing each second that passed, all four men becoming human missiles.

The team, who'd never jumped as a group before, knew when to give each other space, when to pull, and how close to come back together as they released their parachutes just in time for a nice cushy beach landing approximately two miles from the house. Normally they'd have landed in the water and come in slowly, no one knowing they were in the area, but that wasn't necessary on this operation.

"Let's roll," Eyes said, their faces glowing green through his night vision.

The team bundled their parachutes and jogged toward the house. It was an easy trek, the silhouette of the house appearing in fifteen minutes.

"Smoke, Green, split off to the east side of the building. Sleep and I will circle around until we meet. If you see a target, let the others know. All but one person here is a friendly, no lethal force. Understood?" Eyes asked. They each nodded.

Sweat started to bead up around the brows of the team members. Their packs might be light, but the humidity on the island weighed heavy on each of them. That's why they trained in multiple environments.

Through the shadows of the trees surrounding the massive home the men shuffled past doors and windows, silently creeping to each of them, reviewing the contents of what they could see. Only two individuals were seen in the downstairs, two women in a kitchen, cleaning pots and pans.

"Smoke climb to the second floor. They aren't on the ground," Eyes said.

There was only a ten second delay.

"Got them. No time to wait. Must make contact now," Smoke's voice cracked back through the earpiece.

"This isn't good. That's rage in your voice," Eyes said. "Smoke, neutralize, don't kill."

"I'll try," Smoke said.

Smoke's call sign had been given to him because he moved fast. When he was in action all that was left was a trail of smoke behind him. If he didn't want to be seen, he wouldn't be.

***

Smoke didn't care right now who saw him or what sounds he made. The sight before him enraged him. He knew better than to lose control, and he held on to it by a thread as he pushed his way through the open patio door. His frame was large, and he was moving fast, so he didn't make a graceful entrance.

Steve, their perp, was sitting on the bed with Darla tied to it. The creep's hand was sliding down her chest and moving lower. There was a bedpan in his other hand, and he began to place it beneath her. She was turned away from him, humiliation clear on her face as tears flowed down in rivers.

"Please, please just let me get up. This is humiliating," Darla said.

"Shut up and do what I tell you," Steve replied, gleeful in her humiliation.

An explosion of glass and wood ripped into the bedroom as Smoke made his entrance. His momentum didn't stopped. He met the man in four solid strides. He didn't stop as he pulled his arm back, seeing nothing but his fist smashing into the scumbag's face. His body was so fast it was a blur of motion.

The utter disgust Smoke felt, and the scream of fright from Darla, threw off Smoke's aim and he punched Steve in the ear instead of the face, making the man stagger back. Not receiving the full power of Smoke's punch, he managed to stay on his feet.

"Who in the hell are you?" Steve screamed.

"Your worst nightmare," Smoke said.

"No, you stupid asshole, I'm yours," Steve yelled. The man made a dive to the chair, and Smoke watched as he reached for a gun. Damn, this gave him a legitimate reason to take the man out. He wanted an excuse to kill him. Only his iron-clad control kept him from snapping the man's neck.

He moved in a blur just as Steve's fingers closed over the gun. Smoke grabbed the back of the man's shirt and threw him against the closest wall. A low painful growl escaped the kidnapper who surely had a broken nose and jaw from the force of the hit. The gun went skidding across the floor and Smoke grabbed it in seconds and disarmed it before tossing it over the balcony.

The man who'd taken Darla started to get up only to receive a heavy knee into his jaw, sending him spinning backward. He moaned, but he still wasn't passing out. Damn, he could take a serious beating and not die. Smoke was almost impressed.

"How dare you treat a woman this way," Smoke growled through his teeth as he picked the man up off the floor, and again threw him, but this time it was into the area of the room with shattered glass. He was quiet for a second before he looked up, blood pouring from his nose and mouth and a slash on his cheek.

"I . . . I'm sorry . . . I thought she loved me," the attacker said. He was no longer angry, just looked absolutely terrified.

His words set fire beneath Smoke's skin. This disgusting idiot thought he could treat women that way; he thought that was love. He was stepping toward the beaten man to start another round when Green walked through the busted door.

"He's down, Smoke," Green said.

"Come on, just one more hit," Smoke requested.

Green laughed. "I think one more hit will send him to the afterlife."

"That's not a bad thing," Smoke told him.

"No, Smoke, he's done. I'll take care of him. You go get Crew up here now. Their boat just arrived, and after the hell Darla's been through, and the scene she just saw, she's going to need Crew badly," Green said.

Smoke instantly defused. Darla was safe. There was no more reason for the rage. He wasn't sure why it had hit him so hard. He'd always had a thing about men hitting women, but he didn't usually go off so hard. He moved over to Darla, who still looked terrified. After what she'd just seen he could understand why.

"It's okay, Darla, you're safe. Crew's on his way. He'll be here any minute. He's gone through hell trying to get to you," Smoke said.

Tears rolled freely down her face.

"He'll never be the one for you," the kidnapper croaked, his hands now zip-tied behind his back, his face bleeding, and at least a couple of bones broken as he sat slumped against the wall.

"Go to hell," Darla whispered, her voice filled with emotion.

"I'll take you there with me," he said.

Smoke moved over faster than Green could stop him and knocked the man out. Enough was enough. He wanted to do more, but held back as Green lifted the man and Crew rushed into the room. It seemed Smoke didn't have to go find him.

He looked at Green who nodded toward the door.

"Yeah, yeah, I'll go walk it off," Smoke said. True to his name, he vanished like a puff of smoke, launching himself over the balcony and deciding it was a good time to run off his aggression.

Chapter Twenty-Eight

Crew rushed forward, his heart in his throat at the sight of Darla tied to the bed. Her eyes were wide, her skin pale, and sweat dripped from her forehead. The second she saw him, tears flowed down her cheeks as she gave him a wobbly smile.

"I prayed you'd find me. I don't know how you managed to do it, but I prayed you would," she told him.

He ran to the bed and sat, reaching out a hand and cupping her face. "Of course I'd find you. I got the best help the second I knew you were gone. I'm sorry it took so long," he said. He leaned down and gently brushed his lips across hers. He was so upset he was shaking, but he was trying to tamper that down.

He knew victims of violence needed someone to talk to, needed a calm, rational person to tell them it was all okay. She didn't need him punching holes in walls and personally strangling the man who'd dared to touch her.

"Will he get out of this, Crew? Will he get away with it?" Darla asked. It was one of the few times he'd ever seen fear on her face. It nearly broke him to see that look in her eyes. She was a woman full of life, and anyone who wanted to squash that should be lined up before a firing squad.

"He'll pay, Darla. I won't stop until I see him pay," Crew promised. He gently brought his hand to her cheek where he saw a bruise forming. It made him want to walk outside and put a bullet in the man who'd put it there. "I shouldn't have left you alone. I should've protected you better."

"You silly man. You can't be with me twenty-four/seven," she told him. She gave him a wobbly smile. "I'd appreciate it if you untied me though."

His eyes widened in horror that he'd left her sitting in that bed while she was bound. He immediately reached for her arms. "I'm sorry. I should've done that the second I came in. I was just so focused on your face."

"And I love you that you care so much," she told him. He quickly got the ropes untied, and her arms flopped down beside her. He lifted them and ran his fingers over the ugly red welts. He looked away from her so she wouldn't see the rage in his eyes.

"I'm okay, Crew. I promise. He didn't hurt me very badly." He looked up, hope in his expression. Had they made it in time? Steve had bruised her, so in Crew's opinion that was hurting her really bad, but had they stopped more from happening? He was too afraid to ask.

"You're not okay, but we'll make you that way. Eyes already called in a chopper. They'll be here to take you from the island soon, and then you'll be on the jet. We have a doctor on the chopper. We weren't sure what to expect," Crew said.

"It could've been a heck of a lot worse," she told him. "But you got here fast, much faster than I could've imagined."

Crew gently lifted her and cradled her in his arms, holding her loosely as she wrapped her arms around him. She sobbed against his shoulder and he rubbed her back, so grateful she was alive. They could face anything if they did it together.

"He didn't . . . rape me," she finally said after several moments of silence. "He was promising to make us official tonight, but he didn't have a chance to do it yet." Her words grew smaller as she continued to talk.

Crew felt tears in his own eyes at her words. He squeezed her a little tighter, so thankful for Brackish's excellent skills so they'd been only hours behind the criminal who'd taken her.

"He did hit my head a few times and filled me with drugs. I want to be checked at the hospital. I'm still a little fuzzy."

"Of course, baby, we're going to run everything on you. Who knows what that sicko was able to do in the hours he had you," Crew told her.

"He wasn't able to break me, which is what he wanted to do. He wanted me convinced I was in love with him and that you were nothing but a distraction. He never came close to breaking me. Even if you wouldn't have gotten here until tomorrow I wouldn't have let him break me. I was working on figuring out my own escape."

Crew leaned back and smiled at her. It was a smile filled with pain, but a bit of happiness too. "Of course, you were planning your own rescue. You're the strongest, smartest, sassiest woman I've ever met. Nobody can keep you down for long," Crew told her.

"I take pride in my strength, but I've learned being with you that it's okay to lean on someone else too. I love that we can be there for each other when we need one another the most. I think that's the healthiest part of a relationship."

"I agree with you. You make me a better person," he said. He tightened his hold on her and stood when he heard the approaching helicopter. "Your chariot is landing," he said.

"I told Daisy long ago that the final test in a relationship was to ask yourself if you like who you are better with the person or without." She paused as she leaned forward and gently kissed his neck. "I've found that I definitely like myself better when I'm with you. You make me a better person. I hope I do the same for you," she said. His heart swelled.

"I like myself a heck of a lot more with you in my life," he told her.

They stepped from the house in the middle of nowhere just as the chopper landed. A doctor rushed from the plane with another man carrying a gurney.

"I don't need that," Darla told Crew.

He smiled down at her. "Humor me, please. I know my hell is nothing compared to yours, but I need to know you're being fully taken care of."

She smiled up at him, her lips turned up in the way that had made him fall in love with her in the first place. He was so glad to have her.

"Then I'll gladly go on the stretcher," she told him. "I want you nice and healthy so you're around for the rest of my life. I can't have you having a heart attack or a stroke because of me."

He was utterly amazed by her. "I don't know how you can make jokes after all you've gone through. You completely amaze me," he told her.

"We need to get this bird up. We'll load her. Are you coming with us or the other chopper?" the doctor asked.

"I'm coming with you. Give me just a minute," Crew said. The man nodded, then walked away.

Darla couldn't see him as they took her away from him and he walked over to where Smoke was standing, the man beside him properly tied up.

"You piece of shit. I'm going to sue the hell out of you. You have no right to be here," Steve said through swollen, broken lips. He spit on the ground in front of Crew. Smoke just shrugged as if he'd been listening to the vile from this man for the past ten minutes Crew had been with Darla.

Crew didn't say a word, he just stepped a little closer then punched the asshole right in the nose, hearing the satisfying crunching sound as blood squirted out. Now it was broken in at least two places.

"I didn't see a thing," Smoke said as he gazed out over the ocean. He let Steve crumple to the ground. He wasn't going anywhere though, because Smoke pushed him onto his back, then used his huge foot to hold him against the sand.

"Thanks, Smoke. Truly." Smoke nodded again. "I want to kill him, but then this scum gets off easy, and I go to jail and can't be with my soon-to-be fiancée."

"Congrats, man," Smoke said. "Just say the word and he'll disappear."

Tempting. It was so tempting. Crew looked at the pathetic man whimpering on the ground, then back at Smoke. "I believe in our justice system. Until they fail me, I'll continue to do so. If this scum gets out, *then* we'll talk." Smoke nodded.

Crew turned and ran to the chopper. He'd already been away from Darla for too long.

It was too loud in the chopper to talk, so he sat at her side as they lifted into the sky and flew over the ocean. The moon was shining down, and he could see the reflection on the water, but he didn't care. All he cared about was the woman he'd come too close to losing. If that didn't shake him up, then nothing would.

He felt better the farther they got away from the prison this man had made for her. He could try to get out of this one, but Crew and the rest of his family would make sure he paid.

The chopper landed at the small local hospital and Darla was rushed inside. He didn't take his first full breath until they told him she was bruised, had a slight concussion, and would need to be watched, but there wouldn't be any long-term effects. She needed plenty of rest, fluids, and food, and then maybe some therapy. Well, he was just the man for the job.

It was less than four hours before their private jet was back in the skies. Darla slept in his arms on the big bed in the back of the jet while the special ops team stayed out front. There wasn't a chance

Crew was getting sleep anytime soon — or so he thought. He closed his eyes, feeling comforted with her in his arms.

When he awoke again they were close to home. He led her to the front of the jet, and she ate breakfast, moving slowly, but her smile returned as she joked with the men who'd rescued her.

When they landed, and emerged from the jet, Crew was stopped in his tracks. Darla's eyes were wide as she looked out at the huge mob of people standing there to greet them.

"I wanted to come," Daisy cried as she rushed from the crowd and threw her arms around Darla. "I wanted to be there, but I knew Crew had to be the one to save you. I'm so sorry, Dar, I'm so sorry. I can't believe that man got his hands on you. I should've done more."

Daisy and Darla were both crying as they stood with their arms wrapped tightly around each other. After a minute or two they pulled back.

"You're always there for me just as I am for you, but sometimes bad people get through our fences. Then we have to be there for each other to make the repairs," Darla said. "Thank you for being my best friend and my family."

They cried some more as Finn, Noah, Brandon, and Hudson surrounded them too.

"Thank you all for putting your lives on hold for me," Darla said with a sniffle.

"We take care of family, and you're family," Hudson said. He did feel like a brother to her, Crew was sure, since he was marrying her best friend.

"I won't turn down an offer to be a part of your group," Darla said with a laugh. "I guess I made it to the *in*-crowd."

"Ah, sorry, darling," Brandon said. "We've got you fooled. We're really the nerds who've made everyone think we're cool."

Darla smiled at him. "You silly man, don't you know the true *in*-crowd are the nerds. We're the ones who rule the world. You don't see the cool kids with all the bright ideas, you see the people with compassion, caring, and dreams worth following making it to the top of the ladder. That's the crowd I want to be in."

"Damn straight," Noah said. "Then I guess we *are* the cool kids."

"No one's going to call any of you losers kids. Maybe me since I'm the youngest," Brandon said.

"You're not that much younger," Finn said.

"I don't know, big brother. I'm starting to see a few grey hairs on that head of yours," Brandon said. "I don't have a single one."

"Marrying these women gives us all grey hairs. They tend to put themselves in situations that scare the living hell out of us," Noah said with a laugh.

"I'd toast to that if I had something in my hand," Crew said. "I think I got a few hundred greys in the past twenty-four hours."

"No doubt about it," Finn said, patting his brother on the shoulder. "But it all worked out in the end. You got your woman back and the world is once again spinning in the right direction."

He turned and looked at Darla. "Almost," he said. He shocked all of them when he dropped to his knee in front of her.

"This is the worst possible moment, but I need you to marry me. I want you by my side for the rest of my days, and I want a full head of grey hair because I'm so full of worry over you. I was going to take you to a mountain top, but I can't stand not calling you my wife for another single minute. Marry me, Darla. I'll do a much better job of protecting you from this moment on," Crew said.

There were sniffles behind him as the night grew very silent, everyone stepping a little closer to listen to Darla's answer. She dropped down to her knees with him and took his hand.

"It's about time," she said with tears falling down her face. "We belong together." Of course that's what she'd say.

He pulled the ring from his pocket he'd been carrying since just before they'd left for Italy. He'd never found the perfect moment. He'd given up searching. The perfect moment was any time and any place he was with this woman he loved. He placed the ring on her finger.

"You're wrong about one thing. This is the perfect moment and the perfect time because everyone we love is right here with us," she told him.

Then he leaned in and kissed her, sealing their promise to each other for eternity.

Epilogue

Joseph Anderson looked down into the crystal blue eyes of his beloved Katherine. She was fixing his tie that was off center. He'd been knotting a tie for more years than most, but maybe he'd never done it correctly because he wanted his wife's finishing touch.

"Where are we going my love that I need to be in a suit and tie?" Joseph asked.

Katherine finished what she was doing, then patted his chest and gave him an angelic smile.

"You will soon find out. It's not quite as fun being the one without the answers, is it?" she asked him with a musical laugh.

He grumbled. "You know I'd walk over coals for you, so it doesn't matter where you're taking me."

"So, if I told you I want to become Bonnie and Clyde, you'd hold my hand and jump into a convertible?" she asked with a laugh.

"I'd walk through fire for you, so doing a little shootout mission would be a new adventure," he said.

"Joseph Anderson, I don't think it's possible to love a human being more than I love you," Katherine told him. She wrapped herself in his arms and he held her, so grateful for the doctors who'd helped her, and so appreciative for every single moment he had with her. He didn't want to face the day they might have to part for a while until they met again in their afterlife.

"I guarantee you there's no greater love than mine for you," Joseph told her.

She took his hand and led him from their bedroom, down the enormous staircase, and through the halls. A limo was out front waiting, the back door open.

"It's not my birthday and it isn't a holiday, so I'm completely perplexed," Joseph told her as they slid into the backseat.

"I know. I love it. After nearly fifty years together I've finally managed to surprise you," she said with glee as she poured each of them a glass of champaign. He held the delicate stem in his huge hand and waited. "To love, laughter, heartache, and success. May we have many more years to come," she said.

He gladly clinked to that.

An hour later they pulled up to a private residence in the country outside of Seattle. Katherine slipped a blindfold over his eyes.

"Now Katherine, this is just silly," he said.

"I know. But you'll grant me my fun and games," she told him. She was absolutely correct. He wouldn't deny her anything, especially something that was bringing such joy to her voice.

He took her hand and trusted her to be his eyes as they walked down a path. It was oddly quiet out, and he had no clue what to expect at the end of the journey. What a ride the two of them had been on together. It hadn't always been easy, but it had most certainly always been an adventure — and he wouldn't change a single day.

"We're here," she said as she reached behind him and undid the tie.

It wasn't often that Joseph was stunned into silence. That might've happened a handful of times in his life. The first time he'd been speechless had been the moment his soon-to-be-wife had stepped to the front of the aisle and he'd looked up, knowing they were about to be united for all time and eternity. He'd nearly fainted at the raw emotion raging through him. He'd wanted to rush down the aisle and pull her into his arms. He'd wanted to shout to the world that she was his — and he was forever hers.

The next moment had been when he'd held his eldest son, Lucas, for the first time. He'd been so in love and awe he hadn't been able to say a word as tears had fallen down his cheeks. He'd been just as mesmerized with his next two sons, Alex and Mark.

The day his first grandchild, Jasmine, had been born, he'd once again been awestruck at the perfect tiny human who'd so lovingly and trustingly been placed in his arms. He loved each and every one of his grandchildren, but that first moment with Jasmine a bond formed that words couldn't describe.

Now, as he stood next to his beautiful Katherine and looked out at a crowd of hundreds of people all beaming at him, Joseph was at a loss of words.

"Surprise!" the called as they lifted glasses into the air. Someone handed Joseph one and he was so in awe he didn't think to raise his to toast them back.

"This is for you, my love," Katherine whispered.

"For what?" he asked, his voice a bit choked with tears.

"Let's find out," she said. She took his hand again and led him over to where two huge throne chairs were set up. He smiled as he and Katherine sat.

Jasmine, Jacob, and Isaiah came out with crowns on pillows. They stepped in front of Joseph and Katherine.

"Grandfather, grandmother, we bow to thee," Jasmine said with a little giggle as the three of them did just that. They placed a crown on Katherine's stunning white hair and another on Joseph's equally white locks.

Joseph was getting his breath back and laughed. This was silly and beautiful, and might go down in history as one of his all-time greatest moments.

His grandchildren bowed again and walked off the stage. The crowd of family and friends all bowed while they giggled.

"What is this?" Joseph once again asked his wife who was grinning ear to ear. She didn't answer as Lucas stepped up to a podium. Silence settled upon all of people before them. Joseph looked out in awe. This was his family, his friends, his loved ones. Each person there was special to him in many different ways. Lucas looked at his father and smiled before he began speaking.

"Thank you all for coming today on extremely short notice. As we all know, my father has a way of figuring things out, and if we aren't fast and sneaky, he'll bust us." Laugher followed Lucas's words, and Joseph shrugged. It was true. He was shocked he hadn't figured this out anyway. They must've planned and implemented in less than a week. That was the only explanation that seemed plausible.

"Dad, we've all gathered today to . . ." He gave a long pause and Joseph found himself confused. "To thank you." Joseph's heart swelled as he felt stinging in his eyes.

"What are you thanking me for?" Joseph asked.

"As we all know, this giant of a man has meddled in each of our lives." Joseph looked down. He didn't meddle. He just pushed people along.

"And each of us fought you every step of the way, but what we finally realize now is how grateful we are for what you've done for us. We're stubborn and set in our ways — we are Andersons after all. We couldn't see what we truly needed or what value there was in true love. But you never gave up hope, you never gave up on us."

There were many agreements from the crowd.

"We wanted to gather here today and let you know you never fooled us, but we appreciate you anyway. We appreciate what you've done for us."

"Well, I didn't do too much," Joseph said, slightly embarrassed, though he didn't understand why. That made the entire crowd laugh hard. Joseph sent them a glare.

"Ah, the famous Joseph Anderson started with me, at least we believe it all began with me. He decided Amy was my perfect wife." Lucas stopped and looked at his wife who was beaming. His daughter Jasmine was next to Amy, their arms wrapped around one another, both so beautiful.

"He knew we were a perfect match, and he gave her a job where we'd be side by side. He knew the moment we met it would be fate. And he was one hundred percent correct. Because I not only got Amy, but I got my children too, and I've never been happier in my life," Lucas told them.

Amy and Jasmine both blew him a kiss. His boys stood with their shoulders back looking like such fine young men. The next generations of Andersons were well on their way to a beautiful success story.

"Once my father matched his three stubborn sons, he knew he wasn't done. Uncle George had moved away years earlier, and my father made sure to bring him back to Seattle where the two of them put their heads together, doubling the trouble. My cousins didn't stand a chance," Lucas said.

"Not a single chance," Trenton said with a laugh as he stood with his arm around his wife, Jennifer.

"And we were furious at first, but now we realize that not only did you help us find our way, but you brought us all back together. We were floundering, and now we're home," Trenton told him.

George stepped up to Joseph and put his arm on Joseph's shoulder. They both looked like extremely proud and humbled men. All of them knew the humbleness would wear off quickly.

"But we decided to share something with the two of you today," Lucas said with a wicked smile.

"I don't trust that look," Joseph said.

"Me neither," George said.

"You shouldn't. I got it from you," Lucas said, making the crowd laugh again.

"Not only did Uncle George have one love of his life, but he's been lucky enough to have two," Lucas said. He looked out at Esther and smiled. She blushed.

"You see, we knew before you told us that you two were in love. We knew you were fighting it just as much as each of us did. So, we gathered together and did some meddling of our own."

"What are you talking about?" George asked.

Bree stepped up to the podium next. "You see, Dad, we figured out real quick that you and Uncle Joseph were meddling in our lives, so we decided to have a bit of fun of our own. Do you remember when you couldn't get a single moment alone with Esther?"

George's gaze widened in realization that he'd been tricked by his own children.

"You monsters did that on purpose?" he gasped.

"Yep, we took turns to make sure each of us had a problem needing solved. We loved the annoyance on your face. We did feel bad about doing it to Esther, though. Sorry about that," Bree said, looking toward Esther.

"I forgive you. I know what a terror your father can be," Esther said with a laugh.

"I'm a terror but I sure love you," George said.

Bree stepped back and Lucas took the podium again. "But we all knew my father still wasn't done. Oh no, he had many more lives to mess with."

Katherine took Joseph's hand and squeezed his fingers. "We all knew," she whispered. "And we all loved you in spite of your meddling. But now, we realize what a blessing you have been to this family and how you've helped it thrive and grow. We all love you."

Joseph felt those dang, irritating tears stinging his eyes again.

"My father paired up with his long-time family friend, Mr. Martin Whitman." Martin laughed as he waved to Joseph. "The two of them decided it was high time to marry off his children as well."

Spence Whitman, who'd been invaluable in helping Katherine with her brain cancer stepped up next to Lucas. "Yes, we were lucky enough to be saved by our father, Martin, when my brothers and I were young punks in foster care. And then we were saved again when Joseph and our father knew we were once again heading down a wrong path. We didn't think we needed rescued, but we realize that's when we needed it the most."

Joseph looked out as Martin discreetly wiped his own tear away. These children of theirs had grown into such fine young men and women. It was impossible not to get emotional.

"There's nothing I wouldn't do for you, Spence, after what you've done for my beautiful wife," Joseph said respectfully.

"And my family and I feel the same toward you. Thank you, Joseph for never giving up on us."

Spence stepped down after giving Lucas a hug.

"Our wonderful father then discovered a long-lost brother." Richard stepped up next to Joseph and George and waived to everyone who cheered. Their family had grown and grown, and it was all for the better.

"Uncle Richard came into our lives without knowing he'd been stolen at birth. It was a magical moment for all of us. We added five more cousins, and Father and Uncle George were ecstatic to find more unruly children to meddle with."

More laughter erupted. Crew stepped up next to Lucas and smiled at the crowd.

"My sister, brothers, and myself were a mess. We were entitled, spoiled little brats, and then we met all of our family. Our father gave us a choice to shape up or learn the realities of the world. He gave us projects, and with the help of his brothers, helped us find true love. We couldn't be happier."

Joseph, George, and Richard all sat there, looking regal and humbled. They couldn't be happier for their children. They couldn't be happier with their lives. This was family, and this was what it was all about.

"I think I was the brattiest of all," Brille said as she joined her brother. "And I'm so glad no one gave up on me. Thank you, Uncle Joseph, Uncle George, and most especially, thank you, Father. We all love you very much."

Now all three men looked as if they were going to cry. They looked down and all of their children gave them a few moments to get themselves together.

Lucas once again took the podium. "My father, the wonderful Joseph Anderson, still had more up his sleeve. Damien Whitfield came into our lives. He didn't want to do it in a boring way. No, he had to bring his brothers along with him and my father clapped his hands in glee to have a new generation of Andersons to meddle with."

Damien stood next to his brothers, their relationship growing slowly, but the bond truly beginning. They might've gotten a late start, but there was no doubt they would flourish. Joseph knew beyond a shadow of a doubt, that love would unite them all, and nothing in this world could tear them apart, not even those who'd been trying to bring Damien down. Joseph had faith in his bloodline.

"So, once again, we're here to celebrate decades of love, laughter, and the blessings that have rained down on this family." He paused and lifted his glass. Someone came out and handed glasses to Joseph, his brothers, and their spouses. Lucas lifted his glass high in the air. "To family."

"To family," the chorus of voices called. There were a lot of happy tears and hugs throughout the clan of Andersons and friends.

Crew placed his arm around Darla, noting the tears streaming down her face.

"I guess my uncle's meddling hasn't been such a bad thing since each of us have found love," he told her.

"I think we should buy him many thrones," Darla said with a giggle.

"He lives on one. We can't let his ego get too big."

She laughed. "I think it's too late for that," she said. "But I do have a surprise for you."

"Oh really. What is that?" he asked.

"You get to have your little girl or boy," she said.

"What do you mean? We know that was fake."

She took his hand and placed it on her stomach. "Trust me, the morning sickness isn't fake."

It took him a few seconds to realize what she was saying. Once it sunk in, his lips turned up so big, it made his cheeks hurt.

"Really?" he asked, awe and joy flowing through him.

"Truly. We're going to be parents."

"I adore you," he said, not trying to hide the emotion flowing through him.

"And I you."

Daisy stepped up to them. "I guess, then, our children will be as close as we are," she said with a sweet smile.

Crew was confused, but his brother was grinning as wide as he was. Darla gasped then let out a cry of delight as she grabbed Daisy.

"Oh, this truly is a day of celebration," she said as the girls held each other tight. Finally, Crew realized what Daisy was saying.

"Congratulations," he told them both.

"I guess love really is enough," Daisy said. "I went from being adamant that I was never having children to needing to have a little one that's half me and half Hudson. I think she'll be incredible."

"Or he," Hudson said. "Or maybe both."

Daisy laughed. "Don't you dare put twins out in the universe. I'm already going to get too fat."

"Nothing could alter your beauty."

"What's this I hear about babies?" All four of them jumped as Joseph spoke over their shoulders. Crew turned and laughed.

"Can you hear the word babies from a mile away?" he asked.

"I sure can," Joseph said, beaming down at them. "This world goes round and round with new generations born."

"Well, it looks like this time next year you're going to have even more babies to spoil," Crew said.

"That's the best gift you can give me," Joseph said. His smile fell away as he looked out over the massive crowd around them.

"What's wrong?" Hudson asked his uncle.

Joseph smiled a bit. "I just realized everyone's married," he said with a bit of a pout.

"Isn't that what you wanted?" Crew asked.

"Well, of course, it is," he told him as if he was daft.

"Then why are you so sad?" Hudson asked.

Joseph looked around again. "I don't know what to do next."

Those words made all of them crack up with laughter. Katherine stepped up beside her husband, wrapping her petite arm around him.

"Oh, Joseph, don't you fret. I'm sure something will happen to foster your meddling ways," she said.

He instantly cheered. "Of course you're right, my darling. Something always happens," Joseph said.

Just then fireworks were set off in the air. The timing couldn't have been more perfect. They all turned and watched the show as they celebrated together: a life of love, a life of union, a life of immortality. Each member of their family had found their happily ever after in their own unique way. And that meant the Andersons would live on for eternity.

Note From Author Including Anderson World Read Order

If you enjoyed this new spin-off from Melody Anne's first series, *The Billionaire Bachelors,* then you can catch up on all of these characters you're going to see in and out of the series in the books listed below. Any of these series can be read alone, but it's also a lot of fun to read them in somewhat of an order. Each family has their own unique dynamic, and Joseph is the key character that pulls them all together. His meddling knows no bounds.

Also a side not from me. The Andersons originally began as a three-book series when I started my writing career. But I fell in love with Joseph and the Anderson dynamic. I went on to write other series, but I found I was bringing Joseph along, wanting to take him with me to all of the worlds I was creating. So in came his twin brother George, who just happens to be one of my favorite uncles. He lived in Cordova, AK, where I spent a summer when I was sixteen, which is why I sent my couple there in *Blackmailing the Billionaire*. I loved that town. He moved to Anchorage, and I can't wait to go there again and do some fishing which I've become addicted to.

Well, at the end of book seven of the Andersons, I thought it was all finished once again, and then a fan wrote me an email and said they'd had a dream that Joseph and George were staring at a newspaper, and they saw a man who looked just like them. And I was in love with the idea of a stolen baby plot. So in came Richard, who is another favorite uncle of mine. Richard was stolen at birth as their triplet. Back when Joseph's mother had her babies, fathers weren't often in the delivery room, and the doctor just figured she already had two babies, and wouldn't miss a third. So in came five more kids for Joseph and George to play cupid with.

At the end of that story, Joseph would go on to meddle in the lives of his friends children, and so his legacy has continued to grow. I left openings in many of my books because I can never truly say those magical words of "*the end*" and so a new branch of Andersons were found in my Montlake series, *Anderson Billionaires*.

Then I with friends, and we were storyboarding about possible ideas, and that's how this newest spin-off happened with *Anderson Black Ops*. This series has been so much fun, because I'm co-writing it. I have a friend who knows the world of black ops, so he's been giving strong outlines, and chapters for these new men we've created in this fun new world. We have a lot of ideas of where this will all lead.

Now, I'm getting a lot of emails, asking about the order to read. I've created so many stories at this point, that even I'm a little lost on the order, but I'm going to list it as best I can with staying in the right timeframe. The newest, of course, are easiest to keep track of, but since I bring in so many other series in the middle of writing these books, it does get a bit confusing.

So here we go. And as always, I love to hear feedback from you. After all, I can't do this job, can't write these fantastic stories, and can't live in my dream world, without your support. You make the magic happen. You give me a voice to put onto paper, and you make my dreams come true. If the order is at all messed up, then please let me know and we'll adjust.

I have a fantastic team I work with, and we're constantly changing and fixing things. It's amazing this digital world we now have, that we can fix things so easily. Before the world of epublishing, if there was a mistake, it couldn't get fixed until the next set of books were printed. Now, it's just a few hits on the keyboard, and woola, we're good to go again.

Thank you so much for your support. And I hope you are well, are enjoying these stories, and are making magic happen in this crazy world we've found ourselves in in the parallel universe that some call 2020.

Read Order for The Anderson Empire

Billionaire Bachelors

1. The Billionaire Wins the Game
2. The Billionaire's Dance
3. The Billionaire Falls
4. The Billionaire's Marriage Proposal
5. Blackmailing the Billionaire
6. Runaway Heiress
7. The Billionaire's Final Stand
8. Unexpected Treasure
9. Hidden Treasure
10. Holiday Treasure
11. Priceless Treasure
12. The Ultimate Treasure

Now, you can read the Tycoon Series, which Joseph's in, but only one of the books is truly relevant to the continuation of the Andersons. I'll list all of the Tycoon books here, but highlight Damien's story, which will come up later on in a twist for *The Billionaire* Andersons listed below.

Billionaire Bachelors

Book One: The Tycoon's Revenge
Book Two: The Tycoon's Vacation
Book Three: The Tycoon's Proposal
13. Book Four: The Tycoon's Secret
Book Five: The lost Tycoon
Book Six: Rescue me

And here we go again, with another insert. So, the next series Joseph is in is my Heroes Series. We have a visit from *Dr. Spence Whitman* in this book you've just read, which is in this series. You can read this series next to know Spence's story, but you won't be lost if you don't. So I'll list the entire series here, and again highlight the story that has Spence in it, adding it to the list. All of these books can be a stand alone, but I do bring my characters in and out of most of my series because I can't let them go. So if you read *Her Hometown Hero*, it's a complete story, but the brothers will be all throughout it.

Heroes Series

Pre-Book: Safe in his arms (in an Anthology called *Baby it's Cold Outside*)
Book One: Her Unexpected Hero
Book Two: Who I am with you
14. Book Three: Her Hometown Hero
Book Four: Following Her
Book Five: Her Forever Hero

And now, we come up to Sherman, who will play a big roll in this series. Sherman's another of those characters I seriously love! And when I came up with Bobbi, Avery's mother, I knew right then and there, she was going to be a match for Sherman. By the way, Bobbi is named after my best friend's mother, who I absolutely adore! She mirrors some of her character traits too, and we'll be seeing a lot more of her. In real life she's married to Hal, who happens to be a fantastic man.

After I wrote the Bobbi character, I was telling her what she's saying and doing, and I might've made her blush. Hal's okay with it, though. If he's gonna lose his wife, at least it's to Sherman, who just so happens to be a pretty great guy. We just spent a long weekend at their house in Northern Cali, and had a refreshing, fantastic time. And I was putting them under the microscope for my upcoming stories. I use real life in my books all of the time because family events are definitely story worthy. So, Bobbi, beware cause I'm gonna have fun with this character.

I'm going to list the Billionaire Aviators here, but not number them because you don't have to read the books to read all the rest, but if you want to get to know Sherman, then I'd dive on in. This series was one of my fav to write, because I love the characters, love the journey, and I was really growing in my writing at this point, getting a little more courageous with what I was doing within my fantasy worlds.

Billionaire Aviators
Book One: Turbulent Intentions
Book Two: Turbulent Desires
Book Three: Turbulent Waters
Book Four: Turbulent Intrigue

Now, you will also see Joseph and other Andersons appear in my Undercover Billionaire world, where I also really started adding more suspense into my writing. Some of these characters will pop in and out of this world as well, because, like I said, I love to bring these characters into each world. So you can read this series, but again, won't be lost if you don't, so I won't number them.

Also, on a side note. *Owen* is my *favorite* book I've ever written. I lost my dad in 2018, and it nearly killed me. I write men like Joseph, George, Sherman, and more because I'm a daddy's girl, through and through. He raised me with so much more love than I can even begin to explain, and he also taught me how to be independent and strong. He's the reason I'm an author, the reason I'm so strong, and the reason I still cry because I miss him so much.

He LOVED UFO stories, and when all of the news broke that they were releasing the government files on UFO's, my heart was breaking again, because he would've been so excited, and absolutely glued to the internet. But I know he's up in heaven laughing because he has all of the answers now, but I sure would love him to be here with me so we could talk and wonder, and laugh, and so his arms could be wrapped around me.

My heroine loses her dad in Owen, which I'd begun writing before I lost my dad. I had to stop, and when I came back to the book, I cried my way through a lot of it. A lot of those lines she uses when she's talking about her father were things I asked and said. I was so lost for a long time losing him. And writing Owen helped me heal. My heart will never be truly full again, but my dad loved me, and I love him, and I know he'd kick my butt if I didn't live my life with love, laughter and triumph. He raised me to be a powerful woman, and I won't dishonor him by being anything less than that. So I'm gonna highlight Owen, not because it's needed for the Andersons, but because it's needed for my soul. ☺

Undercover Billionaires

Book One: Kian
Book Two: Arden
Book Three: Owen
Book Four: Declan

And now it gets a bit more confusing as I'm finishing out my Montlake series at the same time as we're doing *The Anderson Black Ops* series, so you get to go back and forth a bit if you want to stay exactly in the timeline. We're finally making it to the end . . . for now. But I guess I'll have to stay on top of this because I have no doubt that the Anderson world will continue to grow and grow and grow, even as I take time to visit other worlds in between. Thank you again for all you do. I hope you fall in love with these characters over and over again, just as I do each time I dive back into the Anderson Universe.

The Billionaire Andersons

15. Book One: Finn
16. Book Two: Noah

Anderson Black Ops

17. Book One: Shadows

The Billionaire Andersons

18. Book Three: Brandon (October 20, 2020)

Anderson Black Ops

19. Book Two: Rising

The Billionaire Andersons

20. Book Four: Hudson

Anderson Black Ops

21. Book Three: Barriers

The Billionaire Andersons

22. Book Five: Crew

Anderson Black Ops

23. Book Four: Shattered (Coming April 2021)
24. Book Five (Coming June 2021)

Printed in Great Britain
by Amazon

68908391R00173